THE WITCH'S DIARY

by

Rebecca Brae

THE WITCH'S DIARY

by

Rebecca Brae

TYCHE BOOKS LTD.

Published by Tyche Books Ltd.
Calgary, Alberta, Canada
www.TycheBooks.com

Cover Design by Indigo Chick Designs
Interior Art by Sonny Tamko
Interior Layout by Ryah Deines
Editorial by M.L.D. Curelas

First Tyche Books Ltd Edition 2020
Print ISBN: 978-1-989407-21-9
Ebook ISBN: 978-1-989407-22-6

Author photograph: Stacy Kreger

This book was funded in part by a grant from the Alberta Media Fund.

For all the beautiful souls in the corners and at the margins. Persevere. Be you. This world is interesting and magickal because of you.

Forward

I WAS SURPRISED and honoured to receive Dean Peuturella Bloodroot's request to provide my old diary and letters to Grimoire College as a reading aide for first semester students. I had not thought my troublesome entry into professional life of interest to anyone, save myself, but I would never refuse an appeal from my favourite potions professor and good friend.

Though it has been many season cycles since the trials depicted herein, I hope they are of some use to you, my beautiful budding Scion of the Moon. If nothing else, let these pages stand as an example to never give up on yourself or your dreams. I started out doing everything wrong, but I learned and improved, and in doing so became a stronger person and witch.

Special thanks goes out to my talented friend Magda, who generously offered to replace my atrocious sketches with

hers. If it were not for her, you would all be very confused and possibly slightly nauseous. I have left in two of my original drawings so that you are aware of the depth of service she has done you.

If you find yourself confused by any of the characters or terms that follow, please refer to the reference sections at the back of this tome.

Have fun, my witches!

Hester Digitalis Wishbone

Moondias, Wolf Moon 15, 209

I NEVER SHOULD have left my hovel this morn. You know that funny tingly feeling you get when pondering a decision? The itchy, crawly sense that whatever you decide will profoundly affect the rest of your life? Well, trust me, spend more time thinking about it than it takes to suck down your gruel. And don't ever forget to check the expiry date on your prosthetic adhesive. When that stuff goes, it really goes.

Everything was going so well. I was the ugliest, filthiest, vile old hag this village had ever seen. One of the peasants told me so.

The crone who previously held my position had no work ethic. Her curses were generic and lacklustre. She never bothered to learn about her subjects. For instance, Abathonda is terrified of finding loose hairs and Markus is obsessed with counting things. I can get them both at once with a hex that causes people's hair to fall out whenever they are around!

She also had no pride in her appearance. Would you believe there was only one crook in her nose? I have three. That's how dedicated I am. And each of them is a marvellously bent specimen of hag-tastic art.

There's a fine line between a sinister, imposingly crooked nose and a nose that looks like it was accidentally slammed in a door. When peasants see mine coming around a corner, they quake down to their very souls. I've heard them say it feels like it's hunting them, following their every move, aiming ominously at them, thrusting threateningly at their tender bits, just waiting for them to take their eyes off it for an instant, and then twitch, bam . . . done in by the nose. If my nose alone inspires that much respect, imagine what chaos my halitosis wreaks on this sleepy village!

Ah, but the higher you fly, the farther you fall. And I'd be surprised if the grubs in the Ascariim deep mine didn't hear my splat.

It all started last eventide when I wagered a bet with my best friend, Magda, that I could make everyone in the tavern think their skin was melting. She was a little too skeptical, which raised my hackles. Admittedly, I had unsuccessfully attempted a similar spell last season cycle, just after our graduation ritual—let's just say our graduating class had a distinct "eau de rotting flesh" that would not quit—but I've learned a trick or two since then.

There is a chance I was a bit short-tempered and not as careful as I should have been. It probably had something to do with my consumption of a few too many fermented ghoul eyes. I must have accidently added a pinch of powdered albino salamander livers instead of ground rat bones (*NOTE: Remember to label my spell component pouches*).

I ended up summoning half a juvenile phoenix that was understandably confused at its sudden change of location, not to mention its lack of a left side. Creature summoning never was my best subject. Anyway, the long and short of it is that I burnt out the Resplendent Toad tavern . . . and my magick.

I didn't even notice the latter until I arrived home and unsuccessfully tried summoning a fire elemental to heat my tea. You hear horror stories about this kind of thing happening to your third cousin's friend's brother, but you always think, "not me" or "I bet So-and-so was just being dramatic." Here's hoping my life doesn't end up as a moral fable to keep young witchlings on their brooms. I'm sure it'll be fine. This has to clear up. At some point. Right?

I was hoping my magick would return after a good sleep, but it didn't. This morn, I tried to put on my hag glamour . . . and . . .

nothing. No cracked, sallow skin. No stringy grey hair rearing like angry snakes in a malodorous wind. No boils erupting with puss. Not even a measly wart.

In times of crisis, it's best to fall back on what you know. So, ultimately, I blame Grimoire College for the following debacle.

Our teachers constantly hammered into us that old-fashioned costuming and theatrical makeup should underpin every glamour. It was an archaic concept, as outdated as our prehistoric Profs. After all, weaving a quick, clean illusion was far more efficient than spending an hour individually gluing on moles and warts. Nobody understood why they wanted us shackled to these ridiculous magick training wheels. We weren't toddlers. So, most of us ignored our kits. I certainly did. Until this morn.

Stratified layers of dust slid off the case as I yanked it out from under my pallet. This should have tipped me off that maybe, just maybe, my plan needed some rethinking. But, no. I was so intent on getting out and pestering the peasants that I didn't pay any attention to my gut.

When I glued the kit's nose on, my enthusiasm waned. It only extended about an inch past my real nose and was more hooked than crooked. Every time I inhaled, the sides of the prosthesis clamped my nose shut like a vise. After experimenting for a while, I decided I could make it work. The nose looked like it was pulsing—in and out, in and out—and it produced a memorable, wet, sucking hiss.

I slapped on some wrinkle cream and stuck a huge hairy mole on the apex of my chin. If I crossed my eyes, I could just see the hairy bit over the tip of my new nose. I was quite pleased with it, but the standard boil needed work.

After staring in the mirror at the craterous red-blue mound on my cheek, I decided puss would improve its lacklustre appearance. I mixed a glob of adhesive with the yellow skin paste and created a reasonable likeness. I spread the milky-yellow substance over the boil and down my cheek, and had to admit it wasn't bad. I mean, it wouldn't ooze or anything, but it gave the impression that it might if it felt like it.

My look was starting to come together, but I had to do something about my hair. No self-respecting village hag would be seen in public with fiery red locks . . . unless they actually were on fire, which wasn't a feasible option. I dug through my supplies. A palmful of crude oil darkened my hair. After dusting on a combination of flour and cremated toad feet, I managed to create a suitably repulsive stringy nest.

I had a spot of trouble getting the red contact lenses in. It feels decidedly unnatural to stick something in your eye on purpose. The eyebrow was much easier. One glob of adhesive and voila: Instant Menace. There's nothing like a thick mono-brow to really freak people out. It occurred to me that it was possibly meant to be a moustache, but it worked well enough as an eyebrow.

I donned my hag rags, popped in a set of uncomfortable dentures, and studied my new visage in the mirror. A hunched, putrid old creature peered back at me, and I felt confident I could pull it off. I smiled and took a closer look at the sharpened brown teeth. Someone had done a smashing job on them; there were even bits of food stuck between the incisors.

I slid two blood capsules and a fake severed finger into my belt as I hobbled outside. I believe in being prepared. Plus, it's always fun to have a piece fall off while accosting someone.

As I'm thinking back now, I do remember noting a faint vapor rising from my boil, but I was so focused on getting to work that I ignored it. It must have been an interesting effect—a smoking boil has an element of surprise over a regular old purulent one.

I practiced a few intimidating scowls on my way to the village square and realized I couldn't move my brow or lips. My face felt like rawhide stretched over a drum. The wrinkle cream was clearly not all it was cracked up to be. Figuring it was too late to do anything about it, I scrunched up my face as much as possible and hoped that I at least gave an impression of supreme pain and misery.

I arrived late because of my additional morning activities, so the first peasants I came across were already hauling wheat bales out to the fields. I sidled up to a young girl and pulsed my nose at her. During one particularly vigorous inhalation, my left contact somehow lodged itself on top of my eyeball. I tried ignoring it, but it is overwhelmingly irritating to have something stuck in your eye—especially something you intentionally put in it.

Squinting as threateningly as I could, I pointed at her. "You are a wicked 'irl." Enunciating the words around my bulky dentures and tight lips was challenging. "May your sp—"

It was at this point that my teeth hurled themselves at the startled kid.

Stunned by their desertion, I struggled to salvage the hex. "May your spiteful tongue split . . . and your teeth fly from your deceitful mouth."

Bending to retrieve the mutinous dentures, which now lay at the girl's feet, I slipped both blood tablets into my mouth and came up drooling. As I rose, I noticed thin trails of smoke curling around my head.

This was when everything else that could go wrong, did.

Whoever made those stupid capsules should be transmuted into an incontinent worm and left in a puddle. There was so much blood in my mouth that it surged down my throat and up my nose. My spluttering cough liberally sprayed the girl, and although that temporarily emptied my mouth and allowed me to breathe, the froth trapped in my prosthetic nose continued swelling to volcanic proportions.

Then the infernal itching started. The insidious burning spread everywhere I had applied that blasted adhesive. Not only was my nose drowning me, it felt like a thousand fire ants had crawled in and started a disorganized conga line. Incidentally, this is also when a rather large crowd of villagers gathered—it wouldn't be inaccurate to call it a horde or mob.

My choking and snorting morphed into a gurgling screech as the steaming latex boil caved in and fused to my skin. I managed to rip most of it off before I inhaled another snootful of the ever-expanding blood goo.

I tore the prosthetic nose off with a howl of pain and threw the wretched thing as hard as I could. It sailed in a perfect arc through the air, spewing pink foam, and landed point down between the ample breasts of the village baker, who promptly fainted.

Next to go was the mole. It offered little resistance, but the mono-brow was another matter. That thing was determined to stay on. It took three determined yanks to free the furry mound. I'm glad it got caught in my rags when I dropped it. I think I'll keep it in case I find a way to re-attach my real eyebrows.

What the peasants thought was happening, I'll never know. You'd think someone tearing bits off their face would be terrifying. But, no. By the time I raised my smarting head from the horse trough, the villagers were guffawing so hard that some were literally rolling on the ground. I've never been so humiliated.

I know it's usually better to face your mistakes head on (though, I have also proved that facing your mistakes can occasionally be foolhardy: For instance, when a mistake involves a roided-up orc in heat or a dragon experiencing severe intestinal disruptions), but this was more than I could bear. I turned and ran. Adding insult to injury, the severed finger chose that moment to fly out of my pocket. I didn't stop to pick it up. In retrospect, I probably should have, because I later heard a kid asking someone to pull his finger; which in actual fact was more my finger than his. I'll never get it back now.

As soon as I closed the door to my hovel, I had a good cry. The activity proved more useful than usual. It finally dislodged the contact from my eye. I spent the next several hours washing my hair. The combination of flour, cremated toad feet, and crude oil creates something akin to cement. I eventually removed most of it with a mixture of liquid ammonia and sand. This did nothing to soothe my stinging face.

And that awful wrinkle cream took its time wearing off, but I am happy to report that I have now regained control of my face. I read the label and, would you believe, it's actually meant to get *rid* of wrinkles. Why is it called "Wrinkle Cream" if it's really *anti*-wrinkle cream? I'd like to kick the alchemist who came up with that gem.

I also found a warning on the adhesive bottle (in tiny print) advising immediate disposal once past the expiry date. That stuff must be designed to expire quickly. I've only had it for four season cycles. And I don't remember a single teacher warning us about that.

The union scryed me while I was cleaning up. I didn't answer and they left a message asking me to contact them. I just know they're going to tell me I've been fired and I can't deal with that right now. I'll scry them back next sun. Maybe by then I'll figure out some way to explain what happened.

ADDENDUM: I just tried a minor illusion and found out

my magick is still kaput. How long is this drought going to last? I'm a witch. What am I supposed to do without magick?

Tydias, Wolf Moon 16, 209

So, AFTER CONFIRMING my magick was still defunct this morn, I scryed the union back and made a complete ass of myself.

Turns out, they weren't contacting me about what happened last sun, they wanted to inform me that my familiar has been selected and will arrive shortly. This would have been a relief, except I'd already launched into an explanation of the unfortunate incident. Everything snowballed from there . . . down a really steep hill . . . collecting more and more crap as it went . . . and then it careened off a cliff . . . and went *splat*. Again. Which pretty much describes my life at the moment. Splattity-splat-splat.

In the middle of my recounting, my union agent transferred me to a job satisfaction agent who, after hearing the details, transferred me to a job security agent, who then transferred me to a work equality agent, who transferred me to a job safety agent, who gave me the choice of being transferred to a job suitability agent or a work placement agent. I chose the work placement agent, who suggested I speak with a job mediation agent to assess whether my current position was salvageable.

At this point, I began to wonder if I was being passed around the office like a five-legged frog in show-and-tell. At least the job mediation agent kept things short. My story must have gotten around to him already, because I didn't even have to tell him who I was.

He told me to cool my broom, in my hovel (he was very explicit about that part), while he contacted the village council. He muttered something about no direct contact between parties during mediation, which sent me into a tizzy wondering how I was supposed to host a party if I couldn't leave the hut to get supplies. With no finger food and only half a jar of fermented ghoul eyes, it would be a pretty miserable gathering.

I didn't panic for long. I hadn't even finished polishing my scry mirror when his face popped back into view.

The news was not good. The town council wanted me gone. The mayor said there was an opening for village idiot, but I agreed with the agent that it probably wasn't a sincere offer.

Thus began another long series of transfers around the union—back to the job safety agent who recommended I consult a specialist about my loss of magick; to the job suitability agent who suggested finding a position more in line with my age (ageist much?); and finally, to a particularly patronizing hedge witch who advised me to attend therapy until I was able to effectively deal with my "ghoul eye habit."

After saying "no" to the hedge witch four times with no indication she heard, my frustration boiled over and I terminated the scry. I do not have a fermented ghoul eye problem. I was just out with a girlfriend having a bit of fun. Even a hag has to let her hair down once in a while. Terrifying the masses is surprisingly stressful. It was just plain old bad luck that my slight overindulgence ended so disastrously. It could have happened to anyone.

When my head stopped spinning, I contacted the union job bank in Aestradorra. I thought adding my name to their list would be simple. Not so. Turns out, new clients have to book an in-person appointment with an employment counsellor.

I scheduled a meeting for next sun but I don't know how it's going to go. What work can I do if I can't cast spells? And if I can't work, I can't pay down my student loan. And if I can't pay the loan, I'll end up assigned to some government-run love potion sweatshop. And that damn rose puree is impossible to wash off your fingernails. I don't want red nails. It's so . . . vamp.

This has been the most depressing sun of my life. Well, maybe it ties with when jerky-Justin and I broke up. Haven't thought about him for a while. Isn't that just the soggy slug on my pizza. I desperately need a cathartic junk food binge, but all I have is one pathetic Mean Cuisine meal left over from my failed diet last moon. Yet another reminder of how much I suck. And I really don't fancy downing a bucket of water to dislodge the fungus-stuffed bat wings and dry-grilled spider eggs from my throat.

I think I'll skip the meal and curl up with a hot cup of nettle tea (with just one fermented ghoul eye to calm my nerves) and watch other people be brain-numbingly foolish. At least there's still some charge left in my crystal ball. There must be someone out there having a worse sun than me, and I'm going to find them and watch.

That brings up another issue. If this magick funk goes on much longer, I'll have to pay someone to charge my ball. How embarrassing. And if I can't find a job, I won't even be able to afford a recharge. Great Galloping God of Thunder, what if my scry mirror goes dead? I'll have to rely on carrier pixies or air elementals to deliver messages.

Even if pixies manage to deliver a message, you can never be sure who received it or when. I bet the little buggers have notes stuffed in tree crevices all over the countryside. And air elementals—don't get me started on them. I heard about a witch who used one to tell her Outerplane cousin she was coming for a visit. It sucked up some kid and her dog and then dropped a house on the poor witch. Now that is a bad sun. I suppose I should be thankful that I'm stuck in my hut and not under it.

There was one faint ray of hope this sun: my familiar should arrive soon. I wonder what creature I'll get? Magda received hers last moon. An asp isn't terrible, unless you're like her and are afraid of snakes. Funny how that worked out.

I'd love something traditional like a raven with one eye or an extra-large rat. They have the whole harbinger of death thing going on which totally fits my current mood.

Here's hoping next sun's forecast is fairer.

Wendias, Wolf Moon 17, 209

I'M FEELING BETTER. I relaxed last night, had a nice long sleep, and woke up with a refreshed attitude and a wicked idea.

REGARDING THE ATTITUDE:

If this village is fickle enough to terminate me after one accident (okay, so it was numerous accidents, but they all happened at once so I'm counting it as one), then it isn't somewhere I want to work.

Accidents happen. It's kinda their deal. Everything is rolling along fine and then, *wham*, you're suddenly having one.

Actually, I'm thankful I found out how intolerant this village is before something really bad happened. This kind of environment breeds angry mobs and everyone knows what happens next: the witch is always the scapegoat.

REGARDING THE IDEA:

It came to me while I was sleeping, as all inspired thoughts do, and will be my fond farewell to the villagers. My last act as their hag. Let it be known that Hester Digitalis Wishbone held up her duties as village hag to the bitter end.

Besides, who knows when another witch will be dispatched. Best to channel any loose misfortune to my own ends before it grows strong enough to blaze its own indiscriminate path through the villagers' lives, like a lightning bolt of misery.

People are starting to forget what happens when there isn't a hag around to balance out all the healing and abundance spells. The giant sucking pit that used to be the village of Ghee'im'Oro should be a required field trip for all grade school students. Maybe then, hags would be treated with the respect we're due.

Before first light this morn, I brewed a special concoction and dropped it into the village well. No magick required, just straight-up hedge-witchery, baby! And it worked like a charm . . . well, almost.

It was probably the trampled dragon entrails that complicated matters. I had to guess the quantity because there was something spilled on that section of my potions tome. The tincture was supposed to turn the well water blood-red, but nothing happened. I gave it up as a lost cause until I saw a field worker run by sporting bright scarlet skin.

Instead of turning the water red, it seems my potion turned whatever drank the water red. I say "whatever" because as I was flying around, I saw a rather handsome cherry-red cow with a milkmaid lying under it in a spilled bucket of pink milk. She must have fainted. They're usually hardier than that. I'm sure she'll be fine.

Ah, nostalgia. It hit me then that this was my last panic-inducing act of chaos in the village. I admit, my eyes were misty. I stuck around long enough to soak up the bedlam and then headed to Aestradorra for my appointment.

There was an extra zip in my broom and twinkle in my eye as I flew. The trees, fields, and lakes softened into a patchwork of colours far below, and I suddenly realized how fortunate I was to have invested in a palandar-wood broom after graduation.

My parents scoffed at the expense, saying the higher magick retention was an unnecessary extravagance. My father tried to argue it wasn't safe because he felt the wood hadn't been thoroughly tested. Sometimes he's too traditional for his own good. I'm glad I didn't listen. At least it'll be a while before I have to worry about recharging it.

Surprisingly, the meeting with my union employment counsellor went well. She's an interesting sort—a sentient octopus named Ouleah who sits in a small pool of water behind a desk made of living coral. She's pleasant, thorough, and seems quite efficient, except for the falling asleep part. Our meeting took forever. She nodded off in the middle of handing me a form to fill out (a decidedly damp parchment which I hung on the back of my chair to dry), asking me what I considered my strongest asset to be, stamping three parchments of some description for my file, and offering me a steaming cup of tea (which thankfully ended up on the floor, not on my lap).

She also gestures excessively while talking. Carrying on a conversation with someone who's overly gesture-y with two hands can be daunting, trying to keep track of eight flailing tentacles is downright overwhelming . . . and messy. I left sopping wet. When I eventually left, that is.

Ouleah was sympathetic about my magick burnout. She said I wasn't the first witch this had happened to and recommended I contact a support group if the drought continued much longer.

There is one major (as in *major*-major) issue she brought to my attention: my Adept ceremony is in a little over one season cycle! I had no idea almost nine moons had passed since I graduated and went to work in the village. How time flies when you are busy hexing. And now, by Kyamites' crippling flatulence, I am in trouble!

To become a full union member and work as a professional witch, I need to have both an employer and mentor swear an oath that my craft practice is in good standing. The union requirements state that, "A witch must work for an employer over one complete season cycle." There is no wiggle room. The time can't be split between different employers. And there certainly can't be any breaks.

If I don't find steady employment within the next three moons, I won't be eligible to attend my Adept ceremony and I can kiss my career goodbye. No one respects, let alone hires, a witch who fails their Adept rites. I'll be the laughingstock of my graduating class, the loser of my family, and I'll have to pay to retake my last two semesters of college. The pain doesn't end there either. I'll also have to wait another two season cycles before I'm eligible for the next Adept ceremony.

I can't even begin to imagine the horror of explaining all this to my parents. My parents, who graduated top of their classes and passed every rite as easily as thread gathers on the Fates' spindle.

To make matters worse, now I need to find a position for a witch with no magick. Despite the absurdity of that notion, Ouleah thought it was possible. I hope she wasn't pretending to be optimistic. She did warn me that such placements were geared toward junior-level Apprentices—meaning they won't pay well—but that is the least of my worries right now.

I told her I'd take anything, which seemed to cheer her up. It did the opposite for me. The desperation of my situation hadn't truly sunk in until I heard those words come from my mouth. I can't go home to my parents like this. I'd have to explain what I did at the pub and what it might cost me. The thought is like a red-hot blacksmith's vise clamped around my innards.

All I ever wanted to be was a village hag. As a child, I would follow ours around in awe. But, in the joy of my triumph and cursed youthful ignorance, it never occurred that I could lose the ability to weave hag illusions around my thrice-blasted unsuitable form.

As angry as I am, I can't fault the villagers for firing me. They were right. Without a sure way to hide my curvy, bright-skinned youth, even I have to admit I'm not suitable. A hag's appearance is too vital a part of the role. If only I was naturally boney and pale! It would be so much easier to don the guise of a hag with some prosthetics, carefully applied makeup, and artful acting.

No. My anger now rests with myself, where it belongs. I spent six season cycles immersed in intense training to become a professional witch, landed my dream job right out of college, spent seven glorious moons as a hag, and then botched everything in the time it takes a handful of sand to fall through

my fingers. Hester, you are a bloody fool.
Where do I go from here?

Soldias, Wolf Moon 21, 209

IT HAS BEEN a few suns since I last wrote because a lot has happened.

I bunked in Aestradorra at an inexpensive but respectable inn called The Hunter's Hofas. I spent most of my free time trying to distract myself from depression by wandering the twisting lanes of the metropolis. Returning to my college town churned up an odd mix of feelings. The landmarks, the crowds, and the atmosphere of the place brought back many memories—some good, some not so good.

I spent an eventide with Magda, not demolishing a tavern for once. It was lovely to see her again, though I wished it were under better circumstances. I felt like such a dunce telling her what happened in the village and my subsequent predicament with our Adept rites. Her life is so together and drama free.

Thankfully, I didn't have much downtime to fill. Ouleah scryed me about a new opportunity that opened up in a midland forest. I don't care how soaked I was after our meeting or how many times she fell asleep on me, that beautiful tentacled soul is a lifesaver!

I am now the Assistant Witch at a Gingerbread Hut. There's only four such huts for unwanted or lost children. I've never heard of positions in any of them becoming available before. My luck has finally turned.

As suspected, the pay is abysmal, but I'm not complaining. It's a job! My worries about only having three moons to find employment were all for naught. Go figure. Now, I just have to stay here for one season cycle and I'll be set for the Adept rites. It seems like a long time, but I spent almost that long in the village and the suns just flew by. After that, hopefully my magick will have returned and I can look for better-paying employment.

Room and board is included, such as it is, which is good because my savings are meagre and I'm sure I couldn't afford three meals a sun on this wage, even if I went back to eating as badly as I did in college. The food is hearty, but a bit too rustic for me. There are only so many suns in a row I can stomach boiled bratwurst and gingerbread.

I'm also not used to having a roommate, let alone one who snores like an apple-drunk bull moose in mating season. It's no wonder pieces of the hut collapse "for no apparent reason" (her words). The maintenance on this place is daunting. I can see why she needs an assistant.

Mostly what I'm expected to do is bake, so at least I'm safe on the no-magick front. The old witch, Althea, won't even let me feed the kids—like it takes some kind of special skill to toss gingerbread cut offs and sweets into their rooms. Sheesh.

Althea's pretty cool otherwise. She's a true, old-school, shrivelled-up, crabby crone, full of wicked cackles and sinister schemes. She terrifies the kids who sneak illicit nibbles off her hut. Of the many effective hexes and threats I've heard so far, my favourite was when she promised to bake this one kid into the walls if she caught him at it again. Poetry in motion. She's been at this job for a hundred and forty season cycles, so I should be able to learn a lot from her.

I've already discovered that I need to be careful around the ovens. Apparently, the last assistant accidently fell into one and it didn't end well for him. I also found out, the hard way, that wearing robes with droopy sleeves is a bad idea. Althea cooks naked. Says it cuts the cleanup time in half. I think I'll keep my robes on (minus the dramatic sleeves). I'd rather have a burnt bodice than a singed nipple.

The baking is more challenging than I anticipated. Keeping the huge wood-burning ovens heated evenly is next to impossible. So far, I've either burnt or undercooked everything. And there are endless shapes and toppings and presses and ingredients for the hut pieces. It's hard to keep them all straight, especially when the sole hint as to what piece is needed is a half-eaten hunk of soggy gingerbread or a random hole in the wall.

Althea saw how lost I was and brought out a massive leather-bound tome (volume One of Seven). It must have been at least five inches thick. Turns out, the hut has a blueprint. A dense, confusing, multi-volume blueprint. It breaks the structure down into oven-sized pieces with maps, diagrams, dimensions, recommended ingredients, approved substitutions, baking times . . . I'd go on, but after a while of staring at the thing, my eyes gave out. I'm not even sure I understand how the indexing system works. How am I supposed to bake a particular piece if I can't even figure out how to look it up?

And there's no way I can guesstimate anything. The recipes change based on whether the piece is external or internal, whether it's supportive or decorative, whether it's laid vertically or horizontally. And don't get me started on how to colour match decorative details.

Althea doesn't understand my confusion because she's done the baking for so long. She thinks I'm a complete idiot.

Apart from zapping ready-made meals and char-boiling the occasional stew in my cauldron, I don't cook much. Like most modern witches, if I want a decent meal, I go out. I didn't exactly tell my new boss that. I glossed over my cooking skills in the interview. Actually, I just replaced it with my potion brewing experience, which I figured was essentially the same—transferable skill sets and all. Turns out, not so much.

For now, I'm job shadowing as Althea fixes the hut, but I can tell she's eager to get back to dealing with the kids. They do seem to be piling up. She considers keeping them in line and finding them permanent homes advanced tasks, so it'll be a while before she trains me to handle that.

After my last few suns, I could be discouraged, but I'm going to view this as an opportunity to tap into expertise that has thus far remained hidden. Who knows? Maybe there's a gourmet chef trapped inside me.

I'm going to start by studying the blueprints. Maybe they'll make sense if I stare at them long enough.

Moondias, Wolf Moon 22, 209

MY FAMILIAR ARRIVED this morn and I'm still bristling. So is he, though I'm not sure cockroaches can bristle.

Before I had a chance to introduce Herman, the old witch mistook him for common vermin (a reasonable mistake) and tried to drop a pan on him. When I explained who he was, she apologized for the misunderstanding . . . once she stopped laughing.

Herman was not amused and has taken to hissing whenever he sees Althea. I doubt he will ever forgive the affront to his dignity.

So far, all he's done is eat everything in sight and poo all over my stuff. I had to bake the same piece three times because the little jerk decided to express his displeasure all over it . . . repeatedly. And this eventide I found that he had expressed himself all over my pillow.

I don't understand how I ended up with a cockroach. The union gave us a list of approved familiars with their accreditation package before we graduated, but I don't remember "cockroach" being an option. I'll have to find the handout and double check. I'm doubly suspicious because he's not even a remotely witchy creepy-crawly (there are many decent ones like tarantulas and scorpions on the list).

There's been rumblings in our community since I was a young witchling about how the familiar assignment process has become corrupted. The union tries to hide the fact that they use them as a hierarchical totem of merit, but most of us know better. Piss off the wrong person, and you're screwed. I wonder who has it out for me?

Herman is clearly meant as an insult. A very public one. "Look at that witch. She must really suck. Her familiar isn't even ranked."

From the way Herman acts, you'd think the assignment was an insult to him. I suppose it could be worse. I could have ended up with a dung beetle.

Herman hasn't said one nice thing since he came. He won't stop complaining about where we live. I guess he's more used to a metropolis. The "ass-end of nowhere" (as he refers to this forest) doesn't appeal.

You'd think the countryside would offer endless opportunities for a cockroach. There's ample rotting vegetation to wallow in and lots of nooks and crannies to explore. And yet, he refuses to go outside. Says too many dangerous creatures are lurking.

If you ask me, the average metropolis would be worse. Thousands of grumpy people trying to coexist in a warren of closely-packed passages and residences, most of whom would react the same if a roach crossed their path. *Smack. Splat.*

Unfortunately, my housebound familiar is also easily bored. I caught him eating the kitchen table. Actually, I didn't so much catch him as put a book on the table and witness its collapse. I deduced the rest from the neat cockroach sized holes in the gingerbread legs— just enough to compromise the structure, but not so many that you'd notice them on a

cursory glance.

He's going to get me fired if he keeps this up and I *cannot* let that happen! I promised Althea that I would replace the table, and she whipped out another set of tomes (volumes One through Four) describing how to construct gingerbread furnishings. How many books can there be about gingerbread? I mean, come on!

It took me most of this sun to bake it. I followed the recipe and instructions as best I could, but Herman kept distracting me with unsolicited advice. He claims to know about cooking from his stint as a chef's assistant—said nothing left the kitchen if he hadn't first tasted and approved it.

I wasted a fair amount of time shooing him off the pages. He has a knack of sitting right where I'm reading. And pooing. That's definitely one of his talents. Possibly, the only one. I stared at this one section of text for the longest time, trying to identify the language, only to discover when I moved the book that he had left a trail of poo across the words. It was slightly more understandable after that.

I eventually managed to shut him up by asking him to read out the instructions while I baked and assembled. We worked pretty well together after that. Maybe we just need time to get used to each other.

The new table seems sturdy, though it's heavier than the old one and its surface is quite tacky. Hopefully that will decrease once it's fully dried. Herman claims it should be better than the old one because of the extra binding agent he added. Somewhere, in the back of my mind while I was mixing, I knew beetle spittle shouldn't be in the list of ingredients, but I was too tired to argue.

Guess we'll see.

Tydias, Storm Moon 2, 209

NOTHING MUCH TO report over the past while, except lots of baking and reading. It's like being in college again, only more boring and with worse food (didn't think that was possible).

Most of Althea's tomes are old. I mean, really oooold. The ink is faded (though from the smell and what's left of the colour, I believe some passages were written with something of a more biological origin), the parchment is foxed and delicate, and the handwriting is scrawled to a degree I suspect a number of the contributors must have been writing it on their deathbed. I'm going to need to see a hedge witch for sight correction soon.

One tome is even written in an obscure language. I tried to ask Althea about it, but she just told me to use a translation spell. I think she's forgotten that I'm sans magick. I dropped the subject. If nobody's bothered to translate it in however many hundreds of season cycles it's been around, how important can it be? It's probably just another recipe book and I have more than enough of those.

I'm not even certain where she keeps them. The hut isn't big enough to hold the inexhaustible volumes that keep materializing. She stores the baking supplies in the first basement and the kids' rooms are in the second basement. Maybe there's a third basement? If so, perhaps there's room for me to put a cot down there. Althea's snoring and the subsequent lack of sleep is starting to get to me. My temper is shorter than usual.

It doesn't help that Althea orders me around like a first moon Apprentice and then, whenever I break down and ask for help, all she says is, "Look it up." She treats her familiar's meals with more respect (never thought I'd feel lower than a mealworm). Oh, that's another thing. Her familiar doesn't get along with Herman.

If Sophie was just a regular bat, I could understand there being confusion about whether Herman was food or not. He is a pest in every sense of the word. But she's *not* a normal bat. She's a familiar and bloody well knows that Herman is one too. And yet, she persists in terrorizing him.

Herman keeps muttering about job safety regulation breaches. He left a section of the union policy manual open on my scry mirror documenting how and when to report an antagonistic workplace environment. I managed to close it before Althea saw it. I think. I've spoken to him about how important it is that I keep my position here, but I fear my pleas are ignored.

He still refuses to go outside, and now he's moaning about not being able to stay inside because Sophie is Hel-bent on making him bat brunch. I don't think she actually would, and I told him as much, but he disagrees. According to him, all bats are devious brutes.

I don't know what to do about Sophie. I tried talking to Althea about her companion's behaviour, but all she did was laugh and say, "They do have their little games." I told her that Sophie's "game" wasn't one Herman wanted to play, but she laughed that off too.

I also caught Althea using my toothbrush this morn. She didn't even bother to be sneaky about it. Given my precarious employment situation, I decided not to say anything. I have a spare in my broom bag. I'll make sure to keep it out of sight from now on.

Althea spent a good portion of this sun rummaging through an old chest, taking out all manner of strange garments, and trying them on. One of them was an odd kind of shirt, covered with garish flowers. I can't fathom what purpose she has for it.

No self-respecting witch would be caught dead in such a thing. I got woozy just looking at it.

I'm starting to get an uncomfortable feeling that something is up, but the old witch is staying mum and I know better than to ask her about it.

There is one positive thing that happened recently. The table Herman and I made is still sound, albeit stickier than I'd like. At least we managed to do something right.

Cerridias, Storm Moon 11, 209

Well, Hephaestus's proverbial anvil has dropped and it has landed squarely on me. I awoke this morn to find a note from Althea stuck to the kitchen table . . . and I do mean stuck. That parchment is not coming off.

It read:

Gone to Hawaii. Maintenance instructions in the [illegible] [illegible] [illegible]. Back in ½ moon. Don't screw up.

No "please." No "thank you." Just "don't screw up." Without those thoughtful words, I might have botched everything. But now, I'm safe for sure.

What was she thinking? I'd like to believe it means she has confidence in my ability, but I know that isn't the case. I can barely bake basic bricks, let alone the numerous other hut pieces. So far, the table is my greatest accomplishment, and I'm starting to worry there might be something wrong with it. It shouldn't still be this sticky.

What am I going to do? I can't even read part of the note she left, though the characters do seem vaguely familiar.

It took me a while to find out where Hawaii is. It's a popular Outerplane vacation spot where people go to cook their skin and stare at what can generously be described as the island's occasional flatulence and fiery reflux. What is the appeal? It's not as if Althea doesn't experience an abundance of personal flatulence. And she certainly doesn't seem that excited when I join in. Maybe it's different when it comes out of the ground?

Most witches wouldn't consider visiting the Outerplane because it's a Level Seven Null Zone. Elementals are rare and our spells don't work properly, if at all. This is of particular note for me at the moment because it also means communicating with someone on the Outerplane is problematic. Especially when you don't have contact information for scrying, which Althea conveniently failed to leave.

If something goes wrong, I have no way to reach her. Pixies charge an exorbitant long-distance fee for Outerplane message deliveries, and air elementals need specific arrival coordinates— which wouldn't be a problem if I was familiar with the area she's visiting (I'm not) or could cast a location spell (I can't). I'm totally on my own. Well, sort of.

That's really the worst part. Sophie didn't go. Althea told her bats weren't allowed in Hawaii without something called "vaccinations" and a "quarantine period." Personally, I think she made it up to get time away from the little terror. Sophie's in a right snit about the whole thing, not that she has even a passing acquaintance with a good mood as far as I've seen.

What is it with familiars? Herman and Sophie seem to go out of their way to disrupt what I'm doing. I thought familiars were supposed to be helpful.

I don't know how much longer my sanity can withstand Herman, let alone Herman and Sophie together. I went to open the basement door this morn and the damn thing disintegrated as soon as I touched it. It's Herman's fault. All he does is eat. I've put out piles of gingerbread rejects for him, but he isn't interested.

If he keeps this up, the hut will be a pile of rubble by the time Althea gets back. I'm going to have enough trouble fixing it as it is.

The pressure is really starting to get to me and this was just my first sun alone. I should be sleeping, but every time I lie down, I start thinking about everything I need to do and everything that could go wrong.

If I fail at this and Althea fires me, what are the chances of

Ouleah finding another employer willing to take on a magickally-impaired witch? Not great. I was surprised she found this job. Then I'll have to move back in with my parents and endure their disappointed sighs and desperate advice about how to properly adult. Good goddess, what will they think of Herman? Their daughter couldn't even manage to get a normal familiar.

Freydias, Storm Moon 12, 209

I HATE GINGERBREAD. That is all.

Pandias, Storm Moon 13, 209

Dear Magda,

How are you? Are you still enjoying working for the Magick Emporium's Hexes and Vexes Division? You must love being somewhere you can make a difference. Nothing makes a wrongee feel better than inflicting a few well-placed boils on the wronger. You've always been such a giving person. I knew you'd end up doing something amazing.

You are probably wondering why I scribed a letter instead of scrying. Truth is, I'm broke. I need help and you have always been my truest friend.

My boss unexpectedly went on a vacation without leaving contact information, and I have no idea where she keeps the hut funds to cover our operating expenses. Certain events arose that required creative problem solving and I had to dip into my savings . . . actually, I exhausted my savings. I don't even have enough left to pay someone to recharge my scry mirror. (I won't go into how embarrassing it is to have to pay another witch to do something so basic. I'm sure you can imagine.)

Without going into too much detail, let's just say the Gingerbread Hut isn't all it was cracked up to be. Whoever thought it was a good idea to build an edible hut should be forced to work here for eternity. I can think of no more suitable punishment. Everything I own reeks of vanilla and sugar. It's disgusting.

A princess happened by the other morn. She looked pale and exhausted, so I offered her an apple, thinking she might be concerned that the gingerbread would affect her ability to fit into the ridiculous corset she was wearing. I must have said something wrong because she became quite upset and accused me of trying to murder her. Princesses! Always so dramatic.

The diet of fatty bratwurst, gingerbread, and frosting is certainly wreaking havoc with my figure. My robes are tight in all the wrong places and I don't think it's because they shrunk in the wash. My stress eating is out of control.

Also, I'm getting a toothache. The nearest tooth fairy is two suns away—I'm obviously not the only one who can't stand the noisy kids gallivanting around these parts. Ever see an overpopulated anthill with a spoiled apple beside it? Yeah, it's like that. The woods are crawling with the tiresome little twits; kids, that is, not ants. Someone must be importing them. I ran out of rooms a few suns ago and had to double bunk the last batch. I can't take in any more.

I tried everything I could think of to stop the kid gangs from tearing the hut apart (at their current rate, I have no hope of repairing the place before Althea gets back). I hung no-trespassing signs around the forest, laid a few skeletons around the hut clearing, and attached a poison symbol to the front door—all of which did nothing to dissuade the cheeky vandals. I even put out a "trespassers will be baked and used as building material" sign, but to no avail.

Then it hit me. This was like any other hostile invasion. What I needed was a strategy to prevent their advance across the clearing to the hut. I spent a sun scrying for supplies (which is how I depleted my mirror's charge). I'd forgotten all the wonderful things you can find in scry markets. Unfortunately, I also forgot that what you see isn't always what you get. I thought the festering snot beast was cheaper than it should have been. It turned out to be a miniature replica. Nicely painted though. In retrospect, the FSB was probably overkill. I managed to acquire a number of exploding cycadia scum pods, rodithium vitriolic creepers, and purple heathtrobe fungi—you remember, the bouncy ones we accidently planted in the school herb garden.

Long story short, the clearing is now sufficiently battle hardened. All I have to do is fix the existing hut damage before Althea gets back and my job should be safe.

The only downside is that everything was more expensive than anticipated. Delivery fees are astronomical out here.

I used the last of my funds to get this message to you. I know you'll help if you can. If you can't, I'll understand and make do with what's on hand.

Your best friend forever,

Hester Digitalis Wishbone

P.S. Sorry about the air elemental. Hope it didn't cause too much damage. I tried to hire a pixie, but all the union ones were too expensive and the only freelancer who responded ran afoul of a scum pod.

P.P.S. If you hear about a familiar being murdered, send bail. Another of the hut's walls is looking wobbly, and I'm not sure if it's because of Herman or the elemental's arrival and departure.

Moondias, Storm Moon 15, 209

I'M HUNKERED DOWN in the hut flipping through old issues of *The Burnished Cauldron* and *Modern Hag*, hoping to wait out the remainder of this Moondias without more serious incidents or injuries than I have already endured.

Moondias is a rest sun for good reason. No hag-born hex or pestilence can compete with its intrinsic malice. Witchy blessings and charms fall flat. One person's folly becomes a problem for everyone near and possibly far. And when those affected take steps to fix things, Moondias makes sure that doesn't happen. Thus, the curse passes, spreading as fast and wide as the most virulent of plagues.

Of all Moondiases I have survived, I really felt this one had potential to not be awful. Sophie took off two suns ago and hasn't been home since. She must be seriously miffed about Althea leaving her behind because she's never been gone for more than a night at a time. Herman and I have been enjoying the peace and some much-needed uninterrupted sleep. Hence my incautious optimism.

The first catastrophe hit before I even made it out of my cot. I awoke in a pool of sweat staring at the ceiling until my brain registered that a scum pod explosion had interrupted my usual stress-induced nightmare about leaky cauldrons. The explosion knocked down a wall I'm rebuilding and blew in the front door (which is now stuck to the table).

After burning my breakfast and wrestling my bowl, utensils, and sleeve off the kitchen table (it keeps getting stickier), I decided not to clear the rubble or attempt any reconstruction.

Herman, however, had other plans. He insisted it was too drafty with only three walls and that if I wouldn't fix it, he would. His strategy consisted of trying to eat his way through the wall debris, which predictably led to more collapses. I had to rescue him. Twice. Cockroaches have a very poor grasp of natural consequences.

So now, I am staring out at the forest where a wall used to be, hunched over my lap as I scribe, unable to use the kitchen table because a door and everything else is stuck to it. I will be very grateful to see the backside of this sun.

Tydias, Storm Moon 16, 209

LAST NIGHT WAS mercifully Sophie-free. I woke up this morn rested and ready to work. I spent some quality time baking bricks to fix the collapsed wall, hoping I might actually make some headway.

As I baked, a prickling sensation started at the base of my neck—the kind that happens when your body knows someone is watching but your brain hasn't caught on yet. I felt a presence, but couldn't tell what or where it was. Then my nose twitched and I knew something sinister was afoot.

It warned me just as I bent over to pull a rack of gingerbread bricks from the oven. This was the first batch I hadn't burnt and I was feeling rather proud. I turned around with deliberate slowness, certain someone or something was behind me but there was nothing.

Assuming my nose was on the fritz like my magick, I went back to work. I jumped slightly as it gave another great jerk. This time, I spun around quickly and caught a grey blur of movement outside the collapsed wall.

I threw the full tray I was holding at the opening out of shock, but there was nothing there. How I miss my magick, those blissful suns when I could conjure up an illusionary dragon to scare away my foes. Will I ever get used to this mundane existence? Will I have to?

I double-checked the clearing to make sure the hut's perimeter defences were active. They were. Then, I set out to find my scattered bricks. Thankfully, they had bounced nicely and were only minimally injured. I believe I've finally mastered the recipe!

As I gathered my little beauties, I kept my head down and surreptitiously examined the woods. There were a few areas of deeper shadow in the cloaked browns and greens. I could not make out any details.

I returned to the hut and kept half an eye on the shifting voids while I baked. They changed locations, sometimes closer, sometimes to one side, but always there.

Whoever or whatever they were, they never ventured into the clearing, so I logically assumed my intruder calming measures were keeping them at bay. That's the tricky thing about logic. Something can be perfectly logical, but also perfectly wrong.

I turned around after checking the oven temperature and found the answer to my uneasiness crouched on the counter. A gargoyle stared back at me as steadily as only a hunk of stone can.

There is a raw, primitive awareness born of fear and burned into our bones that takes over when our mind goes into shock. By completely bypassing mental processing, our body is usually able to respond more effectively to dangerous situations. I say "usually" because sometimes it backfires. At least that's what I choose to believe happened when the pathetically shrill scream burst from my lungs and I threw a handful of kelp essence.

Don't get me wrong. Kelp essence would have been an effective binding agent, if I had access to my magicks. And screaming can be a perfectly reasonable response to danger. It warns anyone near about a potential threat and lets them know that someone is in need of help. Unfortunately for me, the only relatively friendly being nearby was a cockroach, whose response to my cry for help was to leave a trail of excrement from one end of the hut to the other as he scuttled under my cot.

The gargoyle remained unmoved. My kelp essence harmlessly cascaded off his rocky face and down the carved lines of his limbs.

I felt around for anything resembling a weapon, but there are surprisingly few lethal tools in a baker's kitchen unless you want to viciously sift or whisk something. The best I could do was an old wooden rolling pin and a pot of caramelized sugar.

Aware that I'm not the most coordinated of witches, I decided against brandishing the molten sugar. I stepped forward and waved the rolling pin at the gargoyle. It stared impassively back at me as if it belonged in the hut, as if it had always been in that very spot on my counter and how dare I question its presence.

I glanced around, trying to think of a way to evict it, and noticed another one perched in the rafters. I looked back at the gargoyle on the counter and saw that there were now two. No whisper of sound, blur of movement, or tiniest displacement of air had betrayed the newcomer. Who knew something made of stone could be so silent and quick?

There was a fluttering noise near the collapsed wall, and closer inspection revealed a parchment tacked to one side of the opening. One of the counter dwellers had relocated to the kitchen table by the time I retrieved the note. Its previously impassive face was now a puzzled grimace as it stared at the door attached to the end.

To my dismay, the parchment turned out to be a Notice of Condemnation. It explained that the building commission had received a complaint about the state of the hut and had carried out an inspection.

My flinty interlopers suddenly made sense. They were building inspectors.

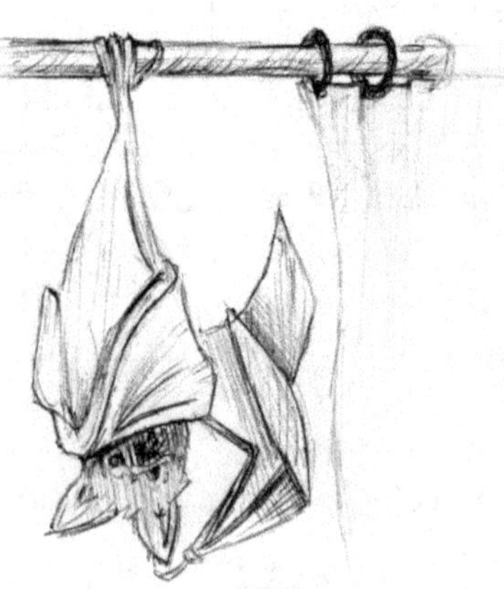

In retrospect, their career choice makes perfect sense. The little buggers are all over buildings in every metropolis.

Two of the three inspectors disappeared shortly after I read the notice. However, the one on the kitchen table doesn't appear inclined to follow his comrades. I hope it leaves soon. I don't think I'll be able to sleep, knowing it's there, crouching and staring and not blinking.

We also had another unwelcome arrival this eventide. Sophie came home. She won't say where she's been, but I smell fermented berries on her batty breath and she's fallen off her rafter twice.

The mini vacation hasn't improved her mood. She's just as ill-tempered and snarky as before. She keeps looking at the collapsed wall and snickering.

Herman unilaterally refused to come out from under my cot. This was a happy occurrence until I went to lie down and found myself sprawled on the floor. He must have gotten hungry during his self-imposed confinement. My only consolation is that I landed on him when the cot collapsed.

So now, I'm sleeping on the floor and need to find the blueprints and recipes for gingerbread cots. Could my life get any worse?

I hope Magda received my letter. I still haven't heard anything from her. Not being able to scry is very isolating.

Wendias, Storm Moon 17, 209

I STARTED THIS sun with every good intention, determined to keep my nose to the grindstone. Not that my nose needs sharpening or polishing per se, but I unearthed an old grindstone in the basement and decided it might enable me to sculpt some of my deformed gingerbread products. My output will vastly improve if I don't have to discard as many lopsided bricks, shingles, legs, etc. If I increase production, I can whip the hut back into shape in no time, or at least maintain some hope of fixing it before Althea's homecoming.

After I dragged the heavy stone up from the first basement (oh, how I long for the suns when I could cast levitation or conjure a handy imp butler), I started right in, re-shaping my pile of rejects.

It was slow going. Concentrating with a glaring gargoyle crouched in the centre of my workspace is difficult. I suspect he would leave if he could, but I think he's stuck to the table. In any case, he looks very disapproving. He must have been carved that way. His eyes had a slightly nervous wideness about them when I brought out the grinding stone, but that could have just been wishful thinking on my part.

Unfortunately, I have no choice but to use the kitchen table. I wasn't concentrating on what I was doing last eventide and accidently laid the pastry board on it to dry. That thing is not coming off. I tried to pry it loose with various knives, bars, and spatulas, but that was a monumentally bad plan. Now I have to figure out how to get those off as well.

Even with all the gingerbread dust flying around from my vigorous grinding this morn, the reek of kelp essence was overwhelming by mid-sun. That stuff does not age well. It's stuck in the inspector's nooks and crannies. I threw some buckets of water over him and hung pine boughs and cinnamon sticks from his ears (they were the only convenient outcropping to tie things to). It's hard to tell from his flinty expression, but I don't think I've improved his mood and I can't say the "eau de seaweed" has lessened.

Sophie discovered that the table is tacky and is amusing herself by dropping things onto it to see if they'll stick. Most of the items she's experimenting with are mine. *(NOTE: Add knickers to shopping list.)* Herman must have hidden himself well, because I don't see him stuck to the surface yet and I'm sure he's on the top of that winged hellion's hit list.

I stopped baking long enough to tie down everything that was important to me. It was a quick endeavour as my broom was the only thing of value not already stuck to the table.

It's hard to believe that this is my life. I had so many dreams, so many hopes. And now, I've got one pair of knickers, an errant cockroach, a chained broom, and the imminent threat of professional humiliation hanging over my head. Little did I know, this was just a taste of the troubles to come.

A swarm of irate storks descended on the hut shortly after mid-sun and took all the children. I wish they'd taken me too.

I asked under whose authority they were acting and they advised me to read the fine print on the Notice of Condemnation. Some minuscule lettering at the bottom, which I initially mistook as a streak left by a crash-landed aphid, stated that the occupants had one sun to vacate the premises. You'd think they'd make such a time sensitive condition more visible, but noooo.

They gave me no time to arrange alternate accommodations for the little tyrants (not that I even knew where to begin with that). All I could do was watch as the storks flew off with them.

It's my understanding that the kids will be returned to their parents. Given their past level of care at home, I have no doubt I'll see them again, but if Althea comes back before they do, I'm done for.

In order to remain on the property, I had to sign a form stating that I understood the premises was condemned. The last stork refused to leave until I set up a lean-to at the edge of the clearing and agreed to wear appropriate protective gear while working near the hut. I have no clue what type of gear that is, but I'm sure some creature will show up and fine me when I'm not wearing it.

ADDENDUM: Raining heavily this eventide. River running through lean-to. Very uncomfortable. Festering snot beast is not an inanimate model and appears to be water activated. FSB is also grumpy when woken. Moving back into hut.

Cerridias, Storm Moon 18, 209

THE FESTERING SNOT beast is an invaluable addition to my defensive perimeter. It can best be described as an enormous (the rain also stimulated significant growth), bipedal virus which zeros in on anything that moves and encases them in a snot cocoon. It's formidable, to say the least.

Owing to the recent monsoon conditions, there have been no child trespassers, but the FSB handily dealt with a gnome who was pilfering mushrooms from our garden. The only issue is that it either can't or won't differentiate between friends and foes. It's making excursions difficult, which exacerbates another major issue.

Our roof icing is disintegrating at an alarming rate. The hut looks like it's melting. According to the books, icing should be replaced every moon, but I just redid the south side and it's already half gone.

Herman saw me investigating ways to make the icing more water resistant and, in a rare flash of helpfulness, offered to assist me in developing a new recipe. Turns out, cockroaches exude water-impermeable grease when they are cold.

We experimented and came up with a concoction that nicely repels water. I taste-tested it and it's not too revolting. Admittedly, I'm not the best judge as I find regular icing disgusting, but with the kids gone, I'm the only game in town.

I only had a pinch of grease, so my test batch was small, but it was enough to ice one roof tile. I'll keep track of how well it holds up. Hopefully, it'll do the trick and I can approach Althea about investing in a tub of cockroach grease when she gets back.

ADDENDUM: The new icing recipe is a no-go. Cockroach grease is a very effective laxative. I am extremely uncomfortable. I don't even know where all this is coming from. It's not like I've been eating much lately. Yeesh. I can only imagine how awful the mess would be if the kids got at it.

NOTE: Scry the info imp once my mirror is recharged and see if it can find contact info for Prof. Bloodroot, the hedge witch who taught potion classes at Grimoire College. I believe her first name was Peuturella. See if she's interested in a partnership to patent the laxative icing formula.

Freydias, Storm Moon 19, 209

IF ANOTHER INFERNAL Demon ever shows up on my doorstep with an envelope marked "Defendant", I'm not only going to lodge it up the fiend's rear end, I'm going to personally shove the little devil up his supervisor's posterior.

Imagine waking up to a knock on your doorframe. You pull aside the tacked-up blanket where your door used to be, expecting to find an elemental bearing much-anticipated funds, and instead, a flaming jerk in a gaudy tie shoves a sheet of white-hot parchment in your face. I mean, come on. The letters were still aflame, for Goddess' sake.

The worst part is, Infernals sound threatening even when you don't understand what they're saying. And you know what they're saying must be important, otherwise someone wouldn't have hired them to stand there charring your doorframe. It was just dumb luck that the recent rainfall rendered the gingerbread damp enough to be flame retardant. Sadly, bats are not. Sophie is singed and seriously ticked off.

I tried to read the parchment, but all I could make out was *Defendant*, *the*, and *and*. I had the option of taking an Infernal language course in college, but I couldn't fathom what good it would do me. Nice one, Hester. Now, I can't even cast a measly translation spell (not that it makes Infernal that much more understandable, but it's better than nothing).

But, hey, I'm fluent in ancient Trakak—a dead language. That's sure to come in handy. Curse my short-sightedness. What was I thinking? Actually, I know exactly what I was thinking. I'm terrible with languages and needed a course I could coast through. It was a common tactic. Anyone learning a dead language was allowed to summon their own testers. It's amazing how pleased thousand-season-cycle old ghosts are to come back, even for one sun. Very good for the marks.

I've never heard of Infernals using a language other than their own, though they're perfectly capable. It's a calculated move so that you have to hire another Infernal to act on your behalf in negotiations. Once they're involved, nobody has any hope of figuring out what's happening. You inevitably end up with two or more demons, depending on how many parties are involved, furiously arguing with each other . . . or so their tone and manner suggests. For all you know, they're exchanging old family recipes.

Regrettably, festering snot beasts are not effective against demon intruders. Fire trumps snot. I'm sad to report that the FSB is no longer with us and my rodithium vitriolic creeper has thus far been unable to digest its remains. On the plus side, they are considered a cockroach delicacy (I suspect very little isn't). After Sophie's smoky departure, Herman ventured out from under my cot long enough to scamper under the expired FSB.

Nothing in my tactical flora buffer zone slowed the Infernal. There's a burnt trail leading right up to the hut and the jerk had

the gall to munch on a scum pod as he left. Tossed it into his mouth like a giant piece of popping candy.

I have no idea what to do about this Infernal situation. What did it want? Was I the intended recipient, or was it looking for Althea? The timing of her vacation suddenly seems suspicious.

I talked it all through with the gargoyle and haven't come up with any conclusions or solutions. Although it felt good to get my anxieties about what's happening out in the open, my stress level remains astronomical.

I've decided to name my stony guest Bob. He's a fantastic listener and I'm starting to appreciate his presence. At least he doesn't interject snide comments when I talk to him about my problems, unlike Herman.

My bowels seem to have settled, though even the thought of sugar sets them rumbling and the smell of it makes me dry heave. Hopefully, I'll get a better sleep this eventide. I spent most of last night wallowing in misery in the outhouse.

In the meantime, I will keep on, keeping on. Or rather, keep on, baking on. By the Triple Goddess' six breasts, I'm tired of slaving over a hot stove and digging icing out from under my fingernails.

NOTE: FSBs give cockroaches gas that would curl a Gorgon's hair. Herman has been banished to the lean-to for the remainder of this eventide.

Pandias, Storm Moon 21, 209

Well, I figured out why the Infernals were summoned. I received a letter this morn.

To: Gingerbread Hut Managing Witch

United Parents of Unsupervised Roaming Spawn (UPURS) has filed a lawsuit in the Infernal Court against the Gingerbread Hut and Staff (Gingerbread Hut et. al.) for contract violations regarding the substandard housing and unlawful return of children.

A verbal contract that children be provided accommodation in a safe and timely manner has existed between UPURS and Gingerbread Hut et. al. for two hundred season cycles. Due to building code violations, a full baker's dozen of children were returned to UPURS and members have incurred significant expenses.

Gingerbread Hut et. al. is directed to reimburse UPURS as outlined in the attached invoices (including but not limited to general maintenance, room, board, entertainment, Infernal fees, etc.) and for damages resulting from emotional distress and physical hardship.

Any delay in reimbursement will be met with strict

measures, up to and including fines and termination (assassin contract fees to be added at the time of court settlement).

Sincerely,
UPURS

This is the beginning of the end, for my career and possibly me. There's nothing quite like receiving a death threat thinly veiled in official language. And their group's name . . . it's possible I'm paranoid, but UPURS? Really? Well, I say UP THEIRS! The Gingerbread Hut provides a useful public service and all we get in return is grief. No "thank-you for the two hundred season cycles of service." No "can we help." Just "fix it or die." Same old, same old.

Despite how I feel about UPURS, I also know I have failed here. All I can do about it is keep patching the hut. If I get it back in shape, I can at least petition the storks to return the kids, but there's no way they'll be back before Althea. This isn't a mess that can be swept under a carpet and ignored.

I don't think I can save my job at this point, but maybe fixing the hut will make me feel like less of a loser and distract me from my crippling fear about the future. I still don't have access to my magicks, and after Althea gets back, I'll only have two moons to find another job.

One task I'm not looking forward to is disarming my defensive perimeter. It was an inspired plan, but perhaps it worked better in theory, than in practice.

And I really must do something about the kitchen table. Bob the gargoyle is still stuck to it and Sophie keeps filling up any bare spots she finds. I caught her affixing a pair of my stockings to the edge and using them as a slingshot. I don't think Bob appreciated being the subject of her target practice.

Herman also lost a leg on the table while evading his dive-bombing tormentor. He doesn't seem overly upset about it, more irritated. I don't have enough magick to re-grow it, or even give him the use of an illusionary leg. Luckily, he has a natural excess of them and it's not hindering his movement too much.

Ooo . . . interesting thought. When/if I get my magick back, I could cast a transmutation spell and transform Herman into something less buggy. That would solve his leg loss and my cockroach issues in one fell swoop. I remember there being rules about not altering your familiar to look like another type of familiar (especially one in a higher tier, which they all are since cockroach isn't even on a tier), but I don't remember if there are rules about turning them into creatures that aren't on the union's approved list. Interesting. Definitely warrants further investigation.

The only good thing that happened this sun is that the same elemental who brought the UPURS correspondence also brought a much-needed care package from Magda. She is such a good friend. She sent enough coin to recharge my scry mirror and added in a few extra goodies. I've never been so happy to see spiced grasshopper poppers and kartak larva tea. It's the small things that bring the greatest comfort. That, and actually being able to call for help in an emergency.

Moondias, Storm Moon 22, 209

Sooo, I'm writing this entry from the job bank waiting room. Big surprise.

As much as I tried to ignore it, I was not cut out for the Gingerbread Hut. That's what happens when you're desperate and take the first job that comes up. Crappy thing is, I'm still desperate. More so, actually.

I spent my last sun in a whirlwind baking binge. It was all gingerbread, all the time. I even managed to repair the hut enough to pass a building inspection. Having Bob around proved quite handy.

Then this morn an albino raven flew over me seven times and dropped a dead frog on my head. You know things are about to get real when that happens.

The portent became clear once Althea showed up. She swooped in before I could finish dismantling my defensive perimeter and landed on a scum pod. It's a good thing the building inspection forms were already submitted, because she made another hole in the wall.

She also managed to get herself stuck to the kitchen table. I even moved the damn thing out of the way, or so I thought. After trying my best at candy coatings to mask its stickiness and failing, I gave up and stuck it in a corner, literally. It was a little-used corner. Bob seemed right at home and I thought it would be safer. I chose wrong. The only luck I seem to have is bad.

NOTE: Try to recreate the recipe Herman and I used to make the table. If I can, and its glue-like properties hold true, remember to talk to Peuturella about that formula as well as the icing laxative.

Thanks to Magda, I was at least able to scry an emergency crew to help with Althea. I barely managed to disarm the rest of my anti-intruder measures before they arrived.

Althea could have attempted to be understanding, but no. She didn't even ask if I was okay or how things had gone while she was away. Admittedly, she was having a hard time talking as she was stuck face first to the table, but she never really tried.

Things caught a severe downdraft from there. Althea saw a somewhat inflammatory letter I received from a group of environmentalists, thanks to Sophie, who stuck it to the table in front of her nose. They were upset about me introducing invasive flora to the local ecosystem.

I had ignored the note, as there were more immediate concerns and I had no idea who this group was, but Althea was well acquainted with them. Turns out, she's on their board of directors and the project head for their renewable housing and recycling initiatives. She's even won awards.

Sophie was ecstatic to have Althea home, mostly because she was eager to rat me out. She told Althea everything that happened, glossing over all my hard work to rectify things and exaggerating anything that didn't go as planned. I tried to explain things properly when Sophie became overly creative in her recollections, but that just stoked the witch's irritation. She cast a silence spell on me, so all I could do was listen to the traitorous winged menace skewer me.

I did glean one interesting tidbit. Sophie is the one who started this whole mess by informing the building inspectors. I should have known.

I accept responsibility for my good-intentioned, but ultimately ill-advised defensive perimeter, but I'm not solely responsible for this disaster. My boss abandoned me after minimal training and her assistant, who could have helped, did everything but. Getting the building inspectors involved directly led to the stork guard reclaiming the children, and then the

Infernals and environmentalists jumped into the action and . . . *aargh*!

Well, it looks as though my writing time is at an end. I've just been summoned into the employment counsellor's office. I was smart this time—I brought a graphite shard so my signature won't bleed on the wet parchment and I wore my traveling cloak. Any splashes should roll right off. Here's hoping my intrepid eight-limbed union representative can find me a more suitable job.

TECHNICALLY, I'M STILL in my meeting but I have to do something while Ouleah naps. I don't want to wake her up prematurely in case I get slapped (eight times) for my trouble. She can be disoriented when she first comes to.

The good news is, she's positive she can find me a new job. The bad news is, she seemed positive last time and that didn't work out so well. I think she might be one of those types that are positive about everything. I wouldn't be surprised if she could find something good to say about being swallowed by a regurgitating aktar (because there's nothing like being eaten, partially digested, and thrown up ten times before dying).

I don't know how to take her. She was hanging from the ceiling when I came in. I had no idea octopodes were so agile out of water. Having suction pads and eight arms would be useful, but I can barely manage my two at the best of times. I can only imagine how clumsy I'd be with another six to organize.

Oh. She's back. And she's picked up the conversation right where she left off. I had no idea what was going on before, and I still have no idea. So much for *her* being disoriented!

ADDENDUM: Weirdness abounds! While I was talking to Ouleah, I noticed a gargoyle sitting on the balcony outside her window. I know it's Bob because he still has the pine boughs and cinnamon sticks looped around his ears. He disappeared after the emergency crew used their special Benuverium slime solvent to release him from the table, so I figured he was long gone. I wonder what's up with his sudden reappearance.

Tydias, Storm Moon 23, 209

I SPENT LAST night at the cheapest inn Aestradorra has to offer,
The Balding Bull. It's all I could afford. And by that, I mean I
have no coin, so I agreed to clean the second floor and muck out
the stable twice a sun in exchange for a room. And by room, I
mean closet. Seriously. I'm sleeping with buckets and brooms,
and it's so small I have to fold myself into the fetal position to lie
down. Not that I wouldn't end up like that anyway. It's freezing
at night.

Herman got so cold he asked if I wanted to harvest his
grease. I did. The smell of it still makes my nether region seize
up, but another night or two of this and I'll have enough to
make a small batch of laxative icing to send to Peuturella.

So far this morn, I've finished the stables, barely, and am
taking a short break before I start on the rooms. I miss magick.
There's no mundane way to add flair while raking hay, cleaning
troughs, scooping feed, and shovelling manure. It's all exactly as
glamorous and exciting as it sounds. On the plus side, I did get
to top up my excrement-based spell components.

On the not so plus side, I'm not great with animals. It took
me half the morn just to coax their geriatric milk cow out of its
stall. That thing was stubborn . . . and heavy. I tried to get
behind it and shove it out of the paddock, but the beast sat on

me.

Oh, and I think I might be allergic to hay. My nose is sniffly and there's a constant tickle in my throat.

NOTE: Scry Magda ASAP and see if she can put me up until I hear back from the employment counsellor.

People are pigs. No, people are worse than pigs. I've seen tidier sties than the rooms I cleaned. It was so bad, Herman felt right at home. Said he hadn't been anywhere that snug since his youth in a metropolis called Nooyork. His family had a place in an alley behind a restaurant.

I wasn't familiar with Nooyork so I asked where it was and, in his exuberance, he let slip that it was in the Outerplane. He clammed up as soon as I enquired whether he had temporarily lived in the Outerplane or if he was originally from there.

His cagy reaction doesn't prove my suspicion that he's not native to this plane, but it certainly indicates a need for further investigation. If he is an Outerplane native, it means the Witch's Union is outsourcing for familiars. They aren't supposed to do that.

I have half a mind to report this to Althea's environmentalist group. If they were up in arms about my intruder calming flora, surely they would be interested in a major organization like WU introducing off-world fauna. I guarantee they'd be concerned if they met Herman. It doesn't take long to see how much damage he's capable of. Problem is, how do I stop Althea from discovering who the tipoff is from? It's a conundrum. And I'm getting ahead of myself, as usual.

NOTE: See if Magda can magickally determine whether Herman is from here or not.

The good news from this eventide is that I have eliminated any worries of hay allergies. The bad news is that I'm getting sick. I've caught some kind of mucus plague. Yay, me. My nose is a fountain. Even Herman is keeping his distance. That cow had better follow his example next morn or by the moon's tides, I will . . . oh, who am I kidding. In my state, the worst I could do is sneeze all over it, and I doubt that would make much of an impression. *Bah!*

To top everything off, I haven't been able to contact Magda. She must be out or something. I think I got through once, but her asp must have answered the scry because all I saw was a black blur and a tongue.

Familiars! They aren't remotely helpful. Or sympathetic. Herman refused to come into our closet this eventide. Said he'd prefer to sleep on his own. I would be hurt that a cockroach rejected my company, but I don't have the energy.

I only have enough coin to buy meals for another two suns. If Ouleah doesn't find me a job soon, I'll have to scry my parents, and that's a conversation I'd prefer to avoid. The last time we spoke, I was happily working as a village hag. I can already hear Mom tsk-tsking—like she's dismayed that I messed up, but not surprised. There's nothing I hate more. Especially when I know she's right.

Wendias, Storm Moon 24, 209

MAGDA RESCUED ME from having to scry my parents! I'd be so lost without her. I hope I can return all her favours soon.

I finally got a scry through at mid-sun and she said she was happy to have me stay at her place for a while. It's a good thing, too. My nose was so runny this morn I had to stuff cottonweed up my nostrils so I could finish my chores. I was leaking more than The Balding Bull Inn's balding mop.

As soon as I arrived at Magda's apartment, she bundled me onto her couch with a thick woollen blanket, surrounded me with wrapped hot rocks, and whipped up a kettle of her special tea. I remember it well from college. I used to come down with some kind of plague every time Justin and I fought or finals rolled around. Must be a stress thing. No wonder I'm laid low now. There's enough stress in my life to choke a hinge-jawed nether cat.

The tea slowed my mucus production and reduced the crippling iron-bar-rammed-though-all-my-joints pain to a bearable throb. She even added two fermented ghoul eyes. After that, I didn't care so much that it hurt to breathe or that my life sucks FSB butt.

Which reminds me: I was a titch worried that I might have caught this snot disease from the FSB, but Magda looked it up

in one of her many Bestiaries and said it's not possible. Phew!

She has the most impressive personal library of anyone I know. Every wall in her apartment has at least one over-stuffed bookcase. She says she needs them for reference when she's mixing her potions and elixirs, but I know the truth. She's a total nerd and I love her for it.

Her concoctions were always the best in our classes. Actually, they were the best in the whole college. By the time we graduated, she was being courted by the Hedge Witch faculty and several big companies specializing in enchantments and hexes. She's a genius, though she'd never admit it.

I'm glad she didn't go down the Hedge Witch path. She would have been in college for another four season-cycles and then had to work as an Initiate for another two. Her nose would have been so deeply buried in her tomes that I wouldn't have seen her in all that time. I know these thoughts are purely selfish and I'm okay with that. Witches need their best friends. Especially this one. Especially right now.

She must have negotiated a wicked contract with the Magick Emporium, because her apartment is amazing. There's not much space, but I think that's due to all the stuff she's crammed in. If I travelled as heavy as Magda, I'd need a barge to get around instead of a broom.

The neighbourhood is nice too. It's just outside Aestradorra's core, so it's a short broom ride to anywhere worth going and there are a couple of parks nearby for ritual gatherings.

Which reminds me, I've been neglecting my rituals of late and must rectify that. I'm sure Magda will get me back into practice. Althea never once invited me to join her for so much as a simple full moon ritual. She must have been a solitary. I lean that way myself, having a more reclusive nature than most witches, but I do enjoy group rituals once in a while. It's a different kind of energy.

There's so much I want to talk to Magda about, but every time I speak more than three words, it ends in a coughing fit and I have to go pee.

I'm beyond relieved to be here. The inn was horrible. Herman wasn't happy about leaving, but then he complains about everything. At least he seems to be coexisting with Magda's familiar better than he did with Sophie.

Poor Magda is still having a hard time due to her snake phobia. It doesn't help that her asp seems to enjoy popping out of random places. I would think her name was AAAAAAAAAAAAAAA if she hadn't paused her game of hide-and-seek to tell me it was Missera.

Magda's familiar also has a poor grasp of personal space. I jolted awake from a nap and found her dangling off a lantern above me, an inch from my face. In fact, I suspect I woke up because Missera's flitty little tongue was tickling my nose.

On a side note, snakes don't blink. I wish I had known that before I made a fool of myself trying to stare her down. Trust me to find out the hard way that winning a staring contest with an asp is impossible.

Herman may not be the most prestigious of familiars, or even a recognized one as far as I can tell, but at least he doesn't go out of his way to scare the crap out of me. I haven't seen Magda this twitchy since she started dating.

Not that her nervousness was unwarranted. It is how we determined blind dates should never be attempted on a full moon. Let's just say her companion turned out to be furrier and toothier than expected. There's only so much gnawing a girl is willing to put up with, especially on a first date.

Cerridias, Storm Moon 25, 209

I RECEIVED A scry from my amazing employment counsellor this morn. She found me another job! Crisis averted.

Working at Moonbrews won't be exciting, seeing as most of my co-workers are in their first term at Grimoire College, but I'm not in a position to be picky. Staying long enough to be eligible for my Adept rites and making a living income, however lean, are all that matters. I'll just have to ignore the fact that I won't even be able to afford the crappy potions I'm mixing.

So much for my up-and-coming star on the hag track. Manual labour it is. If I think too long about it all, I get an ache in my chest and my mind starts whispering horrible things. If this is where I'm at, can I even still call myself a witch? And if I'm not a witch, what am I? It's all I've ever wanted. I'm lost.

No. I must not go down that path. Not yet. If I can salvage my Adept rites, give myself time to heal whatever is blocking my magicks . . . maybe, maybe I can come back from this downward spiral. I just need to keep slogging on.

I visited the Moonbrews franchise right away and met with the manager. Andreas is all right. He's a typical hyper-positive, sales-driven, micromanaging type, but after being abandoned by Althea, I might appreciate a more diligent supervisor.

I was upfront about my loss of magick and he assured me it

wouldn't be a problem. There are set recipes for all the brews they offer and the ingredients come pre-enchanted. All I have to do is mix them up and serve customers quickly and with a scowl. Customer service is very important. Maintaining a scowl through an entire shift will take a concerted effort. Sadly, my natural resting face has been described as "cheerful" and "pleasant". *Ugh*!

They were super busy, so Andreas put me to work right then and there. I am now an official Brew Master in training. I spent most of this sun with Teagan, an Apprentice witch who's been there for eight moons. She picks up shifts whenever she doesn't have class to help pay her tuition fees. Smart. Her student loan will be much more manageable than mine.

Which reminds me—I'll be getting a payment notice soon. Sigh. I'll have to defer it to next moon. There's no way I can pay it, get an apartment, and feed myself, let alone reimburse Magda for her loan.

Anyway, after being at Moonbrews for a sun, I can confirm that the work is okay. It would be boring but the brisk pace keeps things interesting enough. I should have no trouble learning the recipes. They're simple compared to the Gingerbread Hut nightmare. And, although I wasn't able to talk much because my voice quit halfway through my shift, the co-workers I met seemed nice. Teagan is overly energetic at times, but at least she's eager to help me learn.

Health-wise, I feel better this eventide, though I'm flat-out exhausted. My feet ached before my shift, but after standing on them all sun, they're on fire. I have another shift next morn. I hope they recover by then. The moment I got home, I made a soothing foot soak from the vast array of components in Magda's kitchen. So far, it isn't doing much besides making them smell better, which is something, I guess. Not being able to enchant things really sucks.

Magda isn't home yet. She's working late on a big project. Probably just as well. If she were home, I'd be tempted to talk and I should save my voice for work.

I have to admit that bunking with Magda and witnessing Teagan's bright-eyed enthusiasm as she talked about her classes is making me nostalgic (not in a good way). I remember how I felt, how the world felt, when I started college. The mystery of the future seemed so thrilling and full of possibility. It feels very far from that now.

I'm going to try to keep my depression to myself and enjoy my time with Magda. It's been too long since we had a chance to hang out and connect.

BOB THE GARGOYLE has shown up again. I nearly spat out my brew when I turned around and saw him perched on one of Magda's spell component chests. I hope she doesn't need to get into it anytime soon because he's no lightweight and I haven't been able to convince him to move. I asked him what he wants, but all I got in return was his unnerving, flinty stare.

Missera doesn't seem put out by him. She's currently slithering around his crooks and crags. It's mesmerizing to watch—especially when Herman hitches a ride.

The two familiars are getting along a little too well. I found several snake-sized holes in strategic places around the apartment. It seems I wasn't the only one busy this sun. Herman has eaten passages between the living room and bedroom, and between at least two kitchen cupboards.

I don't know what they're up to, but I don't trust them. I left Herman at home this morn because I figured he'd get into less trouble. Wrong. If he doesn't smarten up, he'll have to come to work with me. I'll have a chat with him this eventide about behaving himself and see that he gives Magda a proper apology for damaging her apartment. Yet another thing to fix and more coin out of my perpetually empty pouch.

Freydias, Storm Moon 26, 209

MY SECOND SUN at Moonbrews went well, with one minor hitch: I accidently switched two orders. They were for identical twins, so I can't feel too bad. One wanted a Mucho Golden Fate and the other ordered a Fat Heart Stopper. If you ask me, I did them a favour. It's not good to be too focused on money or love. You need to mix it up now and then.

They didn't see it that way. Andreas had to smooth things over. Gave them each a complimentary drink card. He is a master at handling disgruntled clients. He wasn't happy about my mix-up but said he understood how difficult it was adjusting to such a fast-paced work environment. He's *way* more understanding than Althea ever was.

I'm shocked at how popular Moonbrews is. Not to throw shade at my new workplace, but come on. I'm not sure whether their potions are specifically designed to expire every sun or if the ingredients are just so weak that they don't last, but it means customers have to come back often to get their fix. Why don't they invest in something longer term? The initial outlay might be higher, but it ultimately costs less. I really don't get people sometimes.

On top of the temporary nature of Moonbrews' potions, there's no innovation, no deviation, no *spirit* in them. Brew

Masters can't tweak them or anything. You'd think our customers would get bored, but I saw many of the same faces this sun as I did last sun.

I suppose it's a case of convenience over quality. Oh well. At least I'll never be out of work here.

I'm feeling almost normal on the snot front, but my feet are still killing me. We aren't allowed to sit while working the counter. Andreas says it looks like we're more alert and attentive if we're upright. Whatever. I saw him levitating. Most of the other Brew Masters do it too, so I think the rule is a little unfair where I'm concerned. I'll wait until I'm fully trained and then approach him about it again. All employees should have equal opportunities to rest their feet, whether they have access to magickal means of doing so or not.

At least I won't have to put up with foot pain for too much longer this eventide. Magda and I are going out to celebrate my new job and I plan to partake in enough fermented ghoul eyes to pickle that judgmental union healer who suggested I had a ghoul eye problem.

Oh yeah! Time to put on my party robes and dancing boots!

WELL. THAT WAS interesting. At least this time I can say it's not my fault a tavern burnt down, or more accurately, exploded. I never even made it to the point of over-indulging in ghoul eyes.

Our eventide started out normal enough. Magda and I decided to visit The Moon's Lament, our favourite haunting ground in college. Not much had changed. It was the same dark, hops-soaked retreat where we wiled away poor grades and whittled rude comments about instructors into the wooden tabletops and pillars. My Dame Dicentra limerick was still visible at our old booth. Someone even added several amusing verses.

We both carefully avoided rehashing anything connected to my disastrous Justin phase. We should talk about it again at some point, even if it's just me making sure she knows how instrumental her support and friendship were in getting me through those dark times. But that is a conversation for a brighter sun. I'm just starting to claw my way out of this current funk. No need to add another layer to my depression.

The tips I received over the last two suns paid for the first round of ghoul eye cocktails for me and Magda—and Herman and Missera, as they insisted on coming. Our familiars quickly lost interest in our conversation and worked their way around the room picking pockets. They spent their ill-gotten gains on some kind of loud mechanical wizard box with blinking lights. I'm sure they were cheating. Every time Missera deposited a coin, Herman skittered into the works and did something that involved a series of bongs and pings. At least it kept them out of our way.

Poor Magda is trying hard to overcome her snake phobia. Living with Missera, who is very snaky and active, has destroyed any sense of calm she had at home. She hasn't even tried to bring her familiar into castings as her fear makes it impossible to hold elementals in balance. I broached the idea of transmutation by letting on that I've considered trying it with Herman, when and if my magick returns. She flat-out refused. She doesn't buy into the theory that it cleverly skirts union policy. Magda always was more of a rule follower. I'll keep working on her. It's not good for her to be this stressed out all the time.

Since my voice had finally recovered, I updated her on the most recent events in my un-charmed life, including the nagging question that consumes my mind: If a witch is magick (our closest held tenet), can there be such a thing as a witch with no magick? Am I still a witch? And if not, what am I?

Her answer was a warm hug and a whisper in my ear, "You are my precious best friend whose humour and love makes the road ahead seem bearable." Those caring words almost made me feel whole. Almost.

I couldn't shake the feeling that I was an outsider to everything that had once been so familiar. Even there, in our pub, surrounded by witches cackling at the same old bad jokes and debating the same tired points of professional contention, I was other. Unnatural. Someone's best friend, which counted for a lot in my heart, but still, my mind screamed that I was lacking. A dusty jar at the back of a pantry where you put unidentifiable things that might be useful at some point, but you should probably just throw out.

Given the staggering number of ill-fated occurrences in my life, Magda was concerned I had run afoul of a curse. She did a quick spell and found nothing active, but promised to do a few random checks to see if someone had cast a hex with an intermittent or situational effect.

If anyone can find out if there's foul play, it's Magda. She was good in school and now she has close to a season cycle of killer work experience. Nothing will get past her.

We spent some time reminiscing about college and I told her about scrying Peuturella. We had her for our first term potions and elixirs class. Magda ran into our flight instructor a few moons ago and said it was weird talking to him as just a regular person and not a teacher.

I commiserated. I'm sure I sounded like a flustered student when Peuturella answered my scry. I muddled through the conversation by skipping pleasantries, which might have led to disclosing the embarrassing horror of my magick-less state, and flying straight to the business at hand. Thankfully, Peuturella was interested enough that her focus remained on the icing laxative and gingerbread glue recipes. She said she'd put out feelers with her business contacts. Things did get awkward when I asked if I could be dismissed, but I pretended there was interference with our connection and ended the scry. Maybe she didn't notice.

Magda was curious about the recipes, but I couldn't tell her much. I have yet to successfully reproduce the gingerbread glue. Everything I've baked is nowhere near as sticky and, to be honest, the smell of gingerbread still makes me gag. The idea of testing the icing laxative is equally appealing, so I'm not all that keen on continuing either experiment.

NOTE: Harvest grease from Herman so I can at least send Peuturella a sample for the icing laxative.

Anyway, there we were, two witches out on the town, reminiscing . . . and in walks a gaggle of uppity young wizards from Primus Magia Seminary and the eventide hits the crapper. Just the name of their school is pretentious enough to set my teeth on edge.

I knew those PMS screwballs were trouble the moment I saw their perfectly pressed robes and oversized staffs. One of them had a horribly gaudy, bejewelled wand and matching scroll case tucked into a blindingly red sash. Wizards! Eyesores, all of them.

Magda and I ignored them, as did most other patrons. We even moved to a dark corner (thankfully, near a window), but nothing dampened their belligerent presence. They were looking for a fight, or they wouldn't have set up at the bar and sung the very offensive drinking ballad, "99 Witches Fishing in Ditches."

The Moon's Lament is a witch tavern. By the Hunter's green bollocks, everyone knows that. It's right beside Grimoire College. There's been an implicit understanding between our communities since their inception: Witches don't go to wizard taverns and wizards don't go to witch taverns. It's less painful that way.

So, imagine my surprise when these imbecile wizards split into two groups, one of which slowly and deliberately sidled up to every witch in the tavern, insulting them in every way they could think of. Most of their insults were either lame or made no sense, but their malicious intent was clear.

Things went downhill quickly. Witches started tossing spell components around like snowballs (they must have been First-Terms). And then there really *were* snowballs, because the wizard with the silly scroll case whipped out a parchment and chanted an equation which created a vortex that turned into a storm.

Meanwhile, the other group of dandies headed straight for the only druid in the tavern and proceeded to harangue her about a non-existent spot of dirt on her white robes. Then they questioned whether her robe was a natural fabric.

Now, everyone in their right minds knows to give druids a wide berth. They're prickly at the best of times. The more you interact with one, the more chance you have of landing on their bad side. And which side is bad changes from sun to sun. To be honest, I'm not sure they even know which is which. They probably have to consult the winds or pee in the ocean or something.

I've never seen a druid go into a full rage before and I hope I never do again. Her answer to their harassment was to call forth a monstrous tree. It sprouted in the middle of the tavern, tearing the floor and roof to shreds. Magda and I narrowly escaped its snaking roots.

Magda, who is a sentimental soul, was upset that our old

tavern was trashed and called in a pack of air elementals to end the fray. It didn't go well.

The water elementals in the storm and the random components flying around mixed with her air elementals in just the right way to channel a powerful lightning strike. It forked right out of the clouds, through the tree, and into the flagstones. Of course, they were soaking wet, so we all received quite a shock. And the tree exploded into a hail of flaming spears.

I'm not sure there's ever been a tavern as thoroughly demolished as The Moon's Lament. Makes my half-phoenix incident seem like child's play. From the look of things during our escape, a good portion of the neighbourhood and at least one wing of Grimoire College will need rebuilding.

We were lucky to get out when we did. More accurately, we were lucky to get *blown* out. A rogue air elemental picked us and a few others up before unceremoniously dumping us in a pile a block away. On the plus side, we were still in possession of our limbs and organs, which is more than can be said for some other patrons. I bet the hedge witches and physickers were busy.

Once we sorted our wits and righted our robes, Magda and I stumbled down the street for home. One of the wizards who escaped with us hollered that he wasn't surprised to see witches turn tail. I yelled back that he had the oratory skill of a yeasty scum pod. Aaand the brawl started again.

Somehow, I ended up wedged under two oversized guys engaged in a wrestling match. That usually wouldn't be a problem after an eventide out, but it was this time. I couldn't move or breathe. My vision greyed as I struggled and a familiar tingle crept from the wet ground into my fingertips. Then, an errant staff caught me in the head and the world went fuzzy.

The next thing I remember is Bob (I didn't even know he had come with us) landing on one of the guys and Magda pulling me out. She's stronger than she looks.

Her timing couldn't have been better. A wizard's ominous-sounding equation ended in a startled scream when Missera popped out of Magda's sleeve and spat a stream of venom into his flapping mouth. It must have tasted bad because there was a lot of spluttering and gagging.

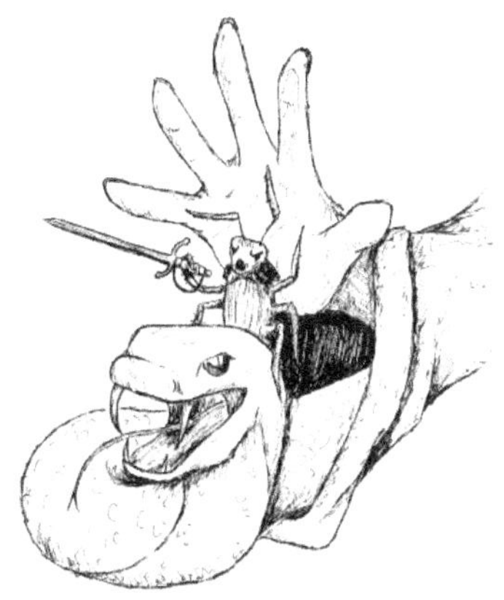

For a moment I thought I was seeing double when I looked at Missera, but then I realized Herman was riding on her head. He was brandishing a bright purple miniature cocktail sword. The rascals were thoroughly enjoying themselves.

Their appearance in Magda's sleeve was a surprise to her as well. Between her shriek and the wizard's, everyone cleared off posthaste. They must have thought another monster tree was incoming.

This eventide is the first time in a long time that I feel lucky. We made it through with nothing worse than singed hair and ruined robes. And none of it was my fault. I'd forgotten how much fun Aestradorra could be.

Due to his heroics, Magda generously invited Bob to stay at her place, as long as he doesn't stare at her too much. My stony shadow was already back at the apartment by the time we made it there. Sadly, Missera and Herman must have hitched a ride with him because they were home as well. I was hoping it would take them a while to get back so we could enjoy a spot of quiet time. I think Magda is losing her voice from screaming so much.

I saw something glinting in the crook of Bob's arm and discovered that he pulled off a daring theft. That wizard is going to be very unhappy when she realizes her bejewelled wand is no longer in her sash. Magda and I briefly considered selling it to replace our going-out robes, but Bob won't let it go. I don't mind. If he gets pleasure from the shiny stick, I say let him keep it.

Pandias, Storm Moon 27, 209

So sore. Must get up for shift at Moonbrews. I hate myself.

NOTE: NEVER get into a tavern brawl when you have to go to work the next sun, Hester. It's a BAD idea. What were you thinking?!

Wendias, Crow Moon 3, 209

OH, HAPPY SUN! My magick is returning. I can't begin to express how relieved I am.

I wasn't certain, but I thought I felt a spark of power during the tavern brawl. It was just the briefest, faintest flicker, but it gave me hope.

Since then, I've been practicing minor glamours, trying to add a little mole to my nose or crow's feet around my eyes, and I finally succeeded this morn! I was so shocked to see the brown spot by my nostril that I tried to bat it off. I thought it was a fly.

When you have a natural talent or gift, it's easy to take for granted. It is always with you, waiting to be useful. And there are many opportunities for magick to be useful. I used it every sun, all sun for small things, medium things, big things. My ability to harness the five elements and weave their energies into beautiful and frightening diversions touched every facet of my life.

Then, it was suddenly gone. Fractus. Mortuus. Finem. The rug was pulled out from under me . . . only it wasn't just a rug, it was a flying carpet and I was dancing in the clouds with no broom in sight. Good luck sticking that landing, Hester!

I've been getting by. Magick isn't everything. I know that now. I still exist without it. I can still work in my chosen field, albeit with difficulty. I still have friends and family. But magick breathed colour and mystery into every moment. A mere scrap of it could craft masterpieces. As a wielder, I was limited only by my imagination and skill.

I miss it so much. I can say that now because there is hope.

I was in denial. Facing a future in which magick had permanently abandoned me was agonizing, so I did my best to live on the surface, in the present, within a sliver of time, not daring to swim into the ocean of my heart for fear that grief would end me.

Sometimes it's better not to know, or question, or plan. Sometimes you have to pretend that now is all there is. That patch of dirt where your next step falls . . . nothing exists outside of it. And the next. And the next. Focusing your will like that gets you through each sun in a crisis, but it only works for so long. Dwelling solely in the challenge of the moment becomes hollow. The absence of your past and future swirl in your mind like great black holes. Steering your thoughts away from them becomes ever more difficult. Eventually, everyone gives in.

I made it through this time. Never has a single mole meant so much or been so beautiful.

I don't know if I'll fully recover. Some, or most, of the damage could be permanent. But even if only a fraction of my talent returns, I will treasure it.

Tydias, Crow Moon 9, 209

I HAD A strange dream last night and I'm not sure what it means. I dreamt I was staying at a country inn. There was a tavern dog—one of those long, sausage-y things with stubby legs. Kind of a helpless-looking mook, but good-natured.

I was polishing off a pint and thinking about retiring when two strangers burst in and ran upstairs screaming about a monster.

Of course, they left the door wide open and a massive black wolf sauntered through. I mean, this thing was huge. It could have carried me in its mouth like a pup.

The little dog was nearest to the beast, and it froze, its peg legs shaking so much I could hear its claws clicking against the flagstones. I ducked in and snatched up the pup as the innkeeper leapt over the bar swinging an axe. I hastily retreated as the wolf turned its solar gaze on me.

It was calm, unfazed by the axe wielding innkeeper and the screaming patrons. Something about its manner, some glint of intelligence in its eyes, made me question whether it was the monster, or simply another creature seeking asylum from it.

I set the dog down and listened as it scuttled away to hide in the kitchen. I nodded to the wolf. The wolf nodded to me. It was all very congenial.

It broke eye contact to wave its nose at the misty landscape outside. I sensed an invitation as it trotted out and glanced back at me. After a moment's hesitation, I followed. The beast did not feel dangerous, but there was a stiffness to its gait that suggested impatience and perhaps urgency.

We travelled over undulating hills while mother moon and her child stars struggled to penetrate the fog. The wolf stopped at the edge of a flat grassland and growled. The ground ahead of us churned and swaths of grass disappeared, sucked into a muddy pool beneath with a great *slurp*. Malicious cackling assaulted me as the soil beneath my feet heaved. I turned to run but the earth had already swallowed my feet. Roots snaked up my legs, pulling me deeper into the fetid gullet.

Then I woke up. I wish there was a sure way to interpret dreams. Am I supposed to re-evaluate a first impression? Perhaps it was a warning not to plan any country rambles. Maybe it was showing me that I'm afraid of something unknown . . . or that I should be afraid of something that hasn't yet revealed itself. Then again, it might just have been the ghostly remnants of that slightly expired stew I brewed up a few eventides ago. Argh.

There are only a few aspects of witchcraft I dislike. Dream interpretation tops that list. It's always so obvious looking back, but gleaning the meaning before something happens is like staring at a puzzle with millions of pieces that keep changing shape. Sadly, dream interpretation isn't Magda's strong suit either so I'll just have tread carefully for a while. And stay away from old stew. I suppose the last is a good plan in general. What can I say? I was hungry.

I have been practicing minor rituals and spells every sun. Working with the elements again feels like coming home. I can only draw a shallow stream of the power and even that exhausts me to the point of collapse if I do it for too long. But it's a start. An amazing, beautiful, thrilling start!

So far, I've told Magda, Missera, and Herman about it. Nobody at Moonbrews knows. I can't do much that's useful yet anyway. Levitating with my co-workers is a long way off as it sucks too much power. I need to build up my channelling stamina first.

I tried sitting on my broom behind the counter to alleviate my aching feet. I was able to keep it hovering low enough that it looked like I was standing, but there just wasn't enough room for me, my broom, and another worker. I kept jabbing Teagan in the hip and I accidently knocked over a tray of drying beakers.

After that, I decided on a more mundane solution and borrowed a pair of Magda's old field boots. The heels are lower, so my feet are slightly less throbby at the end of my shifts. Thank the Goddess her feet are just a half size larger than mine. Best friend to the rescue again.

Work is going okay. Well, at least it's going. It's a good thing my co-workers are interesting, because the job sure isn't, especially now that I've memorized all the brew recipes. I can pretty much switch my brain off. Occasionally the customers are also interesting, but sadly most are simply vexing.

I never realized how disheartening it is to work in the service industry. I interacted with the public as a village hag, but that was on my own schedule and I only approached whomever I felt like cursing that sun.

The more I interact with customers in the regimented Moonbrews environment, the more I see the benefits of being a solitary like Althea. After a sun of dealing with petty, nitpicking complaints, hanging out alone in a forest is incredibly appealing. I'm sick of hearing about not enough foam on a potion, or too much slime, or they are busy and don't we know their time is money—like ours isn't? My mandated customer service scowl is genuine by the end of my shift.

I get no rest at home either. Herman relentlessly badgers me to try a transmutation on him, even after reading the approved familiar list and declaring, "All the good forms are taken." I guess he's tired of being a cockroach.

INTERESTING SIDE-NOTE: Cockroach is definitely not an approved familiar. Granted, the list we dug out of Magda's old college notes is slightly out of date, but we didn't graduate that long ago and nothing changes quickly in the union. It's unlikely they added a new creature between then and now. (I have attached the list for future reference.)

I'm not ashamed to admit, the thought of casting a transmutation spell scares me. I've been out of the game too long to just jump back in without hiccups. And magickal hiccups can be lethal.

I can't try anything on Herman until I'm absolutely certain about what I'm doing. He might be a pest, but I do *not* want to be responsible for my familiar's injury or death. There's a section in the WU handbook dedicated to the consequences. Let's just say, they're unpleasant.

I explained that I wasn't ready, but Herman didn't want to hear it. He dragooned Magda in to help me raise the required power and refused to listen when I told him I wasn't just concerned about having enough juice. He said Magda could cast the spell on her own if I wasn't willing to help. I strictly forbade that.

He's been testy with me ever since, but I'm not giving in. I'm angry with him too. It's unfair of him to put Magda in such an untenable position.

Regardless of how skilled Magda is in spell craft, it's not possible to cast a transmutation on a living being who isn't yourself or your familiar. Intimate spells like that are only possible with familiars because of our bond. I've heard tales of witches turning their enemies into toads and such, but I've never seen it done. There's a remote chance a Sage or Elder could, but not an Initiate.

Besides, Magda has always been uncomfortable with alteration magicks. They creep her out and that fear manifests in her spells. The results aren't pretty. So many things can go wrong.

In the end, I promised Herman that I would transmute him as soon as I felt it was safe. That will have to be good enough for him. To demonstrate my concerns, I cast a series of enlargement spells on simpler subjects.

I'm out of practice keeping the energies balanced, so evenly enlarging anything is challenging. The first three fruit I worked on exploded. The fourth was seriously lopsided and the fifth was uniformly larger, but delicate. It dissolved as soon as I touched it. If I had tried that on Herman . . . best not to think about it.

I hope he learned a valuable lesson about accepting and respecting other people's boundaries.

After all that spellwork, I need a full sun's sleep to recover, but that isn't going to happen. I'm covering Teagan's shifts because she has mid-term exams and, in my off time, I plan to look for my own place. Magda says she's happy for me to stay as long as I like, but I know how much of an imposition we must be and I don't want to jeopardize our friendship. I'm not a bad houseguest, but I come with Herman and, apparently, Bob.

Bless her heart. Poor Magda didn't sign on to share her space with three. She caught Herman snacking on one of her tomes last eventide. I've never seen her so livid. Then, Bob perched on an overloaded bookcase, which collapsed and scared the poop out of everyone, literally, for Herman.

So now, I not only owe Magda for all the coin she lent me, I need to replace her bookcase and the tome Herman gnawed on. These guys are killing me. Being a building inspector, you'd think Bob would know what was stable and what wasn't. I'm just glad it collapsed when nobody was near.

I just had a thought. Maybe he did know and that was why he sat on it? It would have been more polite to leave a note, but inspectors aren't known for their manners. Hmmm. I'll have to pass this on to Magda. Might take some of the sting out of the loss of shelving. A bookcase that size could have killed someone.

WU Sanctioned Familiars

Category 1	Category 2	Category 3	Category 4	Category 5
Cerberus	Jaguar	Cobra	Bat	Ferret
Kelpie	Black mamba	Raven	Asp	Donkey
Gryphon	Wolf	Monitor lizard	Tarantula	Newt
Alicorn	Komodo dragon	Horse	Rat	Mouse
Hydra	Stag	Black widow	Hare	Goat
Kraken	Howler monkey	Crocodile	Parrot	Wombat
Phoenix	Great horned owl	Red fox	Toad	Beaver
	Velociraptor	Racoon	Boar	Possum
	Shark	Giant Squid	King Crab	Eel
	White bear	Snowy owl	Cat	Skunk
		Badger	Dog	Great gray slug
		Jackal	Hyena	
			Scorpion	
			Platypus	

Provided to Grimoire College Lotus Moon 206

Soldias, Crow Moon 14, 209

THIS EVENTIDE, FOR the first time in a long time, I'm attending a group ritual. A full moon rite—my favourite! Magda's coven said they'd be fine with her bringing a guest. Yay!

I was worried that I'd want to strangle people after pulling a double shift at Moonbrews, but I'm actually looking forward to hanging out with witchy folk. Especially ones who aren't demanding service or loudly complaining about how hard it is to find competent brewers.

After work, Magda and I baked mooncakes. As this was my introduction to the coven, we made them extra special. Magda had a jar of lotus seeds on hand and I found some iinok eggs and a vial of Skiartian moon dew in an apothecary on the way home. I made enough tips to cover the cost, barely. I'll skip lunch next sun to make it up. It's important to make a good impression, not just for me, but for Magda.

We ground the lotus seeds into a paste and boiled the eggs to stuff the cakes with. As the delicacies cooled, we anointed each of them with three drops of dew. That should raise everyone's energies.

Magda had never attempted such a complicated recipe, but it wasn't too bad, just a tad finicky with all the steps. Certainly, nothing compared to what I did at the Gingerbread Hut. There was only one hiccup. We got chatting, as we do, and forgot about the oven. Thankfully, my nose must be attuned, because it started twitching just as the cakes were on the cusp of overdone.

The only other hurdle was finding something to wear. Most of my robes are un-wearable due to cockroach snacking or are in need of washing. The tavern brawl ruined my last party robe, not that it would have been appropriate ritual attire anyway.

NOTE: Do laundry ASAP!!!

I eventually settled on a robe I purchased in college and haven't worn for a while. The midnight blue, shimmering material has small crystals sewn randomly about. It's a bit flashy and probably out of fashion (fads change too quickly to keep up with, so I've never bothered), but it still fits, albeit more tightly. I thought it was a fun classic look, but Herman, not so much.

It's one thing for a cockroach to eat holes in your robes. It's quite another to have said cockroach scoff at your fashion sense. Apparently, he judged that robe too gaudy to eat. Said even looking at it gave him indigestion. Good thing, or I wouldn't have anything left to wear this eventide.

According to him, just thinking about owning a cloak without silk lining is an affront to all witchdom (I have three). My footwear is uninspiring and grandmotherly. And what did he say about the colour of the cloak I picked to wear? Oh yes, "it makes earthworm brown seem dazzling." How I ended up with a bloody want-to-be stylist as a familiar, I don't know. And a rude one to boot.

My brown cloak is a good, thick, functional covering. Lots of pockets, roomy, billows dramatically when I'm on the broom, water repellent, nice hood. There's nothing wrong with it. And I happen to like earthy browns.

Herman and I were so annoyed with each other that we decided to go our own ways this eventide. Magda seconded the idea, as she wasn't looking forward to Missera tagging along either. We're going to drop them off at The Haunted Bonnet, our local pub, and pick them up on our way home. Magda says the tavern is frequented by a disreputable lot, so Herman and Missera should fit right in.

The bell just tolled half-eleven. Tally ho, witches on the go!

WHAT A FANTASTIC night! My body is still buzzing with power from the ritual. I feel so connected, so grounded (an aspect of magickal workings that I have long struggled with). I can feel the air moving around me, inside me; the earth draws me down as a mother welcomes a child; blood rushes through the river ways of my veins and feeds the fire of passion in my chest. My spirit is bursting with magickal creativity.

I need to practice my magicks, let off some of this energy, or I will never get to sleep. Magda feels the same, though her solution is to read, as always. That doesn't work for me. She recommended I try it when we were bunkmates in college, but one incinerated book is too many as far as she's concerned.

Our mooncakes were a hit. They were by far the tastiest treat. A few witches even requested the recipe.

NOTE: Scry recipe to Abyssia and Hektor in the morn.

Magda's coven was welcoming and open. Well, not everyone was, but some witches walk the shadowed path more than others. It's good. There must be balance.

It's been a while since I've felt this free, unburdened. I must do better at keeping up with my rituals. In all the chaos of finding a job, I forgot how important it is for witches to stop, stretch our roots, breathe in the night, and let the moon's gentle caress wash away what no longer serves us.

I should be stressed about my student loan and job and weak magick and housing situation (oy, the list does go on), but I can't bring myself to worry about any of that right now. It feels odd to not have anxiety plague my every thought. It's not that I don't care. I'm just not expending any energy agonizing over it. The beautiful ritual energy has infused every fibre of my being and pushed out all the negative.

I think I'll work with water elementals this eventide. I'll be casting alone, as Magda's busy with her book, so I'll start small. Maybe try altering a bowl of water to fog and back again. If I get brave, I may attempt water sculpting. It involves a lot of concentration I may not have, but the effort might induce sleep.

I'm happy to report that Herman and Missera survived their night at the tavern. The tavern also survived, which is a bonus.

On the way home, Herman asked how my magickal experiments were going and if I knew when I'd be able to try a transmutation. He was far more polite about it this time. I must be getting through to him.

Right now, I feel as though I could tap into the life force of the Goddess and weave it into anything. Thankfully, I'm not stupid enough to actually try. I told Herman there was no ETA yet. He'll have to wait until Magda has time to help and I've honed my magickal skills a little more.

Speaking of honing, I should get on with that. Have I mentioned recently how happy I am to have even a sliver of my old magick back?

Freydias, Crow Moon 19, 209

BETWEEN WORK AND magick experiments, I'm pooped. The kind of pooped where you're lying on a couch but have to go to the bathroom and start wondering if you could devise a spell to magickally transport the pee from your body to the chamber pot just to avoid the moving part in between.

Herman retained his eagerness to try out different forms, even after witnessing several catastrophic vegetable transformations. I got better after those failures, moved onto more complicated subjects, gained confidence, and eventually felt comfortable enough to try the spell on Herman. Thanks to Magda's infusion of power, we've done two . . . Wait. No, three, but the last one was an accident. It's not a huge deal, but you'd think it was the end of the world if you listened to Herman go on about it.

Let's see. First, we tried a tarsier. I didn't mind the wide-eyed, perpetually terrified look, figured it added to my cred, but Herman wasn't a fan. It freaked him out whenever he caught sight of himself in a reflective surface. Not only did he keep forgetting it was him, but whatever was looking back seemed petrified of something directly behind him, which invariably led to a fear reaction. That wasn't pleasant for anyone. It involved a mad dash and a trail of watery poo (no idea if that's a leftover from his cockroach form, or if tarsiers normally fear-poo).

He also discovered that people consider tarsiers cute. I had to rescue him from an overly cuddly kid at Moonbrews who found him sleeping under a table and tried to run off with him. Eating bugs also proved problematic, given his original form. I never thought I'd see a sun where Herman felt bad about eating anything.

Next, we tried an eagle because Herman figured people would be less likely to molest him if he had sharp bits. He looked spectacular. I really outdid myself on that transmutation. The wickedly sharp talons, the hooked beak, the predatory eyes. He was beautiful. A masterpiece. I'm sad it didn't work out.

He's not fond of heights and that's a bad phobia for a bird. We hoped that particular hang-up was tied to his original cockroach form, but not so. He also had a hard time not eating Missera. His predatory drive kicked in whenever he caught sight of her. The apartment turned into a war zone. Eagles cause a lot of damage when so inclined. The last straw was when he flew by with Missera in his beak.

The asp must be growing on Magda, because she nearly squashed Herman with a well-aimed tome. Eagles are big, but Magda's books are bigger. She apologized for her reaction, but we all understood. In the heat of the moment, everyone does what they can to protect those they care for.

Herman would have been devastated if he'd hurt Missera, so he wasn't offended by the severe booking. Our familiars have become inseparable.

We set up an emergency transmutation spell right away. We should have waited until everyone was less frazzled, but I was focused on preventing another incident. Herman hadn't figured out what he wanted to be, so we ended up having a quick discussion in the middle of the spell (not ideal).

He insists that he jokingly suggested a flamingo because it was the least dangerous thing he could think of, but he said it and I activated the transmutation. Maybe I have a hard time discerning sarcasm in eagles. They do come off as a serious sort of bird. Whatever. It was an honest mistake. I didn't understand at the time why he wanted to be a flamingo, but I figured it was his prerogative. Not my place to judge.

So now, Herman is a flamingo. A bright pink, spindly legged, weirdo of a bird. He constantly complains about how embarrassing it is, but it's not exactly what I'd pick for a familiar either. His cockroach form was better. The only good thing is that he doesn't want anyone to see him, so he stays close to home and has stopped bugging me to bring him to work. The bad thing is that he stays close to home and is easily bored.

I set up Magda's bathing tub with a supply of fish and shrimp. He likes to stand in it and snack, but he splashes water all over and keeps tossing the fish out. He says he's playing with them, but he keeps "forgetting" to put them back in, so I suspect he's doing it to piss me off. It's working.

Between the dead fish and shrimp, the apartment has a distinctive odour. Our neighbours complained about the smell (and occasional ceiling leak) but I baked them some gingerbread cookies to apologize and managed to smooth things over. At least for now.

I tried bringing Herman to work with me once, but he refused to go back after overhearing a customer offer to purchase his feathers. She said they were the perfect hue for her summer solstice wreath. I assured him nobody would be plucking any feathers, but his new, rosy form has not made him any less paranoid or ill-tempered.

Sad to say (for him), Herman looks hilarious when he's mad. He flaps his wings, makes a ridiculous honking noise, and charges at you like a little pink hurricane. He was in a particularly *fowl* mood last eventide and Magda and I almost peed ourselves laughing. Every time he completed a charge, he'd hop back into his tub and wiggle his tail feathers in disgust. I'm sure we'll tire of it, but for now, it's highly amusing. I looked over at Bob and even he was sporting a stony grin.

I'll transmute Herman into another form as soon as I've had

a few suns' rest. I'm drained and sore down to the marrow. Working magicks is getting easier, but even with Magda's infusion of power, it's a challenge to keep my focus up and the elements balanced for the duration of a transmutation spell. They are complicated and lengthy. Thankfully, transmutations primarily rely on water elementals and I've always had a close relationship with them.

Magda and I have been investigating magickal aids such as energy crystals and elemental wells—things I never thought I'd consider using. We came up with a few potentially useful ones, though even remembering I need to use them will be challenging for a while.

Wizards are the ones who fluff around with overly complicated procedures requiring mounds of arcane tools and supplies. Witches are supposed to *be* their spell. It is us. We are it. Magick isn't something external to manipulate, it exists in the elements that make up the oceans and soil and sky. The same elements that make up our blood and bones and soul. We are magick.

Don't get me wrong. I'm ecstatic to be able to work magick again, even on such a diminished scale. It's just that I miss the old suns when all I had to do was think about calling an elemental and there it would be. Now I have to concentrate, visualize them in the environment around me, inside me, and draw each tiny one out. And they are tiny. Barely discernible, really. I feel like a bumbling toddler. I suppose it is making my elemental applications more efficient.

I'm not giving up. Each time I cast, it's challenging and frustrating, but maybe not as much as the time before. Perhaps that's just in my mind, but I'll take it.

Soldias, Crow Moon 21, 209

Goddess preserve me, I've done it again. I am sooo tired of screwing up.

This sun started normally enough. Herman stuffed a fish in my cot to encourage me to get up. It was alive this time—a small mercy. There's nothing worse than waking up to realize that what you thought was your pillow, is in fact a rotting fish. Though, waking up to a fish sucking on your nose is only marginally better.

I cleaned up Herman's briny mess, chucked down my gruel, tossed on a clean-ish robe, and away to work I flew. I did this morn what I always do and spent the trip mulling random things, like do florofians always moult in pairs and does anyone remember that time I chipped my chalice with my athame. That was embarrassing! What I should have been doing is paying attention to my surroundings.

I remember thinking that the Sol-reddened clouds resembled a swooping vulture. And then there was the nicely wrinkled hag in the parking lot who threw the Death tarot at me and yelled, "Doom. DOOOOOOM." Either one of those portents should have been enough to give me pause, but no.

I figured she was just out doing her job, spreading the word and keeping the balance like the rest of us working stiffs. I know what it's like to have to meet a hex quota. I've heard they're set pretty high in Aestradorra. And Death isn't necessarily bad. Usually it just means a change. However, the tarot combined with her words and the clouds . . .

Things started to get weird when a gregarious customer trotted up to my counter. I heard her coming before she even opened the door. She was young and her energies were high. Either she hadn't bothered to control them or wasn't proficient at it, because the atmospheric pressure in the room plummeted. This caused a beaker in the distiller to shatter, all the lids on our display vials to shoot off (followed by their contents), and my ears to pop. Very irresponsible! I've seen Novice witches in grade school with better control.

A sleek black dog trotted in after her and she impatiently shooed it away. There was an intensity in its gaze as it surveyed the shop, implying an intelligence beyond that of a mundane animal. Apparently, the young witch missed that cue. It brushed against her leg and she zapped it without a second thought. It wasn't a powerfully charged bolt, just enough to make the creature yelp.

A bit of fur and mud on your robe are not an excuse to zap things, especially things that are more than they seem. That can really bite you on the ass. I waited for the dog to do just that, but instead it barked once at her and headed for the door.

I slipped it a honeysuckle and urchin cookie before it left, figuring it had come in because it was hungry. It held my gaze for a beat. There was a spark of magick in the depths of its eyes. Staring into them felt like gazing into the night sky—endless and brimming with mystery. I suddenly felt very small.

The customer was ticked off by the time I came back. Teagan was busy running between the back room and the counter, cleaning up the mess created by the vial and beaker explosions, so I figured I had better serve this horror.

She was not one of our regular patrons, which isn't in itself a bad thing, except in this particular case it was. Everything about her put me on edge, from her phony buggy-eyed smile, to her booming voice and exuberant hand gestures. I narrowly saved our potion bottle display.

She wanted a brew that would give her purple dragon wings for some fancy (read snooty) Scales and Tails party. I told her the closest one we offered was our Green Fairy. At which point, she accused me of being inept and belligerent.

I admit, at various crossroads, I have been both of those things, but not this time. I tried to explain that we had a set menu and Brew Masters weren't authorized to deviate from the company's vetted recipes.

She took this as a further invitation to disparage my skills. I suspect she came in knowing we wouldn't be able to do what she asked and just wanted something to complain about.

I can't say for sure why I did what I did, but right at that moment, I didn't have the time or inclination to put up with her. There were other customers in line—customers who, although likely annoying, wouldn't be outright abusive. So, as I did with Herman, I gave her what she wanted. Sort of. Well, not really, so it's actually exactly like what happened with Herman.

I had a limited supply of ingredients to work with, thanks to Moonbrews' unimaginative menu, so I made some impromptu substitutions from my personal stash. It's also likely that at least one of the store ingredients was contaminated (thanks to the vial explosions, which were entirely the customer's fault).

If it wasn't for her uncontrolled energies flying around, I probably would have felt the wrongness in the spell I infused the potion with. Between that and her grating voice, I was barely able to concentrate long enough to complete the incantation, let alone successfully detect its effect.

She didn't know what to say when I handed her the brew. I charged her for a Green Fairy (even though her potion should have been *way* more expensive) and figured that would be the last I saw of her. I was partially right.

She sat down with an offended huff at the most conspicuous table by the front window and sipped her brew. It didn't take long for the spell to hit. One minute she was her normal glaring self, and the next, she was a giant, bulbous caterpillar lounging on the table. A pattern of bright purple striations adorned her back, so at least I got the colour right.

So much for Initiates not being able to transmute other living beings. And with a potion, no less! I was impressed with myself, though I had no idea how I managed it. Unfortunately, the customer's husband immediately hired an Infernal demon, who was not similarly swayed by my awesome transmutation skills.

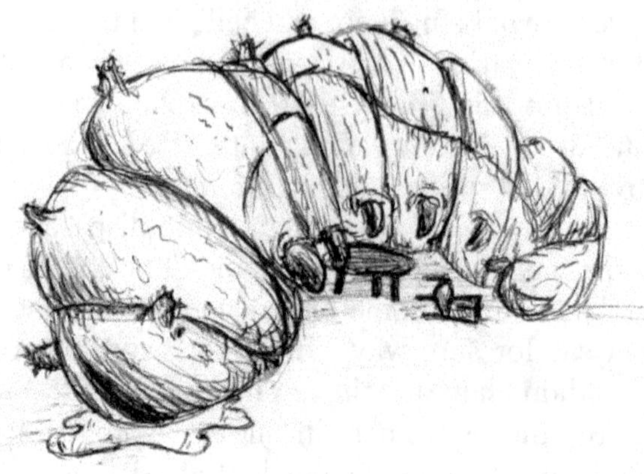

As much as I'd like to blame the customer, I know the responsibility for my actions begins and ends with me. I was the one who allowed her to goad me into brewing a careless potion. Maybe one sun I'll learn to control my temper.

The best scenario at this point is that the effect wears off. But me and best scenarios don't even have a passing acquaintance, so I've already started pondering what to do. I can't reverse the recipe to change her back, at least not until I figure out which components were contaminated and with what. And then I have to recreate her energy vortex, which no doubt affected things as well. That'll be challenging. And there are undoubtedly various unknown contributing environmental factors to identify. Running through the hundreds of experiments required will be time consuming, but I'm determined to fix this mess.

Andreas was all in a flap. Although he handles normal complaints and catastrophes with ease, the Infernal pressure this one brought was a bit much. His face turned ten shades of red. The idea of lawsuits is old hat for me after the Gingerbread Hut. I can't even say I was surprised when the demon portal melted the window.

I am sorry to have caused Andreas so much stress, but based on the testiness of our clientele, he'll have to get used to this sort of thing. I heard that a customer at another Moonbrews got frostbite from a Yeti Punch (a potion which they subsequently discontinued) and is threatening Infernal action.

Ridiculous. It's a Yeti Punch. It has to be cold. You'd have to be a real cracked cauldron to order a lukewarm one.

I'm getting sidetracked again. The long and the short of it is that I messed up and now I'm out of a job. Again. Andreas didn't want to fire me, but the head office didn't give him any say in the matter.

I won't miss the work, but I will miss Teagan and Andreas. Maybe I'll get a chance to have lunch with them once I've found yet another new job, paid off my outstanding debts, and accepted that I'll never be a professional witch and have well and truly given up on having a meaningful life.

Wow. I'm depressed. What I wouldn't give for some ghoul eyes and a bucket of frozen cow juice. I've been skipping lunches to save coin and I'm bloody starving, all the time. I don't want to pig out on Magda's food when I get home either, so I'm keeping my supper portions small. I told her I was dieting. I think she bought it. Herman didn't. To his credit, he has also reduced his fish and shrimp intake.

My trip to the job bank next morn should nicely round out my misery. Ouleah is not going to be happy. The fact that I couldn't keep a job at Moonbrews is more than a little embarrassing. I told Herman what happened and he just stuck his head under a wing and laughed and laughed. Pink, peg-legged jerk.

I'm really not looking forward to telling Magda I was fired again, but I have no choice. I need her help developing the reverse-transmutation potion. I want to put this debacle as far behind me, as quickly as possible.

My head hurts. I'm going to lie-down until I hear Magda come home.

Tydias, Crow Moon 23, 209

WELL, THAT WAS . . . interesting. I'm not quite sure what to make of my latest trip to the union job bank.

I arrived early for my appointment with the employment counsellor and ended up twiddling my thumbs in the waiting room. I don't do well with boredom and figured I'd spend the time getting in some extra practice calling elementals.

It didn't go as planned. My instructions confused the earth elemental and it turned my wooden chair into lead. Both the chair and I ended up in a very startled union accountant's office one story down after the floorboards cracked. In retrospect, I should have skipped earth. Our relationship is tumultuous at the best of times and my cauldron was bubbling over with stress.

Herman and boredom don't get along either. He kept running off with the receptionist's quills. She had them in a pot on her desk and they were just the right height for him to snatch. Between his legs and neck, he's quite tall. I'm not sure if he was offended at the feather use and felt he was liberating them, or if he was just being an ass. He ate the pad off her ink blotter too. That won't be fun to pass.

We were eventually called into Ouleah's office, much to the receptionist's relief, but then we had to wait for "the others" to come. Whenever there was a noise from the main office, Ouleah would duck down into her pool, sending a wave of water across the floor, and then slowly reappear, acting as if nothing had happened. She wouldn't say who we were waiting for, but I understood her jumpiness as soon as a gaggle of infernal demons burst into the room in a showy fireball. They sure know how to make an entrance.

The Infernals talked amongst themselves, talked to Ouleah, talked at me, consulted a mountain of tomes their imps hauled in, and then talked some more with each other. I had to re-explain everything that happened at the village, the Gingerbread Hut, and Moonbrews. It was all very tedious.

Herman's presence weirded everyone out. The demons kept glancing at him, but never said anything. After a while, Ouleah broke down and asked why there was a pink bird following me around.

I've never witnessed a silent infernal demon before, let alone five. Even when they aren't incessantly yakking at each other, there's always a sizzling hiss emanating from them. But when I said Herman was my familiar, the room went so quiet you could have heard a gnat fart.

There were a few guffaws as some of them decided I was joking. The rest showed identical suspicious frowns. One demon nervously edged away. I didn't mind. Being unpredictable keeps people, and apparently the occasional Infernal, at bay. Score one for Herman being outside the norm.

Their final recommendation was to place me somewhere "out of the way," ASAP. If I had to guess, I'd say the union is catching some heat from the Moonbrews incident and brought in this crew to figure out how to best cover their collective asses.

The Infernals took off in short order and so did my employment counsellor. Ouleah said she needed to consult the union placement specialist, but she was gone for a long time. I suspect she had a snooze either coming or going, or both. I've come to appreciate her nap breaks. It gives me a chance to think things through properly, make plans, and get some extra work done.

After the chair incident in the waiting room, I decided it would be safer to spend my time practicing with Water. There was enough of it sloshing around the office. A stack of papers on

Ouleah's desk ended up slightly soggier than it started out when Herman distracted me, but I don't think Ouleah noticed.

I digress. When my intrepid employment counsellor glided back in, she asked me all manner of questions. Am I comfortable working in a team? Would I be willing to work in a multidisciplinary environment? Do I have any divination experience?

I answered as best I could and she said there was a unique opportunity that satisfied the Infernals' requests and accommodated me and my magick disability. The position would involve a certain degree of diplomacy on my part, as the supervisors hailed from multiple disciplines.

A few pent-up tears of relief escaped. I blamed them on the splash from an errant wave but the soggy hanky Ouleah handed me suggested she knew. I could barely believe she found me something, let alone that quickly. The Infernals must have lit a fire under the union's collective bum. Whatever the means or reason, I'm happy. My hope of qualifying in time for the Adept ceremony has been restored.

The only part I wasn't sure about was Ouleah's reference to supervisors. I swear she said it as a plural. Maybe I misheard? One manager is enough. More than enough most of the time. I guess we'll see.

Working with a diverse group could be interesting. I'm sure it'll be challenging, but I'll do my best. I wonder what disciplines? Herbalists, Necromancers, Illusionists . . . though, I can't think of anything that requires all those specialties. Ooo! Maybe we'll be raising a zombie hoard and disguising them as flowery smelling princesses? But then how does my divination fit in? I suppose I could check which nobles can be successfully conned and turned. Now I'm curious. Am I going to be part of some super secret zombie invasion?

Traditionally, witches are allergic to all forms of hierarchy and stay well away from power struggles (our union being the one notable exception and, let me tell you, its utility and authority is hotly disputed). We tend to be a live-and-let-live crew. But, I could be convinced to make an exception for a zombie army.

I will chat with Herman this eventide. He has to be on his best behaviour from here on out. Me as well. And both of us need to work on our diplomacy skills if we're going to be part of a team. That is a top priority. I've never seen him be diplomatic, so I hope it's not a totally new concept.

Ouleah gave us one sun to wrap up our affairs and pack, then we head out to the new jobsite. She didn't offer any further details, saying the team would explain everything once I arrived. All I really know is that it's a rural location. I'll miss Magda and the fun parts of living in Aestradorra, but it will be nice to be in the wilds again.

I'm scared and excited at the same time. I hope this is the job I've been waiting for. The one that has been waiting for someone like me to come along. Ouleah said it was unique. Well, so am I. Perhaps we are meant for each other.

Cerridias, Crow Moon 25, 209

IT IS ONLY through the Goddess's benevolence and the excellent skills my flying instructor passed onto me that I am alive to write this journal entry. I fought Boreas's foul flatulence half the way here and had so many close calls with the ground and other pitiable creatures flung about in the maelstrom that I lost track. Normally, being hit in the face by a fat toad a mile up is a good omen, but it was just really windy. I mean, *really* windy! I had to strap myself in. My goggles were so coated with dirt and bug remains that periodically passing through rain clouds to rinse them off was necessary. Flying blind is no fun.

These blasted moors are treacherous. Had I known about the extreme winds, I would have arranged ground transport and spared the decade of my life I'm sure I lost to fear. That's one detail the union really should have made clear.

The accommodations are rustic. Not that I mind a peat hut, but I'd prefer not to share such a wee space with two other bunkmates. Yes . . . two! The Gingerbread Hut was bad enough with just Althea (and Sophie, but at least that little scamp didn't take up much room) and it was a much larger structure. This is a one-room hut, with three straw bales for beds, and endless piles of random components / tools / tomes / unidentifiable stuff. On top of all that, the whole place is rigged with a complicated structure of tubules, funnels, and beakers. They line the walls and ceiling, with small fire elementals camped under certain flasks to keep them boiling. It all looks very delicate and dangerous. We are screwed.

One room, three people, all sun, every sun. And my bunkmates are . . . interesting, if I'm being generous. This pond isn't big enough for our personalities, let alone all the other crap they have jammed in here.

When I first arrived, I couldn't see through the thick smoke which clogged the hut. Two disembodied voices greeted me from somewhere. I don't mind the smell of peat smoke. I actually quite enjoy it. It's homey. But breathing is a priority. With no windows and a small door (I practically have to fold myself in half and I'm not that tall), ventilation is going to be a major issue. How they haven't suffocated is a mystery.

That being said, I can't be too mad about the smoke. It's the only reason I found the place to begin with. Without that winding trail rising from the bog, I would have flown right over this grassy mound and never given it a second thought. I doubt the smoke was intended as a guide. There's a layer of greasy black residue on everything in the hut, so their hearth fire must be burning constantly. Not surprising given the chill environment.

Another fun fact: Both bunkmates are my supervisors. I did hear Ouleah right. So, now I have two supervisors and we all live together in a one-room hut. What could go wrong?

I'm trying to reserve judgment, but it's difficult. Maybe once I get to know them, things won't be so awkward. So far, they appear to be arrogant and odd (and not in a good way). Their explanation of my position did not endear them to me. I'm to be their maiden, the third wyrd sister (though from the looks of things, they could more accurately be called weird).

I confirmed that as Maiden I don't need magick, though they were very snide about it, as if they didn't expect me to have any talent to begin with. All I have to do is perform some ominous divinations—interpret portents and omens, scare up some gruesome warnings, that sort of thing. They don't have to be true, just disruptive. I can do that. I seem to be disruptive even when I'm trying my hardest not to be.

There is a rumble of disquiet in my bowels and the offal are rarely wrong. I'll prepare for the worst and keep my wits sharp. Despite the apparent ease of my tasks, something tells me that my position here is as tenuous as the glass piping which lines the hut.

I didn't get a warm, fuzzy feeling of welcome from my supervisors, but I'm going to do my best as their "maiden" regardless. I've never been drawn to the maiden aspect of our goddess. I'm more connected to the energies of the crone, which makes it doubly strange that I don't feel any kind of bond to the crone sister.

Crooked, wise, old Sages are usually my go-to peeps, but the only time she pulled her nose out of her cauldron all eventide was when she went to check on her boiling flasks. And the mother sister has an odd way of talking without focusing on you, so you end up wondering if she is speaking to the wall behind you, the vase of wilted heather to the left, or the rug under your feet. It's disconcerting.

They also insist on being called by their position titles and have done the same to me. I am no longer Hester Digitalis Wishbone, Initiate Witch. I'm simply Maiden.

Maiden is not a happy camper.

My apprehension hit a new high when Mother broke out my outfit (read: Uniform). The full impact didn't land until I tried it on. It can best be described as scraps of fabric attached to a tightly laced bustier, all of which seem designed to display copious amounts of flesh.

My flesh does not need assistance. I have, shall we say, generous proportions and I'm not comfortable showing them off. Even in school, I'd throw on a quick glamour and change my appearance to that of a suitably bony old crone. Plump witches just aren't as imposing as ones who are all droopy skin and warts. It's always been an issue. And now I'm being told, nay ordered, to put it all out there. Yeah. I've got a problem with that.

I asked if I could alter the outfit and Mother said no. It's designed to help me "pull" travellers and bring them in for the sisters to work their magicks on. So essentially, I'm bait. A lure cast onto the moors to snag wayward victims. And they said I can't use my broom to fly around either. I'm grounded. Fantastic.

My hope that this placement would be a good fit is well and truly doused. I mean, it is in the wilds and doesn't require magicks, but that is where the good ends (read: Falls off a cliff without a broom).

The incessant winds also make it a bad fit for poor Herman. I'll have to weigh him down or he'll blow away as soon as he sticks a feather outside. Luckily, I managed to grab him before the winds got too bad on the way in, but he was not at all happy about being shoved into my broom bag. His legs and neck cramped up, and he's pretty much all leg and neck, so I can imagine how uncomfortable that was.

He still hasn't gotten used to heights. He has a bad habit of flying low with his eyes closed, which works for short distances in Aestradorra, but not so much in windy conditions on the open moors.

I will have to keep a close eye on Crone. She perked up when Herman popped out of my bag and I later caught her flipping through a recipe tome. When she went to bed, I checked, and she had stuck a dagger in as placeholder for a section on how to cook exotic birds.

Herman is understandably nervous. He asked me to transmute him into something inedible right away, but I can't. Keeping us airborne this morn used up what little magicks are at my disposal and Magda isn't here to help with the power shortage. Given another sun or two, I'll be able to try again, but in the meantime, we'll just have to remain vigilant.

Freydias, Crow Moon 26, 209

Dearest Magda,

I hope you are doing well and that Missera isn't missing Herman too much. I'm sure he misses her, but he refuses to admit it. He asked me again to apologize for the attack. I don't think he'll ever forgive himself. He does have a conscience . . . who knew?! Well, that pretty much concludes the good news portion of this letter.

Last night, I finally got around to asking the sisters what their specialties were. I figured Crone had to be an Herbalist, but I could not for the life of me think of what Mother was. Now I know, and wish I didn't. Though, it does explain my initial misgivings.

Crone is a wizard and Mother is a druid. Can you believe it? Who thought a witch, druid, and wizard working and living together in cramped conditions was a good idea? Even coexisting in the same neighbourhood is fraught with peril. Goddess preserve me, this endeavour has the feel of a sun-bloated scum pod ready to blow.

Mother is obsessed with controlling the weather. She spends all her time brewing up storms and making fancy shapes with the clouds. I caught her using them as puppets to perform a skit (she made up voices and everything). She also seems particularly fond of a type of rain midway between water and ice. It not only drenches you, but with the winds, it instantly freezes your clothes into a hard shell (and I don't have that much fabric, so my skin takes the brunt of the cold).

She carries on conversations with everything. At any given time, she may be addressing a pebble, a dancing flame, a blade of grass, or several of them at once. The other sun she blurted out "well, get yourself washed then" and, assuming she was talking to me because I was right beside her, I took a bath in the peaty brown stream beside the hut. Turns out, she was actually talking to a gorse bush. She said it was complaining that its blooms weren't as bright as usual.

Gorse blossoms are the only thing that's even remotely bright out here. Eternal drabness shrouds the moors thanks to the storms. It's as if the Mystickal Mother of All was a painter who ran out of colour. The sky is a constant shade of grey, ranging from dove grey to soot grey. When eventide comes, the looming greyness is a darker grey, verging on black. But for a few accidental breaks in the clouds, I haven't seen the stars since I arrived. I imagine the great swaths of purple heather and golden gorse would be a beautiful patchwork on the hills if Helios's steeds could break through the gloom.

Thunderstorms are frequent and lightning strikes have set several peat-laden sections of the bogs ablaze. It's a deep, slow burning fire which produces thick bluish smoke that even the howling winds cannot disperse. I intend to stay away from those areas. They're eerie, which is usually a draw for me, but not in this case. I'm afraid the fires have undermined the already negligible solidity of the ground and I'll be swallowed whole, slowly roasting in a pit like a stuffed harvest pig.

It wouldn't be much of a change from the hut. The sisters keep it sweltering. The only relief to be had is outside, and then you're drenched through and half frozen by the time you make it back inside.

I used to love thunderstorms. There is a raw power in them, as if the primal energy of the universe is gathering around you. But, after two straight suns of storms, they're getting old. I counted and there have been twelve since this morn. One winds down and the next one booms to life. They are no longer exhilarating, just wet and cold and noisy.

At least my magick aids are quick to charge with all the energy flying about. And a good crashing storm puts Mother in a half-decent mood. If she creates these when she's happy, what does she conjure up when she's pissed? Here's hoping I don't find out.

Neither of the sisters seem the type to respond well to constructive criticism, so I'm hesitant to point out that more people might venture onto the moors if it wasn't thundering all the time. As it is, there's been nobody about.

Crone is just as interesting as Mother, though potentially less dangerous. Well, less dangerous to me. Herman is another story. I've hidden her exotic bird recipe tome, but that will only slow her down.

She spends her suns experimenting with disgusting concoctions and forcing us to try them. So far nothing has been poisonous in the small doses she's meted out, but I suspect several would be in larger quantities. I've already had to move the straw bale I sleep on because one of the beakers connected to her mass of tubes was overflowing and dripping onto it. I have no idea what it was, but it gave off fumes that made me feel like my head was floating in the rafters.

I would try avoiding her, especially when the vapours coming from her cauldrons and beakers curl my nose hairs, but there's nowhere to go. I wonder if there is some kind of transmutation I could perform on my tongue and nose to dull my taste and smell. If you've ever heard of anything like that, please let me know. It might help.

Crone is very particular about her things. I found out that Mother has the clothes on her back and that is pretty much it. Everything else in the hut belongs to Crone. She has piles everywhere and insists they are organized, though I don't think anyone sane could decipher her system. She tried to explain it, but she veered into complex mathematics and theoretical physics, including something called a Pauli Exclusion Principle, which involved a rather peculiar and ultimately destructive spin-y interpretive dance. Several of her beakers need replacement and the substance from one dissolved the corner off Mother's straw bunk. I was completely lost. She is definitely a wizard.

I fled into a storm and sheltered under that mouthy gorse bush to get away from the lecture. My skimpy clothes offered zero protection against the thorns, so it was an exceedingly uncomfortable hiding spot. I won't do that again. At least not until my magick has improved and I can command the brambles to let me pass without their boon of blood. Had I cast the spell in my current state, it would have taken several suns to recharge my crystals (I'm sure you remember the trouble I have with Earth spells . . . sadly, working with that element hasn't become any easier).

Curiosity got the better of me this morn and I decided to test Crone's organization scheme. When she stepped out to collect water from the stream, I switched a petrified mushroom from one pile with a lump of torpid tusker dung from another. She cast a suspicious eye around the hut (literally . . . there's a wizard scroll for that) as soon as she entered and said, "What foulness is afoot, under cover of squalls, change is come to covet my soot, hurly-burly within these walls."

It may have made sense to her, but I'm beginning to doubt it. She's just as loony as Mother. I'm stuck in the middle of nowhere with a weather-obsessed druid and a neat-freak wizard. It doesn't get any scarier than that. My goal is to survive, but if you don't hear from me again soon, please send someone to collect my body.

Both Mother and Crone have low opinions of witches. Not surprising, but still irritating. They think we're all charlatans pedalling phony cures and hexes to the ignorant masses. Unfortunately, my magick drought confirms their prejudice. During a particularly odorous conversation at supper, Crone equated witches to Outerplane entertainment magicians. Can you believe the gall?

I managed to stifle a rude retort this time, but it was close. There's only so much a witch can take. The employment counsellor was wrong when she said this position required diplomacy. What I really need is a complete lack of all senses, and sense in general.

I've documented the incidents with Mother and Crone and engaged one of the many air elementals partying outside to deliver a letter of complaint to our union. I also sent a copy to my employment counsellor and have requested reassignment. If she can't find me something else within a moon, I'll be stuck here for a whole season cycle. *Shudder.* I honestly don't know if it's possible to last that long with my sanity (and life) intact. I can put up with a certain amount of harassment, but between the epically sparse uniform, treacherous weather, constant insults, and questionable brews, it all feels very much like a deliberate pattern of assault. One that's escalating.

Hold onto your broom . . . there's a commotion on the other side of the hut and I can't see through the smoke.

My MENTION OF assault was timely. Crone was trying to shove Herman into her cauldron. Thankfully, he can be a noisy bugger when encouraged.

After the rescue, His Supreme Pinkness threatened to leave if I didn't immediately cast a transmutation spell. He left me no choice. He wouldn't last long in the storms as is.

Herman didn't know what he wanted to be, so we brainstormed a list of inedible creatures. Our components classes mostly dealt with poisonous, explosive, corrosive, or healthful substances. I don't remember much, or anything really, about inedible ingredients. I never paid much attention to the palatability of my potions. We sure could have used your expertise, Magda! Nobody knows more about esoteric components than you.

We had to be careful in our form selection. If I changed

Herman into something poisonous, he wouldn't be any safer. Crone would invariably find a toxic brew she'd always wanted to experiment with. We needed to find a foul tasting, yet harmless creature that she wouldn't consider useful in any way.

That's when I had a brainwave. Ghost slugs are the ugliest, most unpalatable, non-useful creature I've ever encountered. They have no real predators or purpose. They just kind of undulate about. Even vultures spit them out when they find them on corpses. That says a lot.

Herman agreed, though I can't say he's pleased with the result. He claims I made him look like a ghost turd and he's uncomfortable with people seeing his insides. I'm not exactly excited about it either, but it's the best solution I could come up with.

I pointed out that it should be safe for him to get fresh air on his own now. That perked him up. At least I think it did. His antennas waggled slightly. As a flamingo, I had to tie a rope around him whenever we ventured outside. He found the whole kite setup offensive and complained bitterly that the rope chafed. There's no need for any of that now. He sticks quite firmly to everything.

I'm not sure how I feel about having a ghost slug as a familiar. I think a cockroach may have been more prestigious, but at least he'll be safe. We can sort out a better form once we vacate this deplorable post.

Anyway, I hope you guys are having a better time than we are. I guess at least I'll have a few interesting stories to share when next we meet.

I miss you sooooo much.

Your best friend forever,

Hester Digitalis Wishbone

P.S. I will be drafting my last will and testament and sending it to you ASAP.

Pandias, Crow Moon 27, 209

THE MOMENT I think things can't get more interesting, they do.

Bob showed up last eventide. It was a bit of a shock for everyone since he crashed through the roof during supper and took out a section of distilling tubules. He must have perched on a weak section of the dome. I can't say the drop-in peating ruined supper. Crone had cooked up some kind of stew (the ingredients were unidentifiable as usual). Let's just say it was enough to make me nostalgic for boiled brats and gingerbread.

I was rather pleased to see Bob. He's not much of a conversationalist, but he's friendlier than the sisters. They weren't so happy to see him. Not just because of the cleanup and emergency roof patching we had to do either. I'm beginning to think they don't like having anyone around, even each other. And especially me.

Mother halted her storms long enough for us to fix the roof, which did nothing to improve her mood. On the plus side, I did get to see the stars. I'm afraid I spent more time gazing up at them than patching peat. Finding and tracing the constellations felt like visiting old friends.

I haven't let on that I know Bob. It would just complicate matters. I did point out the carved badge on his chest and suggested he might have been checking hut stability when he fell in. That shut them up.

He's still holding that bejewelled wizard wand he acquired in the brawl. And he kept the cinnamon sticks and pine boughs I hung on his ears. He looks quite bizarre. At least he'll keep the sisters guessing.

They have no idea what to make of him. Is he a building inspector? Is he a wizard? Is he a random gargoyle that was knocked off a building and whisked into a storm? They don't know and I'm not about to enlighten them. Not that I really know either. I mean, he was a building inspector when we first met, but now? Maybe he needed a vacation?

There was a discussion between the sisters about stone soup and rock sculpting, but I doubt they'll mess with him. Other than to move him. I tried to dissuade them from that too, but they wouldn't listen. Big surprise.

I didn't think they'd be able to lift him, but Mother commandeered some loitering air elementals to transport him outside. Of course, as a druid, she doesn't see them as elementals. She calls them nature spirits. As far as I can tell, they're the same thing, only I like to think they enjoy the company of witches better.

True to her usual flighty ways, Mother forgot the second half of her instructions. The elementals didn't know where to put Bob and ended up dumping him a little ways from the hut. It's a boggy spot and he had already sunk a couple inches by the time I made it out. He didn't seem bothered, so I left him. He can relocate himself to wherever he fancies as long as no one is watching.

Crone was livid. She spent the rest of the eventide rebuilding her wrecked tubule maze and sorting her disturbed piles. Thankfully, she was quiet-ish about it and I managed to get a half decent sleep.

I hope this sun is calmer. I checked on Bob first thing this morn and he's still there, wallowing in his bog. He's sunk a few more inches, but is sporting his trademark crooked grin and seems content.

There was a herd of baby hares snuffling around him. All but one ran off at my approach. The straggler hopped up into the crook of Bob's arm and did a very poor job of hiding. I suspect that one won't last long with Crone around. Though, to be honest, I can't confirm if she uses meat in her stews, so maybe it'll be fine.

I've been instructed to spend the rest of this sun drumming up business, which involves flouncing around the moor like an idiot. It won't work. Mother has a wicked storm brewing in the east. I'm sure it'll hit as soon as I'm a fair distance from any viable shelter.

But . . . I have a plan! I'm going to build a lean-to in a patch of trees I found. It's far enough away from the hut that the sisters won't be able to see it, yet not so far that I'll freeze on the way. And the thicket will provide some wind protection. Once it's built, I should be able to weather the storms in damp solitude instead of frozen solid solitude.

Herman hunkered down in the hollow above my collarbone while I slept last night and refuses to budge. It would be fine, except he undulates every so often and it tickles. I keep forgetting he's there and swatting at him. Good thing he's squishy.

Just heard an ominous rumble in the clouds. I'd better get moving. Time to put Operation Alone Time into action.

Tydias, Seed Moon 2, 209

I'M HAPPY TO report that my lean-to is complete and mostly solid. Herman decided to be helpful for once. He apparently picked up a thing or two about structural stability during his adventures at the Gingerbread Hut.

I didn't lose any extremities to frostbite during the construction, but it was close. My fingers were creaky and stiff by the time I finished. Thankfully, we're surrounded by peat (no fuel shortages for me) and it still burns when damp. It's just smokier and takes a while to light.

Once things were set up, Herman ventured into the underbrush. I didn't ask what he was doing. I don't want to know how slugs spend their private time.

It felt amazing to be on my own. I spent some time throwing the bones and reviewing the runic alphabet. I figure if I'm supposed to be reading omens and foretelling the future, I might as well do it right. I don't accept the sisters' "It doesn't have to be accurate" BS. Their tone was so condescending. I'll show them. I'll foretell the crap out of anyone who stops by. They'll be sorry they ever questioned this witch's ability to portent!

I was ordered out on another fishing expedition this morn. I didn't expect to meet anyone, but accidently ran into a maiden cutting peat on the southern edge of the wailing bog (there are no ghosts as far as I know . . . the noise is made by wind playing among the dead trees at its perimeter). I'll avoid that area in future. If only I had read my runes this morn, maybe I could have averted the ensuing fiasco. Then again, trying to prevent it might have made it worse. The Fates are tricky.

As per my orders, I invited her back to the hut and for some unfathomable reason she came. Why are maidens such a trusting lot? I put no effort into hiding my creepiness. Herman said I sounded downright menacing when I told her I had something to show her in my hut.

Anyway, I brought her back, all innocent and unsuspecting, and the sisters descended like a pack of rabid Lederswamp gerbils. They were all over her, touching her hair, petting her arms, shoving a cup of revolting-smelling broth into her hands. I would have freaked out if someone pawed at me like that, but not this girl. She just smiled and placated them, as if they were harmless old biddies starved for company.

To be fair, I suppose that is the vibe they give off. I know them for the dangerous nuttos they are, but I can see how an inexperienced person might be fooled, at least for a while. I don't know. This maiden seemed really slow to pick up on things. I hope this experience at least served to make her more cautious next time.

I did my job. I sat down with her and cast the runes. It was a pretty dull reading. There's a change or journey coming which she may or may not accept (the runes were wishy-washy on that). She has a foolish nature and can jump to false conclusions (no surprise there). And she's prone to emotional instability (duh, she's a teenager) and needs to spend time getting to know herself before she can be truly successful. Nothing world shattering. I cast the bones next, hoping for more drama. There was none.

Crone's attempt to make the reading more interesting was a nuisance. She's been experimenting with alchemical ghost conjuration and hasn't quite perfected the process. Instead of calling up a few dead souls for a nice roundtable chat, she only seems to get pieces. This time her concoction unleashed a fleet of disembodied heads that floated about the hut all muttering to each other. It was less disturbing than other parts she's conjured. Try waking up to a flock of ghost butts in the middle of the night. Not fun.

The incorporeal heads certainly surprised our guest. I shooed away a gentleman with an aggressively bushy beard who insisted on hovering right in front of me and blocking my line of sight to the bones. My hair, which the sisters insist I wear down at all times so that it whips about in the wind and impales my eyes, must have moved because the girl suddenly screamed, pointed at Herman, and fell off her stool in her haste to back away. Admittedly, a ghost slug riding about on a person is surprising, but it hardly warrants such a dramatic response.

Mother grabbed the maiden's hand, under the auspices of reading her palm, and spouted a bunch of nonsense. Seriously, she wasn't even using real words. Some of it was just grunting and possibly farting. To top off her act, she coughed up a baby rat in the girl's hand.

Between the floating heads and mouth-rat, the girl took off. Well, she did her best to anyway. She tossed the rat, which I thankfully managed to catch (Mother is so irresponsible!), tripped a few times on Crone's piles, and got her skirts caught on a section of broken tubules near the door. Her sudden clumsiness made me suspect something interesting had been slipped into her broth.

Mother and Crone melded into the smoky shadows and tormented her with animal noises, evil cackles, and shrieks during her escape. Talk about lame Outerplane magician parlour tricks. One of them even called a pack of small fire elementals that danced and darted around in the murk. Mother is the most likely culprit. She gets distracted at the worst times. A sprite nearly lit my hair on fire and we had several blazes to put out in the hut after. Fire does not go well with some of the things Crone is distilling in her flasks. I would ask why she didn't just summon bioluminescent water sprites, but they wouldn't have been as destructive, so that answers my question.

I have to admit, despite the cliché nature of the sisters' stunts, they were effective. I doubt that maiden will blindly accept invitations from strangers in future.

The poor girl eventually made it out. I watched her weave across the moorland. It didn't look like she headed for any boggy spots, so she must have kept her wits to some degree.

Kudos to her. That's better than most would do under that kind of duress.

When I came back into the hut, Crone sniffed at me with her nose in the air like an irate queen at a guest using the wrong spoon. Mother pulled me aside and gave a stern lecture to a spider dangling a few inches from my ear. Part of it was about the proper way to tell fortunes, but it veered into a treatise on responsive web design. Sounded like a fiddly enterprise. Glad I'm not a spider.

According to her, the only sensible way to do a reading is with entrails. She doesn't approve of the bones, and the runes were inconceivable. She needs to get out more. Her methods are *way* out of date. Nobody uses entrails anymore. Too messy.

When Mother finished that lecture, both sisters harped at me about sticking to luring and scaring, as opposed to actually practicing my craft. Apparently, creating the impression of doom and despair in meetings with clients is their sole concern. So much for my plan of stunning them with my presage skills. Looks like accuracy is just going to piss them off . . . now there's an idea that really stirs my cauldron.

I just let loose an evil cackle and now Crone is glaring. Whatever. If they're going to mess with me, I'm going to mess with them. And if messing with them happens to involve following my job specifications to the letter, so much the better. What did they initially say: No magick required, find victims (they didn't specify that bunkmates couldn't be considered), foretell futures, wear the unmodified outfit (no way around that), and be disruptive. Will do, sisters! WILL DO!

The way they mocked me at supper made me want to shove them in a cauldron and roll it off a cliff. Mother fished a pebble off the dirt floor, licked it, and dramatically proclaimed that she saw a round, iron object in Crone's future. It was black and hot. Oh, it's a cauldron. There's a cauldron in your future!

Very funny. So, the maiden's fortune wasn't exciting. Her boring life isn't my problem. Except when the sisters decide to harass me about it, I guess.

Crone got in on it too and made some asinine prediction about Mother going to sleep or snoring or something stupid. They went on like that for ages, but I ignored them. Gah. They are insufferable bullies . . . which brings me to the starting volley of Operation Sister Torment.

I did some quiet casting this eventide on two cocoons and hid one in each of the sisters' hay beds. A simple spell. That's pretty much all I can manage. From now on, whenever they say anything derogatory, insulting, or mean-spirited, a stream of colourful butterflies will pour from their mouths. I'm balancing ugly with beauty in true witchy tradition. They will hate it and I can hardly wait.

They must have pissed Herman off too because he left a trail of tubular poo on their stools. Took him quite a while. The curmudgeon is starting to grow on me (and not just because he looks like a slimy growth on my collarbone).

He made an unfortunate discovery during his poo mission. One of the sisters has a pet hedgepig and it caught his scent. Those buggers are the one thing that might consider eating a ghost slug. It doesn't help that Herman's new form is slow enough to lose a race with a fossilized turtle. He's scared, to say the least.

The spiky interloper is currently rooting around in my bed. I'll have to sleep with one eye open from now on. The only diplomatic and non-fatal (for the hedgepig) defence I can come up with is to sleep in the nude. At least that way I won't miss it climbing onto me. As long as Herman stays close, it should work. Thanks to the sisters' ever-burning hearth fire, getting cold isn't a worry and it's not much of a change from my prescribed attire. I doubt the sisters will even notice in the smoke.

Cerridias, Seed Moon 4, 209

AH, SWEET SOLITUDE! I never thought I could love a lean-to as much as I love this one. It is an oasis, a saviour, a sanity preserver.

Good thing I built it when I did. It snowed last sun. The flakes melted as soon as they touched the ground, but still, *snow*. And I'm dressed like a lusty wench at a beach party.

It's a cosy place to hide out. I have a small fire going with a cauldron boiling away on a rock. Night has fallen, so the sky is a darker shade of grey. One might call it charcoal. There's a break in storms and it's only misting rain, instead of the usual downpour. It's enough to conceal the smoke, and the trees and lean-to should hide the light of the fire. I'm safe from discovery for

now.

I happened across a healthy grove of nettles in my meanderings last sun and picked the youngest stems for nettle tea. I hung them up to dry in my lean-to. I'm enjoying a cup of it as I write. It tastes of green and hope. And it's hot. Very hot. I'm grateful for that.

The moors have many charming features: the solitude, the abundant peat, the fresh scent of wet heather. You can weave through the lowlands if you want to move about unseen, or climb to the high plateaus and see for miles (providing there's no fog or storms, which is rare but theoretically possible). Even the howling wind has its benefits. You can go for long walks without the constant nip of bugs.

I find the fog to be most pleasant. It can set a damp chill in your bones, but there's something magickal and comforting about the misty veil. It gathers around you like a soft bubble, making it easy to imagine nothing exists outside. There's just you and that little piece of the world. Nobody can see or hear you. There are no demands, or crises, or worries other than those you carry with you. Unless the sisters happen to be in the bubble with you, but even then, all you have to do is move twenty paces in any direction and *poof,* they're gone. Yes, I like fog. Fog is good. Fog is my friend. Fog doesn't fry you like a bolt of lightning.

I was forced to talk to Mother about her thunderstorms last sun. If they want me wandering the moors at all hours, I object to playing dodge-the-lightning-strike. One hit so close that all the hair on my body stood on end and smoke drifted up from the soles of my boots.

I came limping back to the hut to find Mother having a cosy tea party with a ball of lint, a dead sparrow, an aggrieved-looking stoat trapped under a basket, and a skull she kept referring to as Molly Scarhag (I really hope she wasn't their last Maiden).

I felt no compunction about interrupting. "You need to cool it with the bloody storms!" I forced the words out between chattering teeth.

A thoughtful look stole over Mother's face. Her eyes widened and she stood, abandoning her captive guests to stride outside.

Part of me hoped she had seen the error of her ways, but the majority of me knew that couldn't be the case. I followed her and watched as she swayed and chanted and gestured at the sky. She pulled something out of a pouch on her belt and ate it. Then she vomited a tarry substance that smelled worse than fresh troll droppings, coated a twig with it, and pointed the dripping stick at the clouds.

The black mass swirling overhead turned a deep, angry red. Rain pounded down, gathering in great pools . . . only it wasn't water, but blood. Mother spun to face me with an expression of wild elation. Streams of glistening blood trailed down her face and body, turning her white robes crimson.

"Bloody storms!" she hollered over the thunder. "Bloody brilliant!"

I backed slowly into the hut and left her alone for the remainder of the night. A druid lost in the ecstasy of magick is not something to mess with.

My feet were still tender this morn, but the lightning burns looked no worse than a mild sunburn. After confirming Mother had recovered from her bloody revelation and calmed down, I broached the subject of storm moderation again. She grudgingly agreed to tame her storms while I'm out, but I've seen little evidence of that so far. And now, thanks to my incautious wording, I have torrents of blood to contend with. My outfit is permanently stained. I look like I've been on the slaughter for a moon without washing. Given my current mood, I almost wish I had been, but all my new look really amounts to is false advertising. Sigh.

I suppose the thunder and lightning is slightly more distant. That seems to be the extent of Mother's cooperation. I was hoping she'd stop them for a while and allow some blue sky to show. Apparently, that wasn't an option. She muttered something about ambiance, but who really knows. She could have been talking to an imaginary gnat interior decorator.

What the . . . ? Hold on. I need to check something out.

OKAY. THAT WAS interesting.

So, there I was, hanging out, enjoying a peaceful cuppa, when this massive moth nearly blew down my lean-to with the beating of its wings. I went out to investigate the sudden surge of wind and strange humming. It must have been attracted to my torch flame because it dive-bombed me and knocked the torch out of my hand. I heard a sizzle, but it can't have been hurt too badly as it continued flapping around.

I've never minded moths as they eat some of the more pesky bugs, but I've never seen such a monstrous specimen before. Moths are imposing when they're people-sized. And not particularly attractive. There are some things you don't need to see in that much detail.

This one was hairier than a bear in a tornado. I couldn't be certain in the low light, but I swear the fur was mauve. It had long, bristly, wiggling antennae and produced a cloud of musty smelling dust from its wings. And its eyes . . . huge, black, bulbous things sticking out from the sides of its head, reflecting a hundred visions of my terrified face back at me. They offered no hint as to the nature or intent of their host. It was a thing of nightmares.

The moth continued to dive-bomb us (Herman was attached to my collarbone, as usual) even after my torch went out. The cursed thing followed us all the way home. Occasionally, a forceful gust of wind blew it off course, downing it or slamming it into a rock or into us, but it just kept getting back up. Throughout our harried journey, something niggled at the back of my mind. Something about the moth was familiar, but I couldn't put my finger on exactly what.

The sisters assumed I had brought it back on purpose and they were furious. When I tried to explain that it followed me, they accused me of slacking off with friends while I was supposed to be on the job. How they equated me running full tilt at the hut and screaming at them to open the door with a friendly get-together, I'll never know. Sometimes I think they are deliberately obtuse.

They stomped around muttering under their breath all eventide. What they said must have been bad because butterflies quickly overran the hut. Their fluttering appearance did nothing to improve the sisters' moods, but it sure helped mine. The more they insulted me, the more butterflies showed up, the angrier they became, which led to more insulting, and so on. It was fantastic. They were so confused. They couldn't figure out if the butterflies were tied to an illness, the giant moth's appearance, or something else. I'm sure they'll find a way to counter the spell, but I intend to enjoy it while it lasts.

The moth flapped about outside, but lost interest after a while. Good thing too. I don't know whether the winds were battering it against the side of the hut or whether it was ramming the structure in an effort to break in, but Crone's glass instruments were rattling in a most alarming fashion. It also dislodged clods of peat from the walls and domed ceiling. There's a good chance our peat patching was not up to par.

I ventured outside later to check on Bob and there was no sign of the moth. Hopefully it's gone for good.

Bob was not where I left him. Before giving into my anxiety that the bog had swallowed him and digging around in the muck like a crazed berserker, I widened my search. I found him squatting over a rabbit hole dug into the side of a small berm.

The opening and first section of tunnel were neatly shored up with sticks and rocks. A carpet of torn up heather adorned the inside and there was a new stone retaining wall in front to prevent the stream that develops during storms from eroding the hill. A professional reno job for sure. Bob must like those little furballs.

One of them is certainly fond of him. I found a baby hare snuggled up in the nook between his back and wings. I believe it's the same one from before. It has one floppy ear. The poor thing must have had a run-in with something. There's a bald patch on its backside and one of its rear legs was bloody. On closer examination, I determined that it had lost its left foot.

Funny thing, when I reached for the hare, I felt Bob move. It was slight, as if he tensed up, but I've never heard of anyone witnessing a gargoyle move. I mean, you know they do because they show up places and fall through roofs and collapse bookcases and stuff, but this was different. I was right there.

The hare's wound was clean, so I applied some of the salve I had leftover from my gorse scratches. I tore off a strip of material from my skirts (it didn't significantly affect the un-coverage), and fashioned a bandage boot. I'll check next sun to make sure it hasn't kicked it off.

Overall, my patient was accommodating and only let out a slight squeak when I first touched the wound. I wasn't paying close attention, but I also heard a twig snap. I suspect it was Bob shifting again.

I don't know what to make of a gargoyle with a pet bunny. I guess most people wouldn't know what to make of a witch with a ghost slug either. To each their own.

There was another brief break in the storms as I made my way back to the hut. In the shrouded moonlight, I caught sight of a fox pacing the summit of a hill. His gait was hitched, as if he were limping. I suspect I'm not the only creature this sun who witnessed a gargoyle moving.

Good on you, Bob. Sometimes the little ones need a helping hand, or a stone fist.

Pandias, Seed Moon 6, 209

I AM TIRED of being wet. I am tired of being insulted and belittled. I am tired of being moth assaulted every time I step outside with a lantern or torch. I am tired of slipping and falling in the unidentifiable puddles that leak from Crone's mass of tubules. FML

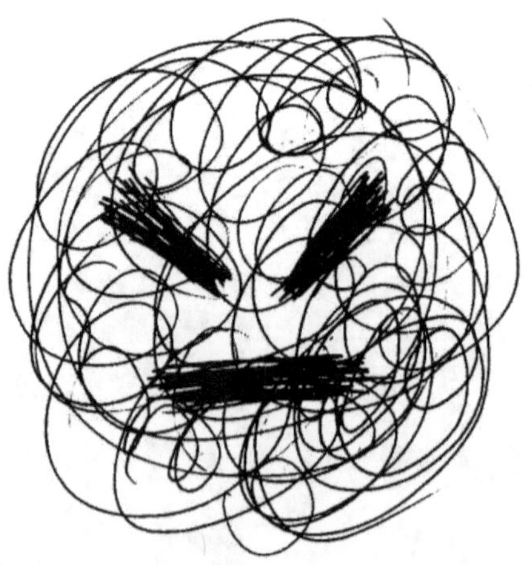

Mood Forecast: STORMY *with a chance of severe cursing!*

Soldias, Seed Moon 7, 209

I PLAYED MODEL for a while this morn. That was as normal as this sun got.

Crone had some crazy idea worthy only of a wizard. Instead of sleeping last night, she wrote out the longest algorithm I've ever seen. She marked up every available surface in the hut, including my body. I object to being used as a scratchpad, especially such a messy one. Even she couldn't tell what she'd written in places. I was blamed for that, of course. She accused me of moving and smudging those sections. Insert eye-roll here.

I had to lay still while she copied everything into a tome—a task that took half the sun. When I asked why she didn't scribe it in there to begin with, she sneered and said, "An artist must be unrestrained by common tools and dimensions while engaged in such a creative process," as if parchment was somehow beneath her. Wizards!

Whatever she used to write on me isn't coming off either. It must be some kind of indelible ink. She saw me scrubbing myself in the stream after and just laughed.

She got Mother too. Crone's scrawl is looped around her white robe in an elaborate diagram that resembles conjoined octopi. Miniature cyclones of insults and butterflies flew through the hut with impunity. Most of them weren't directed at me, so that was a welcome and unexpected turn of events.

I have no idea what any of the scribbles mean. Probably just wizardly nonsense—a formula to make water from water or something equally groundbreaking.

After Crone was done with me, the sisters sent me out onto the moors. Both of them were muttering about an end to strife, but neither the butterflies nor I see an end to it any time soon. Unless the sisters are considering personality transplants.

Before setting out, I popped by to see Bob and his new furry charge. The makeshift boot bandage was intact and the bleeding had mostly stopped so I left it alone. The young hare and its siblings cavorted about their friendly neighbourhood gargoyle and napped on a neat pile of freshly collected grass clippings. Bob's position was unchanged, but his stony expression conveyed contentment. I wished I shared that feeling.

I fought down a surge of uneasiness while trudging across the moors to my lean-to. I didn't know if the monster moth was still around and did my best to follow a concealed route. But, true to form, the Fates wove other unforeseen mysteries into my path.

Two guys appeared over the crest of a slope at the very moment I ventured through a shallow valley. There were no handy boulders for me to duck behind. No fox or badger holes to dive into. I would have even climbed into a prickly gorse bush, but no such haven existed.

After their round of enthusiastic catcalls and earthy suggestions, I hollered at them to shove off and carried on my way. They somehow took that as an invitation to follow and tried to engage me in a conversation about how nicely my hips swayed. Oratory geniuses, they were not.

Their mounts were high-strung beasts, warhorses for sure. Their sword hilts clanged rhythmically against the saddle buckles as they trailed me. With only limited magick at my disposal, no weapons other than my fists, and a ghost slug as backup, I was justifiably concerned for my safety. One never knows what strangers are capable of, especially when they believe nobody is watching.

I gathered power as I walked and muttered a spell to summon a fire elemental under my breath. One wandering sprite answered my call and I kept it in reserve. It was just large enough to create a flash. Flames were the only thing I knew of that consistently spooked horses, though I had no guarantee theirs were not battle hardened against it. Regardless, the activity and plan lent me courage.

The riders were persistent in their lewd suggestions despite my obvious disinterest, so I figured their poor behaviour should be rewarded, if only to spare the next lone woman they came across: A "be careful what you wish for" deal.

I had no intention of drumming up business when I set out, but the soldiers' enthusiasm escalated when I mentioned I had two sisters who would enjoy their company. One of them pulled out a flask and offered it to me, but I knew better than to accept unidentified drinks from strangers. The same cannot be said for them. It is amazing to me that most people survive as long as they do.

The poor sods followed me all the way back to the hut, laughing and boasting and telling rude jokes. All that stopped when they caught sight of my darling sisters. I had a hard time not cackling, but my humour was tempered with relief—an emotion I never thought the sisters would elicit.

After a seemingly endless litany of hails, Mother and Crone swooped in and coaxed the now reluctant men off their steeds with promises of a hearty stew and warm hearth. They never stood a chance. The sisters can be very persuasive.

They set the guys up at the table and Crone shoved bowls of a substance resembling lumpy soup in front of them. To their credit, they started out dubious and became more so after something in the liquid moved. I don't think either of them touched it.

Their hesitation was not lost on Crone. She filled two tankards from a barrel hidden behind a pile of peat logs in the corner and presented them to the guys as "the purest of distilled spirits you'll ever have the honour of tasting."

It's possible she wasn't lying. I've seen her sipping the odd dram of it, but I've never dared try any myself. It is the colour of piss and I'm not convinced she's beyond using that as an ingredient.

Whatever it was, the short hairy guy smelled it and must have judged it drinkable because he downed the lot and demanded more. Crone willingly complied . . . a little too willingly. She's not the accommodating type.

Mother made a big production of saying how skilled I was at reading the future, relating some bogus story about a child I saved from the clutches of death by predicting the sun they would be swept away in a rain-swollen river. She grabbed the head of the taller man and proclaimed that he was a kingmaker. Then, in typical overdramatic style complete with a crack of thunder outside, she dubbed the other a future king. I could swear she muttered "of fools" after, but I may have misheard.

The guys wanted to know more and insisted I order the Fates to lay bare the path of their lives. At this point, I began feeling sorry for them. It was obvious, despite their rough exterior, that these men were as naive about the ways of the wyrd as that first hapless maiden had been. But I had a job to do. I cannot feel responsible for every fool who crosses my path.

I put my (admittedly spiteful but still satisfying) plan to follow my job description to the letter into action and broke out my runes. Hello, Operation Sister Torment . . . you help me slog through each sun out here. Long live OST!

I started with our hopeful royal as he seemed the most eager. It was at least an interesting reading this time: Os, face up and reversed; Manu, face down and exactly between upright and reversed; Wynn, face down and upright.

I told him to carefully ponder his next moves because misjudgement and disaster loomed (especially with the sisters near, but I left that bit out). The runes saw a crossroads. One path led to opportunity, self-betterment, comfort, and material success. The other held unfulfilled potential, greed, and bitterness. Which path he would walk was unwritten. There was also an underlying warning that sometimes, it is best to seek change within oneself, rather than trying to force reform upon the world at large.

The runes revealed in him what could be either a lust for power or a

simple need to wrest some measure of control from the unpredictable Fates. I did not go into that. His companion was listening with rapt attention and I didn't want to prejudice his counsel one way or the other. They were obviously friends, and I am loathe to interfere with such a relationship, knowing its importance in my own life.

He wanted to know more, in the unwise way of those not acquainted with the hazards of plucking on the Fates threads. Most people think of their future as a linear progression, but witches know it is a fluid maze of possible choices and outcomes. The Fates just add the threads we choose to our life's weave. They are traveling with us, not guiding us: A common misconception.

They *can* see slightly farther ahead, given their lofty seat, but when that knowledge is shared prematurely, it mostly serves to complicate matters. Seeing an outcome before understanding how you arrive there leads to wrong assumptions and hasty decisions. This is why I rarely peer into my own future. Been there, done that, got myself kicked out of junior witch camp. It's why I'm cautious with presage advice, both giving it and receiving it.

I may take issue with the Fates on occasion, as cursing them is popular vernacular, but I know that the final umbrage, the real responsibility for what happens in my life, always lies with me. Others have yet to learn this lesson.

I tried to make these concepts clear to our kingly guest, but he was deep into his fourth tankard of spirits and the sisters were not helping. They kept shooting me foul looks and hissing at me to join them for a private council. I ignored them and kept my focus where it belonged, on our guests / clients / victims.

Throughout my reading, Mother whipped up a progressively stronger storm. Cracks of thunder shook the hut, sometimes drowning out my voice for long enough that I was able to brew a cauldron of tea. Wind howled across the moors like a starved wolf intent on breaking in. Swarms of brilliantly coloured butterflies clogged the smoke hazed air. Their incongruous appearance in the ominous setting confused everyone, except me.

Our door finally succumbed to the onslaught and banged open, shearing the bolt clear off the frame. We had to wedge it closed with a stool and a few strategically placed peat logs.

Crone ignored everything in favour of stirring her cauldrons (she had three going). She added mysterious ingredients from her piles and the occasional beaker of fluid from her tubules, all while chanting in the coma-inducing monotone she always uses. Honestly, I don't know how she stays awake. I suppose the shocking pongs and beaker explosions help.

As requested, I threw the bones for our wayward royal and delved deeper. They revealed a woman close to him who was not a good influence. She wasn't inherently malicious, just susceptible to outside influences and perhaps impatient. In fact, most of the people around him harboured ulterior motives and desires. Though, to be fair, that could be said of everyone in existence. The bones indicated a strong risk of him becoming a pawn in someone else's game, that the mask he wore would be all that was left if he ignored his true self and went solely with the counsel of others. That caught his attention.

He began talking so quickly that I was only able to understand parts of what he said. It didn't help that he was so intoxicated his words were a mushy slur. His companion had fared no better and was fully engaged in an awkward battle to keep his bottom planted on his stool and the stool planted on the floor. It was not going well. Mother was behind the trouble, as usual. I saw little roots spring from the wooden stool legs every so often and scoot it to the side.

I gleaned a few scraps of information from King's drunken ramblings. He missed his mother—she had recently died. Hoping to get past his grief, he married impulsively, for what he thought was love, but now recognized as a crush. Nothing I hadn't heard before. We've all been young and desperate to escape something. I suppose some would still consider me young, but I sure don't feel it.

He went on for quite some time about how he'd been pressured all his life to meet people's expectations, to fight, to be macho, but nobody once asked him what he wanted. This appears to be a common tragedy for both the highest and lowest born (though the two groups would never admit to sharing anything).

He was taught how to wage wars, cut his teeth managing armies, mastered battle strategy, became the effective killer his father wanted. But he secretly hated it. It wasn't how he wanted to live, wasn't the legacy he wanted to pass to his eventual children. He was an artist at heart with a passion for painting still life. Said he felt a calling to preserve beautiful snippets of time. Perfect moments. He waxed poetic about it. A lot. At least I think he did. Either that, or he segued into ballad lyrics. Most of it was incomprehensible.

My head was spinning from trying to decipher his speech amidst the random interruptions from the storm and sisters. Mother and Crone kept butting into our conversation (one-sided as it was), but he refused to talk to them. I think he deluded himself into believing I was interested in him. I admit to being interested in his story, but that's where it began and ended. My life is complicated enough without a royal in the throes of an identity crisis.

The sisters were steaming (and not just because Crone constantly stoked the fire, effectively turning the hut into an oven). Crone completely lost her cool when the guy started crying while relating how his father forbade him from painting because it wasn't a manly pastime. That was when she unleashed her floating heads brew. She's unaccountably attached to it and shows no sign of fixing the fact that she can't conjure whole spirits.

Disembodied heads joined the butterflies and smoke. They muttered and nodded and bobbed about the room. Very distracting.

King's friend passed out, either from fright or spirits or both. No doubt it was a merciful oblivion. King held his liquor better and carried on until the giant moth crashed through the door (and part of the wall), landing on the table like an errant mauve whale with wings. It must have stunned itself, because it laid there, flopping in a cloud of wing dust.

Mother launched into a sneezing fit that lasted the rest of the eventide. She must be allergic. I felt no sympathy. At least it kept her from belittling me or complaining about my excellent job performance.

Before the moth's arrival, King had been warily studying the floating heads and butterflies but largely ignoring them. When the monster bug crashed our party, I expected him to slay first and ask questions later, but he sat stock-still for a moment and then carried on with his story. I figured out what had happened when he waved a hand under his nose, said the colour red smelled funny, and then proceeded to dance in a rather suggestive manner with an imaginary fairy.

Crone strikes again. She must have dosed their drinks with something extra, as she did with the maiden.

The moth came to its senses, such as they were, and attempted to take off. Only there wasn't enough room to fly in the hut, so it hopped up, collided with the ceiling, and then hit the table again, sending it flying instead.

King inadvertently stopped the projectile with his head—a fortuitous interception as it was en route to the hearth and Crone's trio of cauldrons, not to mention the terminus beakers of several glass tubule systems. What would have happened when their contents mixed and met flame happily remains a mystery.

The table knocked King out and that's pretty much where I am right now. He's lying on the floor with his friend. They're still breathing (I checked). King will have a ripe bruise and bump on his head in the morn, but I'm sure he's had worse.

Mother ran outside to get away from the moth dust, so she's somewhere, not here—that's all I really care about. The storms have miraculously cleared up, so I'm guessing she hasn't found alternate shelter yet. A thick cloud of butterflies followed her out, so the hut is much less crowded. Crone is blubbering about the mess and straightening her piles. The moth finally settled after the hearth fire burnt down and is now glaring at me from a corner—the one with the spirits, so I guess I won't be sampling them any time soon. The same can't be said for the moth. It has extended a long proboscis or tongue into the barrel and is making slurping noises.

Herman and I are the only happy ones, other than the heads. They're still wibble-wobbling about chatting with each other.

Overall, I count this as an odd job, done well. I'm definitely getting better at thinking on my feet and I'm damn good at throwing runes and bones. Yay, me! The fact that my skill irritates the sisters makes it that much better. I've warned the future king, Mother is out of my hair for now, Crone is in it but preoccupied, and the moth already looks more mellow. This eventide may yet be rescued.

Moondias, Seed Moon 8, 209

MY PEACE LAST night did not last long. Mother came back and insisted we ditch the guys somewhere. I guess she didn't care to wake up next to confused and hung-over soldiers in the morn. Can't really blame her. The only problem was where she decided to dump them.

I, being the unlikely voice of reason, suggested we strap them to their horses and turn them loose (I've heard the beasts are generally smarter than their riders and instinctually head back to where they're from), but as usual I was ignored. Actually, Crone told me to stay out of it as I'd already cocked things up. She's way off base. I'm the only one who did anything useful with the guys.

Mother ordered me to stay and deal with the moth. She probably meant that in the traditional, mortal sense, but how do you swat a bug that big? Even if I could find something large and heavy enough, there'd be guts all over the hut and then Crone would totally lose her nuts.

I listened at the door as they harassed some air elementals into carrying our guests. This was after the sisters went through the soldiers' pockets and relieved them of anything interesting, which wasn't much, judging from their griping.

When they set off with the elementals in tow, my gut

grumbled with concern. I threw a blanket over the moth and followed as stealthily as I could. I wasn't sure whether the moth had passed out, or died. I don't have the foggiest how to check if a bug is breathing, but it smelled vaguely of elderberries, which isn't normally associated with death. In any case, under the blanket it was indistinguishable from one of Crone's lumpy piles so I figured I could "deal" with it later.

Those guys are lucky I decided to tag along. I was so focused on tracking the sisters that I gave little thought to our direction and suddenly found myself deep in the most treacherous bog on the moor. I wouldn't have attempted a crossing in full sun, wearing a cork belt, with a fairy godmother farting magickal glitter at me.

A dead scots pine let out a creaking moan as it slowly sank not ten paces from me. Its gnarled branches grasped at the moon's shrouded light overhead, imploring for help. The tree must have been majestic once, but the ever-expanding bog had drowned it long ago and now, as a final indignity, was wholly consuming it. It was a macabre warning of the trouble I was about to come face-to-bog with.

My body reacted before my mental processes kicked in, and I stepped back, sinking waist deep into a mud pit. No one can be smart all the time.

The soupy, peat-thickened water locked me in a deathly embrace as the last of the tree disappeared beneath the surface with a muffled *glub*. I did not want my life to end like that, sucked into the bowels of the earth, the last sound I made nothing more than a desperate belch of dirt and decay.

I knew moving would make my situation more desperate, so I did my best to stay calm. It was the hardest thing I've ever done. Since coming to the moors, this had been my nightmare. All I needed was an errant lightning strike to ignite the oven.

I also knew stillness wouldn't delay my boggy end for long. There is a hard limit to how motionless the living can be. It is frightening to realize that every breath brings you closer to death. And I'm not talking existentially. I'm talking in a hit-you-over-the-head, thanks-for-playing-but-you're-dead kind of way.

Each breath dragged me deeper and trying to hold it while panicking didn't work well. It was all I could do not to hyperventilate. What there was of my outfit might as well have been a weighted stone belt. It could have been worse. For once, I was grateful for my skimpy garb.

As I sank, my thoughts muddled. Random impressions like how the bog smelled of an earthy tea I once had in Kelospinerre kept sidetracking my escape plans, probably because I had no idea how to escape and my brain was attempting to distract me from inevitable doom.

Herman piped up when the bog reached my armpits and touched his tail end (at least I think it was . . . I have trouble telling the difference between his sluggy nether regions and his head when his antennae are pulled in). He slithered up my face and onto my head, berating me for our dire predicament. Until then, he had been uncharacteristically silent, so I had forgotten he was with me. He must have fallen asleep while I was walking. It happens when he's bored. Slugs sleep a lot.

I pondered whether I could raise enough power to transform him into something useful. A long snake might have been able to pull me out, but it would need to be a *really* long snake as the only sturdy anchor was another dead tree and it was a ways off. A bird could fly and bring back help, but the strong winds were problematic. And the sisters were the only ones close enough to respond. There was an equal chance they'd throw me a lead brick. They were pissed when they left. Butterflies everywhere.

The bird idea got me thinking about the moth who somehow managed to fly about in the gales. Was it conscious? Could I summon it? There was a glint of intelligence in its saucer eyes, but was it benevolent or malevolent? It could go either way based on its behaviour.

Summoning, summoning . . . my mind wouldn't let go of the concept. Mother was good at it. Her control of air elementals was impressive. She could summon strong enough ones to carry a man, but could I? Not right now. I could probably call one large enough to use as an air bubble should I get fully sucked under. It would buy me some time, but not much. And who knew if there were any elementals free. I'd say Air was Mother's specialty, but I had just witnessed her summoning life back into the feet of a stool, so Earth must also answer her call. And then there's the rains, so Water is in the mix, too. She is a veritable elemental artist. I mean, come on. I've never met anyone who could convince dead and burnished wood to grow roots . . .

And then it struck me. Could I gather enough power to tap into the roots of the heather around the mud pit? There was plenty of bog moss and myrtle too. Would Earth respond to my weakened call for aide? My turbulent history with the element was not promising, but I had to try. One braided root system wouldn't be enough to support me, but if I could convince the elementals to knit several together under me? Maybe!

I hurriedly outlined my plan to Herman and he more or less agreed. Mostly he yelled in his sluggish way for me to do something, anything. That was as much support as I could hope for, so I went to work.

The bog was up to my neck. Every time I swallowed, the rotten smell and pressure of it against my throat made me want to gag. I couldn't afford to. I had to reserve every movement and thought for gathering the energies around me. My crystals had some power left, but nowhere near enough. Calling Earth always took twice as much effort for me than the other elements.

There is a surprising amount of power in bogs. The predominant energy is not happy, lively, fun stuff though. It's the kind living things release as they die, and it's laced with their fear and hopelessness. It is uncomfortable to work with (unless you are a necromancer) and especially so if the witch wielding it is terrified and trying to ignore her own looming mortality. And when you then turn around (figuratively, in my case) and use that tainted energy to coax the few living things around you to cooperate . . . you can imagine how well that goes! Bog flora might thrive on decay, but that does not mean it wants a direct channel to the source's death throes.

It was a slow, taxing process. The earth elementals were less than cooperative because of the death energy. Every time I moved my hands and arms, I collected more of the stringy moss that grows in the top layers of the bog. It weighed me down and I had to split my concentration between the spell and keeping my head above the surface.

The bog reached my nostrils before I felt the first twitch under my feet. Herman devolved (if that word even applies to a slug) into a quivering lump of doom spouting swears like a bottomless bucket leaks water. He's usually pessimistic and paranoid, but I needed encouragement, not a slimy blob sitting on my head proclaiming we were going to "rot in stinking ass mud like bloated thrice-cursed swine."

By the time the roots knitted together strongly enough to push me up an inch, I was sneezing out chunks of decomposing vegetation and animal remains. Some roots gave way under my weight and I had to concentrate on reinforcing them. The carpet slowly thickened under me, and my mouth was suddenly clear of the bog. I spat out the putrid liquid and gulped air like a starving bigmouth globhee at an all-you-can-eat inn. My Great Goddess, there is nothing as precious as air when you have none.

With support from below, I worked my way to the edge, half swimming, half walking. I grabbed tufts of grass and hauled myself out of the sucking death trap. There I lay, finally on solid ground, staring up at the circling storm clouds, letting the rain rinse the foul bog from my skin.

Herman apologized for his unhelpful behaviour. His slug form is not fond of deep water (or watery mud pits). Something about breathing out of his ass. I don't know. I pointed out that I am equally opposed to drowning, but he was busy munching on an earthworm. Near death experiences make him hungry.

The sound of footsteps whooshing through the wet grass coaxed me into motion. Crawling behind a patch of heather, I waited and saw the sisters returning. They passed within a few paces, but Mother was conversing with a bat that had attached itself to her hair and Crone was absorbed in counting something. It might have been her steps. Not sure.

After they disappeared, I searched out a long stick. It was probably a branch from the recently departed tree. Morbid, but it worked nicely as a ground tester.

I considered turning back, but I couldn't do it. It felt too much like defeat and I was in no mood to be thwarted. I had tangled with the death bog and survived. I suspected the drunk soldiers might not fare so well. And what with one being potential royalty . . . well, I figured I had better make an effort. Royals have long memories. That can either be a good thing, or a very, very bad thing. I intended to ensure it was at least neutral with regard to me.

What those barmy sisters were thinking dumping them in that bog at night, I'll never know. It's likely to be a death sentence even if you have all your wits about you and the proper training and equipment.

Finding the guys turned out to be easier than expected. All I had to do was stop periodically and listen for their snoring. They could have out-snored a barn stuffed with overfed swine. They may have been worse than Althea, and that's saying *a lot*.

I was completely dry, in a magickal sense only, and had no equipment. The bog had even claimed my boots, so I was barefoot. Thankfully, the stick I'd picked up had a crook partway down that worked as a half-decent hook. I snagged their belts and pulled them out, one at a time.

They were too heavy to carry or drag out of the bog and, as sure as Hermes's pert tush, I did not want to spend the night out there with them. After a bender like this, they'd be looking for someone to blame. Or their wives would. I wanted to stay well away from that drama.

I brainstormed with Herman and he suggested I leave them a note. In theory, it was a good idea, but in practice, I had neither parchment nor writing implements (other than my blood, which is far too dangerous to leave in the hands of those who may not be friendly).

In the end, I left arrows made of twigs and rocks to mark a safe path. I wrote out the word "bog" beside King with pebbles. Hopefully, it was enough to get them out alive. They *are* soldiers, so dangerous situations are probably old hat. And, ultimately, they did get themselves into this mess. I really shouldn't feel responsible.

It took forever to make my way out of the bog and mark the path. I kept having to backtrack and search out new animal trails. There have been many untimely deaths in mud pits. Whenever a track came to an abrupt end, Herman muttered, "Another One Bites the Dust," in a sing-songy way. Sometimes I think he's a bit touched. There's no dust in a bog, only mud. Lots and lots of mud.

The very thought of the stuff makes me shiver even though I'm now dry and bundled up in a wool blanket in the smoking (literally) hot hut. I'm shocked I made it back. I may have hypothermia. I can't stop shivering, although at this point it could also be heat stroke. Can you have both at once?

Crone wandered around sorting through her piles and

checking her beakers, and then went back to stir her cauldrons. I heard her muttering about horse tongue stew, so I slipped outside to release the soldiers' steeds. I may not be fond of the hulking beasts—one of them tried to stomp me when I came too close—but I have no interest in eating them. Messing with the energies in the bog, feeling the moment so many creatures lost their lives, was more than enough death for one night.

The moth is no longer in its corner. The sisters didn't say anything, so it must have left before they returned. Lucky for it or I'm sure Crone would be contemplating moth gut muffins.

The door to the hut is laying about fifty paces from where it should be. I suspect that's how our friendly neighbourhood moth let itself out. The breach has not diminished the hut's internal temperature, so fixing it is a low priority.

I only know where the door is because I tripped over it on my way to see if Bob had been sucked into the earth's dank gullet (it's possible my tangle with the bog has made me more paranoid).

My stony companion was fine. Still hanging out by the burrow. The little injured hare was snuggled up in a dry spot under Bob's potbelly. Its more sensible siblings were fast asleep in their hole.

I mustered enough energy to check the baby's wound and change the bandage. It's healing well, but I don't know how far a three-legged hare will get in life. Out here . . . probably just far enough to fall in a bog.

Sheesh. I'm depressed. No, I'm just exhausted and still under the influence of bog energy. I should stop writing and go to sleep, but it's hard when I'm so angry. How could the sisters be so blasted irresponsible? Four lives were almost lost because of them. Well, two for sure. I need to take responsibility for mine and Herman's close call. I should have been paying more attention to my surroundings.

What a mess . . . and I'm not just talking about what's left of my so-called clothes, though I will be picking bits of bog from my ears and hair and every other nook and cranny for a moon. Those guys could have died. It's unlikely anyone would have even found their bodies. That's how places get haunted by nasty, face-eating spirits. Malevolent ghosts are the last thing that bog needs. It's fatal enough.

The sisters didn't ask why I was covered in mud when I got back. They probably think it's from burying the moth. Bah.

They aren't talking to me—like that's a punishment. The only thing Mother said when I returned was that she'd make sure I regretted coming out here. I told her that broom had already flown. She briefly choked on one of the resulting butterflies, which made me feel slightly better.

Her pinched look implied she hadn't expected me to talk back. Granted, it was more bravado on my part than anything, as she could probably squish me like a normal-sized bug if she wanted. I don't care. I refuse to stand silent while they bully me. I thought if I put up with them for a while, they might get better. I tried modelling appropriate workplace behaviour and that also got me nowhere. So now, I'm giving as good as I get. If I go out, I'll do it fighting like the fierce witch I've always wanted to be.

I haven't heard anything back from the union about my letters of complaint regarding this position or from Ouleah about my requested reassignment. I'm going to take my scry mirror to the lean-to next sun and see if I can directly contact them. Desperation is setting in. There is no way I'll last a whole season cycle out here, which means my only hope of making the Adept ceremony lies in getting out of this job as soon as possible. The time I have left to find a suitable placement is dwindling.

Wendias, Seed Moon 10, 209

Dearest Magda,

How are you and Missera? I hope this letter finds you both hearty and enjoying life. Herman and I often talk of our fun times together. We dearly miss your laughter and company.

I'm sad to report that things haven't gotten much better out here. I won't go into detail as that would take more time and parchment than I have, but I've been wondering if you've gotten anywhere with reversing the potion I inadvertently made at Moonbrews? The one that turned the customer into a caterpillar. I wouldn't trouble you so soon, as I know it's a complicated process and you're super busy at work, but I think Caterpillar Woman might have metamorphosed.

A giant moth showed up a few suns ago and is rather clingy. My supervisors are testy about its presence, among many other things. That's another story I'll tell you later.

I noticed (during a close encounter) that my mothy stalker has a mauve tint. Given the purple striations on the original caterpillar, it supports my hypothesis that this is in fact the second coming of Caterpillar Woman. I suppose it makes sense. I've heard of past mistakes coming back to haunt people, I just never thought it would be this literal.

Any-hoo, the wizard can't have a hearth fire at night, as the light attracts the moth (our roof and door area are less than secure due to some recent unfortunate incidents). And there's no room to spare for an oversized, freaked-out moth. Not being able to experiment with her concoctions is making Crone even grouchier than usual, and Mother is equally pissy. She's allergic to the fine dust on moth wings. It sends her into sneezing fits. I find it hilarious, but Mother, not so much.

Apart from incapacitating her, the moth also creeps her out. She said there's something "off" about it, like nails scratching down a slate in her head. She can't communicate with it either, which she says is odd for a druid, but I'm not so sure. Sometimes I can't understand her and we're supposed to be the same species.

I lured the moth away from the hut this eventide with a torch. It has become a nightly ritual. Although I hate to agree with a druid, there is definitely something odd in how it watches me, as if it's trying to communicate with a stare. Only, I'm not fluent in bug-eye, so the message is lost.

It might be releasing scents as well, but for all I know it could be having intestinal issues. It has been drinking Crone's spirits. Do moths get indigestion? Do they have intestines? Do they normally communicate via smell? Man, I wish I had paid closer attention in our Exotic Bestiary classes. I swear there's a pattern to the odours. Then again, it's also possible the druid's quirks have rubbed off on me. By the All-Mother's swollen cervix, that is a truly frightening thought.

What does the moth want from me? Does it want help changing back or is it out for revenge? Am I going to end up as some hapless victim in a made-for-crystal-ball feature called Revenge of the Mothlady?

Good Goddess! My life gets more complicated with each passing sun.

I scryed the union to make sure they received my complaint about this job, and they had. Their complaints department will contact me in approx. nine moons to collect additional information and statements. Then, they'll decide whether to proceed with my case or dismiss it.

Nine moons! What good is that going to do? That's quite the backlog. Maybe I should apply for a position in their department! Seems like they need the help.

Thankfully, Ouleah was a little more accommodating. She promised to contact the big boss (my supervisors' supervisor) and see if mediation can improve the situation. She's reluctant to just pull me out for some reason and sounded a bit nervous about the whole thing. I hope it isn't because there aren't any other jobs. I'm not overly hopeful about this mediation thing. I don't think Mother and Crone are amenable to change and neither of them seems to want me here in any respect.

Anyway, thanks in advance for any help you can offer with the de-mothing potion. You're a lifesaver as always (possibly quite literally in this case—Mothlady is *huge*).

Much love from your confused best friend,

Hester Digitalis Wishbone

Cerridias, Seed Moon 11, 209

SOMETIMES I SEE disaster looming and still fly full-tilt ahead. I can't really say why I do it. I suppose I'm too stubborn for my own good. Once I set a course, I stick to it from Hades' dark realm to the farthest stars. And I've always been a raze-the-fields-and-poison-the-wells kind of witch. If I'm going down, I'm going down in an age-ending fireball of destruction that will at least be memorable.

This was such a sun. Never again will anyone call Hester Digitalis Wishbone a pushover. Nope. Never. I stood up for myself. Who knew being fired by a goddess would turn out to be such a positive experience?

A midnight black dog, bearing more resemblance to a wolf than a tame pet, announced Her arrival. It strode into the hut and let out a bloodcurdling howl that plucked at the core of my spirit. I clamped my mouth shut to stop myself from answering back with a wild howl of my own. Nobody deserved that warbling catastrophe. I've been told I have the vocal stylings of an inebriated bat.

The sisters and I froze until the howl faded and the dog casually sat down. Its eyes, as bright as polished gold, never wavered from our faces.

Next, a snake slithered in. I had never seen the likes before.

At first glance, it appeared black but its scales flashed deep blue, green, and purple as it moved into the light. It was night personified.

The sisters shared a knowing glance.

Hushed hoof beats sounded outside, as if a horse trod upon the ether of the world instead of solid ground. Mother and Crone cast identical smug looks in my direction. My nose twitched in warning. If they were pleased about something, it didn't bode well for me.

There wasn't long to ponder what might come in next. Witches have a sense of such things. We are naturally attuned to the energies surrounding goddesses. All the hair on my body stood on end as if a spear of lightning was gathering power from the ground to channel through me.

An ancient woman appeared in the doorway, draped in a simple robe the colour of evergreens. She was small, but sturdy, and held herself as someone many eons her junior. Her pale, moon-shaped face was a maze of wrinkles framed by a glorious mantle of white hair which flowed to her waist like a river of spider silk.

She nodded once to the sisters and then her gaze rested on me.

I have never felt so exposed. Her eyes were of the night, stars burning at their core. She peered not at my physical presence, but into my soul, weighing it against some unfathomable measure. I do not know if it balanced out.

She held me in her thrall. For how long, I don't know. Time lost all meaning.

Eventually, she nodded and turned her attention back to the sisters.

I sat heavily on a stool at the table. It felt as though an otherworldly energy had suspended me above the ground and simply let go when she looked away. Even Herman squished himself into as small a slug-package as possible. I could feel him quivering against my collarbone.

There was no doubt as to who our guest was. It was Hekate, *the* patron goddess of witches, and not someone you ever expected or hoped to meet. Magick incarnate.

I had no idea why she was here, but I was suitably terrified. With Hekate, one never knew what might happen. She is my favourite goddess for this reason. Her unpredictability makes people loath to cross her. She is a dangerous wildcard, something I aspire to be.

I listened as she inquired after the sisters' health and choked on my next breath when Crone called her "Boss." After a brief round of pleasantries, Hekate took the stool at the head of the table and beckoned for the sisters to join. They sat together, opposite me, distancing themselves.

I'm recording our conversation in my diary for posterity:

"So," Hekate began, her voice strong and even. "I received a most grievous complaint from our latest client. She's unhappy with services rendered in regard to her husband. Why were we unable to fulfil this contract?"

Mother waded in, pointing the proverbial finger at yours truly. "Hester gave a truthful reading. *Very* helpful, she was. Told him to watch his step and not trust the counsel of others. By the time he, uh," she jerked and glared at Crone. ". . . left, he was prattling on about giving up fighting and painting fruit or some such rubbish."

Hekate's eyebrows rose. "That might explain why he abandoned the lady and enrolled in an art school in Acutaria." Her eyes flicked to me and then back to the sisters.

"How . . . uh . . . I see. So, he's ali . . . in good health, is he?" asked Crone.

Hekate entwined her hands on the table and leaned forward. "I suppose. Though, his mental state is in question among some circles. He claims he was kidnapped and narrowly escaped murder by a 'cabal of foul witches'—his words, not mine." There were hisses of pleasure from Mother and Crone. A slight grin played at the corners of Hekate's mouth. "And that an angel saved him and showed him the way."

"Poppycock! The guy was barmy." Mother scowled.

"That's a rich assessment coming from you," I spoke up, glaring at her. That the royal idiot had replaced me with an angel in his story stuck in my craw, but then what did I expect? Certainly not the truth. It was just overblown enough that he might end up the hero in a ballad or two. And I would be remembered as a pathetic angel with nothing better to do than act as a bog tour guide. Yuck.

"Watch your tongue, whelp!" Mother spat at me. "This mess

is your fault."

"My fault?!" I turned to Hekate, blood pounding so loudly in my ears that I could barely hear myself speak. "Were we contracted to kill the future king and his companion? Because I'm not an assassin. I'm a witch. I was hired as a presage to tell futures, not end them."

"Kill, no. Nudge in a certain fatal direction, yes. A job that required some magickal finesse, which is why we were recommended to Lady Macbeth." Hekate's eyes narrowed. "Why are you confused about the terms of this contract?"

I imagine I must have resembled Herman trying to shrink his body in on itself. "I wasn't aware there *was* a contract. I thought I had stumbled across two random travellers." My voice quavered, but, overall, I think I pulled myself together as much as anyone could under the scrutiny of a goddess.

Hekate turned to the sisters and I was able to breathe again.

Crone cleared her throat. "We keep contracts on a need to know basis because junior members tend to blab about our jobs to all and sundry. It's tedious. Plus, we didn't know how long she'd last. She's even more useless than the last witch. We should consider taking on a young wizard—"

"Or a fledgling druid," interrupted Mother. "Witches are iffy. Maybe we could—"

"Enough!" The ground trembled as Hekate spoke, and I nervously glanced at the patched roof. A few clumps of peat broke off, but the structure held. "Your opinions in that regard have been noted on numerous occasions. I am not here to discuss hiring practices. I'm here to find out what happened with this contract. All parties should be apprised of the terms of *every* contract, so they understand their roles. This is a serious management oversight."

She turned back to me. "Why do you harbour the belief that these gentlemen should have met their deaths?"

I watched the sisters, giving them a few moments to admit their part. They did not. "Because the sisters left them, drugged to the hilt and unconscious, in the middle of a treacherous bog in the dead of night. At first, I thought it was just carelessness, but now I . . . well, I believe it was a calculated effort to kill them."

"We were fixing what you bollocked-up," Mother screeched

at me. An owl outside added its own shrill cry, emphasizing her point.

Crone nodded. "We attempted to correct the witch's mistakes during the reading, but she paid us no mind. Not knowing what damage her insights might cause, we took extreme measures to protect our reputation, and yours, Boss. People go missing all the time in the bogs. Nobody could be blamed for it."

"I see." Hekate let out a long breath.

"She's been nothing but trouble since she came," added Mother.

"I believe that is what I was hired for." My blood was boiling—a state that always frees my tongue. "You said I was here to lure victims, wear this ridiculous costume, tell fortunes, and cause trouble. You got exactly what you asked for. It's not my fault your job description was vague as Hel. And, by the way, I find it vastly amusing that you've done nothing but question my abilities as a witch, yet now you're blaming me for giving a reading that was too accurate. You can both kiss my polished broom handle."

Hekate made a sound that was either a chuckle or a cough.

I turned back to her, reminded that I was in the presence of a goddess and should be more cautious with my words. "I'm deeply sorry for any trouble I caused you. That was never my intention. I have nothing but the utmost respect and admiration for you."

"Noted." Hekate pursed her lips, thinking. A drop of rain landed on her forehead as she gazed up through the shabbily patched roof. "Ladies, your hut is a little more worse for wear than I remember."

Mother left the table and spoke in hushed tones with a green leaf lying on the floor. It was a contentious discussion.

"Yes." Crone scowled. "More damage, courtesy of our new recruit. She can't go anywhere without bringing back a fleet of disruptive friends. Her familiar, and I use the term loosely," she said with disdain and a few butterflies, "has eaten great tunnels under the hut, undermining our floor and causing sinkholes."

She pointed to a repaired section of tubules. "Her gargoyle crashed through our roof and ruined my helliomite distillation experiment. Took me a full sun to fix that and another to set it up again. Her giant moth ripped our door off and batters the hut all eventide if I have the hearth fire burning. It's impossible to work under these conditions, and I am tendering my resignation if something is not immediately done to remedy the situation."

"Moth dust makes me sneeze," said Mother, lovingly caressing her leaf from the far side of the hut. "I'm with Crone. Either the witch goes, or I go."

"Oh, I'll go," I said, shooting daggers at the sisters (with my eyes only, unfortunately). "I have never in my life experienced such a caustic work environment. And that includes the practicum I spent as an aide to foreman Kilbrias in the sulphur pits of Jumerah. I'm sick of listening to you two rant about how useless witches are. At least now I know why you set me up to fail. You each want your own pet Maiden. Well, best of luck." I turned to Hekate. "You are of course free to ignore my plea, but please don't subject another witch to this position. Rabid harpies would make more pleasant supervisors."

I looked back at the sisters. "Just to bring some reality into this conversation—your hut is falling apart because Mother constantly whips up storms and things tend to rot when they never get a chance to dry out. Also, you built it in the middle of a bog, so is it really any wonder that you've got unstable ground and sinkholes? *And* if Herman has been tunnelling under the hut, it's because Mother's hedgepig keeps trying to eat him. Not to mention the fact that Herman is only a slug right now because Crone was thinking of making him into flamingo stew."

Apart from Crone's snort and another strange noise from Hekate, that may or may not have been a cough or laugh, silence dominated the hut.

I took the opportunity to change back into appropriate witch attire and gather my meagre supplies. Hekate's dog picked up one of my books in its mouth and placed it on top of my broom bag. There was a hint of sympathy in its golden eyes. I threw my bedraggled "uniform" at Mother when I was done, never so thankful to be free of a set of clothes.

"Sit," Hekate commanded once I finished packing.

I sat.

She glanced over at Mother, who was still chatting with the leaf. My proto-skirt was half draped over her head, unnoticed. Hekate rolled her eyes and directed her attention back to Crone and myself.

"I am letting you go, Hester, only because it is more difficult to replace two than one. You most certainly made mistakes here, such as ignoring your supervisors while on a job and, presumably, inviting friends to visit—"

There was a triumphant grunt from Crone.

Hekate pointed a warning finger at her and continued, "However, the onus for this contract failure does not rest solely on Hester's shoulders, and I am thankful that she ensured the gentlemen did not meet their deaths in that bog. One botched contract will cause far less trouble than Thanatos hearing I've usurped his authority. As you well know," she said loudly enough for Mother to hear, "I do not determine whether someone dies. I may simply expedite the process for those already slated. And Macbeth was not yet slated.

"Furthermore, I have considered your suggestion, Hester, and have the perfect candidate in mind to fill the position you are vacating. *I* will take up the Maiden's duties until the sisters are better versed in what proper management looks like. It's been far too long since my last jaunt as a youngster."

As she spoke, the webbed lines of her face smoothed, her body plumped in all the right places, and her skin took on the rosy shine of youth. Her hair remained the same luminescent white, but twined itself into an intricate crown of braids and curls. She was the very picture of youthful health, down to the playful smile on her full lips.

Hekate waved a hand and levitated Mother back to the table. The druid stared dejectedly at the newly shrivelled leaf in the palm of her hand and let out a faint whimper as a wind blew through the hut, scattering the dead fragments across the floor.

"Pay attention, Mother. This is important. You two have been warned to play nice—in fact, that is why you are out here—and yet you continually stir up trouble with every new maiden witch I hire. I am the Goddess of Magick. All magick, whether wielded by witches, druids, or wizards. You are all mine, no matter how fervently each of you insist I am your patron alone. It matters not what method you employ to work the energies, or what words you use to describe them. Every scrap of power in you comes from me. You would be wise to remember that what I freely give, I can and will take away if you continue to thwart my wishes."

Her words disturbed me as much as they did the sisters, but the look on Mother's face distracted me from my troubled thoughts. It was worth putting up with their endless barbs and put-downs just to see them taken down a peg. Though, if I ever die in a seriously ugly fashion, I'm certain it will have something to do with a ticked-off druid.

Crone's expression was strangely contented. I suppose she was just happy that I (and my entourage) would be gone and she could safely get back to her experiments.

The conversation seemed at an end, so I bade Hekate a final farewell, assuring her that I had intended no offence and hoped she could forgive my foolishness. She stopped me outside.

"Hester, do not despair. I spoke with your intrepid union representative. Ouleah is a special gift to us all and you are blessed to have her counsel. I understand your challenges. Every young witch must figure out where they fit. For some it is easy, but for others it is a longer and more vexing journey. You have talents. You will find your place."

I should have held my tongue and left, as it is never prudent to question a goddess, but I couldn't help myself. I had to know. "What you said before, about all magick coming from you and that you could take it away . . . is that what happened to me?"

She smiled. "Power should never be wielded lightly, especially in drunken bets. As a Daughter of the Moon, your actions have deep and abiding consequences—for yourself, those around you, and the worlds. You have a much better understanding of that now, wouldn't you say?"

I nodded, aware that far worse could and probably should have happened. What if I had accidently banished half of Magda instead of summoning half a phoenix? I would never have forgiven myself. My suns of drunken spell casting are over.

"By the way, the butterflies are an amusing touch." The humour dancing in her eyes faded and her voice lowered in warning. "But take care to never return to your old ways. Do not step beyond the line of balance with your castings. Magick will equalize itself, either through other wielders or through me. You must always understand what you are doing and the reasons why because they will shade the outcome."

I was silent for a moment, thinking back in time, through my jobs and college and earlier schooling, recalling all the questionable choices made and risks taken. The excuses and reasoning which made perfect sense at the time crumbled under the pressure of experience. Many of the consequences I had viewed as unfair and grossly out of proportion, suddenly felt like a gift, a fair shake at a second chance, and occasionally even a third or fourth. Some lessons took longer than others to learn. Most took even longer to understand.

"Thank you for . . . everything." I checked that Herman was safely positioned and settled onto my broom. "Somewhere, somehow, I lost myself in magick and it became all I was and all I valued. When it was suddenly gone, I felt like I was adrift in a hopeless void. I'm trying to find my way back. I really am. I centre a little deeper in my core every sun. I'm rediscovering who I am, my spirit. There's a special kind of power in that, a grounding completely outside of magick. Without it, I'm not whole and neither are my magickal workings. That truth sings in my bones. It is the piece I was missing. I've been searching for it my whole life without even knowing."

"A-ha!" Hekate clapped her hands in delight. "Then you are close to understanding your place in the worlds. I shall follow your progress, and that of your fascinating companions, with interest."

She absently waved a hand at the clouds and the storms circling the moors dissolved. The moon's rays embraced us and I looked up into the endless twinkling constellations. It was as if the night sky had been washed and polished.

No winds disturbed my journey back to Aestradorra and Magda. Not that I remember much of it. My mind was fully absorbed in the fact that a goddess had just declared an interest in my future. And not any goddess—Hekate, *the Goddess*.

The gods have even longer memories than royals. I am mired in some seriously deep trouble now.

Pandias, Seed Moon 13, 209

I GAVE MYSELF a sun to recover and now it's back to the grindstone.

Magda, being the kind soul she is, welcomed me with open arms, though she could barely believe my story. She wanted to know every detail about Hekate and was most intrigued, yet understandably terrified, about her interest in me.

There's nothing I can do but ride it out. I don't think my life is interesting enough to hold a goddess's attention for long, but Magda isn't so sure.

Missera was happy to have Herman back. She didn't stop hissing all eventide. He has taken to riding around on her again, like a slimy growth stuck to her back. It scared the crap out of Magda. From the amount of amusement our familiars derived, I'm guessing that was the intention.

There is no sign of Bob or the giant moth yet, but I'm sure they'll make an appearance. I warned Magda that Mothlady might show up. The only thing we can do is keep the blackout curtains closed after dark.

Magda is working on reversing my improvised Moonbrews potion, but progress is slow. I'm glad to be back so we can work on it together. Narrowing down the list of ingredients and factors is as headache inducing as the blasted enigmas in our

Magickal Probabilities and Analytical Casting courses. They always felt too close to thrice-cursed wizardry. It's a good thing Magda has never met a puzzle she didn't enjoy solving. I've always been a gut-level caster which is no help in this particular situation. At least I can do the grunt work of mixing and recording results for her.

Speaking of guts . . . mine were decidedly tingly and on edge when I stopped by the WU job bank this morn. For good reason! Justin—my old college boyfriend / nemesis—was there. It was a most unwelcome surprise.

I ducked behind a pillar when I spied him kissing his mother goodbye on the front steps. He left and his mother headed into WU headquarters (a swankier building beside the job bank). She wore business robes and looked mighty comfortable in her surroundings. My offal suggested I follow, so I did.

Lo and behold, what did I find? . . . the reason I ended up with a cockroach as a familiar and Magda, an asp! Justin's mother disappeared into an interior office in the Familiar Department. The fog has finally parted. I knew my familiar assignment was a calculated insult, I just didn't know why. Now, I do. And Justin probably overheard Magda telling me she was scared of snakes and passed that tidbit onto his dear mother. How spiteful!

The department's receptionist stopped sharpening her teeth long enough to curtly ask if I had an appointment. I pretended to be lost. It happens a lot as WU headquarters is a maze, several stories of maze in fact.

I suspect it was designed to weed out inexperienced witches and those with weaker magicks. The union has always attracted a snobbish sort—Ouleah being the only exception I've encountered. It's a challenge to find the office you're looking for without magickal aids, and, if you do get that far, chances are you won't find your way back out. It's fiendishly effective, but easily thwarted if the magickally bereft witch has a spot of common sense (sadly, not as common as it should be).

Not wanting to drain my limited stores of magick as I'm saving up to transmute Herman, I decided to hang around until lunch and follow someone out. Common sense FTW! Unfortunately, this left me with an abundance of time to ponder things.

Actually, I did more seething than pondering. It's painful to recall my suns with Justin and I hate that because a first love should be a fond memory. We met on the first sun of our first semester. I was proud to be a student at Grimoire College and believed myself to be a mature, sharp individual. My mind was full of ideas and hopes and idiotic misconceptions (at the time I thought them utterly brilliant). We snuck out of our last class and went on our first date. Yeah, I was super mature.

In the beginning, it was an enchanting, heady whirlwind. I thought myself blessed to find someone who shared my interests and who was so involved and caring.

Then his attention deepened. Became something ugly. Little by little, gradually enough that I missed the changes, he started taking over every aspect of my life, until I caught myself lying just to spend time with Magda.

I'm an independent person. To this sun, I don't understand how it happened. That's not quite true. At some point, a thousand tiny manipulations piled up enough for me to notice. I remember thinking it was easier to give in than to constantly fight over every little thing. Until then, he'd sneakily run off with whatever bits of control he could, but that was when I gave my power away.

That's no way to live, especially for a witch who's born to be one with the very elements of life. Powerlessness eats away at your spirit, makes you forget who you are and that you have a voice. I suppose that explains why I invested so much of myself in magick. It was my refuge. That connection was the only thing he couldn't touch.

Interesting. I never thought about it like that before. Huh. Score one for writing out your thoughts.

Come to think of it, maybe that's one of the reasons I have issues with authority (or people's perceived authority—there I go again).

When I eventually broke up with him, he took it far worse than I could have imagined. It was beyond embarrassing to tell campus security what had happened and ask for help breaking into our shared dorm room. The force field he erected was maddeningly beyond my ability, and I refused to abandon all my clothes and class tomes and, well, everything, including my dignity. Not sure I entirely got that last one back.

Involving the officials raised his ire, but that was nothing compared to when he found out I had moved in with Magda. From that sun on, he blamed her for our breakup and completely lost it. Everything came to a head when he directed a pack of fire elementals to torch our building.

I always thought he got off lightly, being expelled (I wasn't alone—I've never seen Magda so angry), but I remember his mother sitting behind him as evidence was presented at the college board meeting. She gave me a look that would have curdled the All Mother's milk. I guess it's not surprising that she took up his crusade to ruin our lives. Far be it for her to try to correct her son's atrocious behaviour. He probably came by it honestly. For all I know, his whole family is toxic.

I can't see Justin's mother carrying out this campaign of professional sabotage against Magda and myself without his knowledge. He must be involved. The spite behind it is all too familiar. I'll never forgive him for ruining my last semester of college and nearly causing me to miss graduating with my class, but I had hoped he would at least get past what happened between us. I guess not. In truth, neither did I. That kind of experience isn't something you walk away from without serious scars.

And now here he is, once again, making my life difficult. And Magda's too. She never deserved his wrath (neither did I, though that took me a long time to realize). It makes me sick that her friendship with me has cost her so dearly.

To be honest, I considered not telling Magda about Justin and his mother. It was a short deliberation. I owe her the truth. As thorny and complicated as it is, truth is pretty much all I have to offer.

The best path forward is veiled. We could expose Justin's mother, but that might not go in our favour. It's dependent on who she knows and how much the union cares. I'm not confident they'll care at all. But, doing nothing to balance out their malicious interference doesn't feel right either. I'll see what Magda thinks.

Bouncing off a hungry orc witch who was charging through the hall jarred me out of my thoughts. He stalked past and I followed, seeing my opportunity to escape the maze. Safe to say, our journey was speedy and unmolested. No one alive is stupid enough to get between an orc and their next meal. He led me directly out of WU headquarters and promptly disappeared into the nearest tavern.

After this morn's alarming revelations, my visit to the job bank was positively pleasant, if unhelpful. And to think, that was the part I had been dreading.

As I feared, Ouleah solemnly informed me there were no union job openings at this time. She promised to keep looking and said I shouldn't lose hope. Even she had difficulty giving the situation her usual positive spin. Then, she did something most odd.

She coiled several tentacles around me and pulled me into a corner. In hushed tones, she suggested I might have better luck obtaining freelance work at a non-union job bank. One of her tentacles slipped a scrap of parchment with an address into my hand while her others clapped me on the shoulder, gave me a firm handshake, and shoved me out the door.

Going to a non-union job bank feels a bit shady to me, but my options are limited: I can impose further on Magda and hope a union job opens up soon, give up and go home to my parents in utter disgrace, or take a chance on some freelance work.

I'm not ready to turn in my cauldron yet, but does a non-union job even count as a placement for my Adept qualification? If it doesn't, surely Ouleah wouldn't have made the suggestion. I'll have to look into it.

Now, I have to figure out how to tell Magda about Justin and his mother and our familiar misfortune. I feel so guilty and I seriously resent that. Damn them and their meddling.

NOTE: Ask Magda how Missera came to possess such a prolific collection of miniature hats. She has sported a different style every sun since my return. This morn she proudly slithered around in a jaunty new top hat adorned with a blue feather. It would have been an attractive look if it weren't for the pallid oozing lump on her back.

NOTE II: Do something about Herman's form ASAP.

Tydias, Seed Moon 16, 209

I MUST KEEP my scribing short this eventide. I'm knackered and covet sleep.

I spent most of this morn trying to locate the non-union job bank (not an easy task when their address only intermittently exists), and then I spent the rest of the sun browsing the posted jobs and chatting with patrons. Once I figured out how to get down to them.

The place is massive. Its entrance opens onto a balcony that extends around the perimeter of the building. The main floor below is crammed with makeshift boards and desperate job seekers. And I thought WU headquarters was a maze! There is a dedicated herd of minotaurs taking newcomers on guided tours (for a price). I should have coughed up the coin, but I got stubborn.

Even finding the platform that lowers to the main floor proved challenging. I tried to take the one the minotaurs were using, but I was sternly escorted off and told it was for tour groups only. After circumnavigating the balcony several times, I grew tired of searching and sat on a reasonably clean section of floor. Cleanliness and organization appear to be of equal importance to management.

Suddenly, I was sinking. At first, I thought I was experiencing some kind of slow-motion faint—the air was hot and thick with everyone's combined breathing and sweating and flaring and oozing. After a stunned moment, I realized I had inadvertently sat on an unmarked conveyer.

I've never seen so many different species under one roof. I expected fights but, apart from a scuffle between two alpha scaflags, there was little excitement. I guess the common goal of finding gainful employment binds tighter than speciesist enmity.

It's an old-fashioned establishment. Everything is printed on scrolls and tacked to boards. Nothing is organized. The layout is nonsensical enough that I suspect Crone or a close relative of hers must have had a hand in it. There were job postings for moreuvian apenator shrews in with ones for dighert domers, and everyone knows those two species release gasses that are explosive when in close proximity. I moved the dighert domer postings to a board on the other side of the warehouse.

I should have packed supper for myself. The comprehend lingua charm Magda lent me only works on spoken words, so I had to cast a read languages spell to understand the job postings. There were more languages represented than I believed existed. Keeping the spell active for so long completely sapped my power. *(NOTE: Recharge crystals!)*

There were postings for every profession and species. Finding something in the chaos that fit my particular skill set was a chore, but I ended up with three possibles. Three! My witch-sense screamed that this was one of Hekate's dreaded triple crossroad moments. I pondered my choices very carefully indeed.

I eliminated the first because of the fine print at the bottom: Scythian arthropods preferred. They probably want someone with detachable brain segments, and possibly claws. There's no way I have the skill or access to enough power to pull off that level of transmutation on myself at the moment.

The second posting was for an Apprentice witch. Experience and education-wise, I'm overqualified, but without full access to my magicks I might not be a viable candidate. It also mentioned something about caring for juvenile flying monkeys. I've never been good with youngsters in general, or FMs in particular. I imagine the combination would be catastrophic. Even so, I was reluctant to eliminate the job and took down the information.

The third job posting was the most promising. They want a practicing witch or wizard. I don't know why they didn't recruit directly from the union job bank—perhaps because they couldn't decide which profession was the best fit. Their indecision left a bad taste in my mouth, but I'll apply for it and see what happens. It sounds like an interesting opportunity:

RESPONSIBILITIES:

- Maintaining a house of horrors (love the idea of having my own house)

- Creating new tricks / creatures / scares (oh yeah!)

- Working with the public (not super excited about this, but I did enjoy terrifying villagers, so . . . maybe)

- Assisting with fiscal duties (who doesn't love counting coin?)

- Rotating food prep duties (hope they like gingerbread & Mean Cuisine)

- Managing a small team (they must mean the house monsters . . . they can be pesky, but I'm willing to give it a go)

APPLICANTS MUST BE:

- Independent (you betcha) but willing to work in a team

environment (as long as there's no homicidal druids and wizards)

- Willing to work irregular hours (those are my favourite)

- Open to new experiences (better than the same old crappy ones)

- Accepting of different personalities and customs (after Mother and Crone, I feel capable of handling anything)

- Used to travelling (am I ever)

- Able to think outside the box (I don't know what this means, unless they're worried about Larry Fishbone from Grimoire College applying—he had an unfortunate accident while he was a student, but the faculty managed to salvage his brain and plop it into a jar. For a preserved organ, he was a surprisingly popular and astute professor. Though, I guess in that case they would have said, "able to think outside the jar." So, yeah, no clue.)

- Flamboyant personality and eccentricity an asset (not sure about the flamboyant part . . . I hope they don't expect me to self-combust. I've lost enough robes.)

AFTER I SENT off my application, Magda and I had a good talk about Justin and our familiars. She was shocked at what they had done and agreed that some kind of response was warranted. We gently informed Herman and Missera, who were livid to discover they were pawns in a nefarious scheme to destroy our careers, and then spent an invigorating eventide plotting.

To start, we decided the best revenge would be to ensure everyone knows how wonderful our familiars are. News travels faster than fire in the union, so if we enlist Ouleah's help, Justin and his mother should hear in no time how wasted their efforts were.

Magda feared that anything we did to expose their interference would result in an assignment of new familiars. Despite all reason, we've grown fond of Herman and Missera. Herman is a terrible grump, but so am I. It probably takes one to put up with one. We would never willingly give them up, and we made sure they knew this, as they were both feeling delicate after the whole sabotage revelation.

With that option off the table, we pored through Magda's tomes and came up with an ingenious revenge. I knew the Two-faced Mirror Hex was perfect the moment I saw it. The set-up is extensive, especially since I need to transform Herman into something more mobile. He has to gain access to Justin's mother's office at WU Headquarters and steal items closely associated with her and her son so I can target the spell. Herman is naturally nosy and larcenous, so it shouldn't be too much of a stretch.

I felt it was too risky to send him in alone and Missera immediately volunteered. The two of them will be victorious. Their cunning multiplies exponentially when together.

Magda has all the spell components, which is a stroke of luck. I promised to reimburse her the moment I have coin. I feel bad about not being able to contribute now, but she told me not to worry. She's so excited about the hex and union infiltration that she's bordering on giddy. So are Herman and Missera. I never thought I'd see a sun with all of us happy about the same thing.

As I expended my magickal energy at the job bank, I'm unable to change His Squishiness into something less, well, squishy this eventide. He has to wait until the morn and is sulking on the back of Magda's couch. I can tell because his antennae are droopy and his body is scrunched up on itself (when he's content, he spreads). At least we were able to hash out what form he wants to try next.

A gershuat armadillo didn't make sense to me at first. And then it did. I'm sure being armoured holds a certain appeal, but something tells me the ability to spit acid has more to do with it. It also has a great deal to do with my hesitation. I have only agreed because he solemnly promised not to spit on anything or anyone without my express permission (which will *not* be forthcoming, but I didn't let him in on that). The armadillo will at least be speedier than his slug form, so it should work fine for our plan.

I just had a yawning fit. I thought Missera was joining in, but Herman said she's realigning her jaw after eating a mouse. She's curled up beside me, looking far too cute in her flowered sleeping bonnet to have just killed and devoured a rodent. That must have been one confused mouse.

Wendias, Seed Moon 17, 209

MAGDA WAS SO keen that she couldn't sleep and spent the night gathering and organizing supplies. She also took this sun off work so we could proceed with our plan right away. Yes. Magda played hooky! This shall go down in history (or at least my diary) as the most notable of suns.

Herman's slug to armadillo transmutation went off without a hitch. He waddles in his new form but his mobility is adequate. Justin's mother will never guess that he was the cockroach she assigned to me. Missera is accompanying him through the union maze, but will wait outside the Familiar Department offices to avoid being recognized. She'll only enter if there's a commotion.

It was interesting listening to them develop a plan. They work well together and their sneakiness indeed knows no bounds. Magda and I were quite proud.

Magda sewed Herman a sweet little set of bags that sit on either side of his back and tie together under his belly. She figured he should have something to hide his pilfered goods in. Thankfully, she's more skilled with a needle than I am.

And that brings us to where we are now. Magda and I are hanging out in the pub across the street from WU Headquarters, watching our familiars slither and trundle across the square. I admit I'm nervous, even though I have every confidence in their ability to carry out this mission. They were born to do this kind of thing.

MAGDA AND I polished off a pint of ale each and there is still no sign of our familiars. It's taking too long. What is going on? Are they in trouble? Do they need help? Why oh why did we decide this was a good idea?

It's too risky for us to go in and track them down, as we will surely be recognized, but if they don't come out soon, we will.

May the Goddess watch over them and sweep their path clear of obstacles. If she doesn't, and they are hurt in any way, not even Her benevolence will save the perpetrators from our wrath.

PROBLEM SOLVED. MAGDA wore a ring with a crystal sphere on it and we were able to charge the quartz with enough power to turn it into a mini crystal ball. My eyes hurt from squinting at the tiny image, but it works, much to Magda's surprise. She's never considered improvising a crystal ball like that before.

The union has anti-spy sigils covering various offices, but the Familiar Department must not have been deemed important enough to protect. They obviously weren't expecting trouble from the likes of us. As witches are sensitive to this kind of magickal spying, we're doing our best to avoid detection by limiting ourselves to quick peeks. So far, it's working.

Last we saw, Herman was sitting on a chair in Justin's mother's office perusing a densely lettered parchment. Justin's mother was scowling at the foreshortened legs on his chair. There were small puddles on the floor around each leg from which a vapor rose. I suspect Herman couldn't get up into the chair so he decided to do some spitting and bring the chair down to him. Guess his acidic saliva has already come in handy. This is one time I won't be chastising him.

Our best guess is that he was delayed because he didn't have an appointment. We knew that could be an issue but decided it was better to have the element of surprise on our side. Less time to be found out.

Missera has also been busy. She got into the walls and has worked her way up to the ceiling above the office to keep an eye on Herman.

HAHA. WE JUST checked on them again and our timing couldn't have been better. Missera dropped from the ceiling onto the receptionist. From the looks of things, his screaming was enough to get everyone out of their offices, including Justin's mother.

Herman took the opportunity to knock over her broom and search through her broom bags. We didn't focus on him long enough to see what he found because Magda wanted to go back and check on Missera.

She was fine, already back in the outer hall complete with a wickedly snaky grin. I expect they'll be out in short order.

IT IS DONE. Whenever Justin or his mother looks in a mirror, their reflection will be a giant cockroach. It's a benign hex, no real harm, but it'll be a royal nuisance. They'll know exactly who did it too, but they won't be able to tell anyone for fear of exposing what they did. Balance restored!

Although my magick is beyond drained, I feel energized in a way I haven't for a long time. Nothing is as satisfying as coordinated cursing in pursuit of justified vengeance, especially when it's carried out with your best friends. I'm sure even Hekate would approve.

Herman and Missera escaped WU Headquarters without any major incidents. I have no doubt there were a few minor acid meltings along the way, but I don't care. They were unharmed and in possession of a detailed sketch of Justin and his mother in front of a six-legged horse statue. When I saw his smug face grinning back at me, I wanted to call a fire elemental and burn it to ash. For once, I practiced restraint.

We cast the Two-faced Mirror Hex in one of the groves at the park near Magda's apartment. There were lots of elementals hanging around who were all too eager to help.

The only thing left for me to do is hide the focus mirrors that hold the hexes in place. If I secrete them away somewhere remote, they'll never be able to find them and break the curses. The Gingerbread Hut forest would be perfect. Perhaps I'll make a covert trip there while I'm waiting to hear back about a new job.

Magda insisted we go through a cleansing ritual when we got

home to remove any residual energy from our hexing. She sprayed everything and everyone with a cleansing essence, and filled her apartment with purifying incense smoke. It was like being back in the hut on the moors.

I can't blame her. This may spur Justin and his mother to strike at us again, but I suspect they'll think twice. Magda's magickal prowess is well established among Aestradorra witch circles and no doubt my exploits, no matter how accidental, have been making the rounds at the union. I might not be proud of them, but summoning phoenixes, even in halves, transmuting a witch into a caterpillar with a potion, and drawing Hekate's attention are no small feats. If I knew someone who had done those things, I would certainly keep my distance. In fact, after writing all that out, I really wish I could.

In her usual thorough fashion, Magda also created a Witch Jar for each of us. They act as decoys. If anyone casts a hex on us, the spells will be attracted to the jars and caught in them. I've never seen one made before. After cleansing the containers, she put a lock of my hair in mine, a toenail clipping from Herman in his, some moulted skin from Missera in hers, and a drop of blood from herself in her own. Then she added salt, a length of bramble thorns, and some kind of glowing herb to each and cast a spell. I don't know where she found the energy. She is amazing.

The Witch Jars are now on top of the cupboards in Magda's kitchen. She'll keep an eye on them and know as soon as one catches a hex. We warned Herman and Missera not to disturb them and they readily agreed.

If Justin and his mother foolishly choose to retaliate, Magda said she would set about balancing the equation with the help of her coven. I've never heard her speak in such a deeply serious tone before. She's such a sweetheart to me that sometimes I forget she's also a badass witch.

Cerridias, Seed Moon 18, 209

WELL, THIS HAS been an interesting sun. I wasn't sure I would have time to write in here this eventide as I've been wickedly busy experimenting with reversal potions and dealing with my ever-expanding entourage.

We have been keeping the windows and curtains closed, so as not to attract the moth, but it was a futile effort. Bob showed up early this morn with Mothlady in tow. And the baby bunny.

Magda and I were in the middle of an experiment when a horrible screeching and pinging of metal sounded outside her bay window. We found Bob perched on a small iron balcony with the bunny tucked into the crook of his arm. We narrowly managed to haul them in before the balcony tore away from the wall and clattered to the street. My back may never forgive me. Thankfully, it was early enough that there were no pedestrians. Magda told the landlord it fell off and didn't mention the gargoyle precursor. I doubt it'll get fixed. It's a good thing she doesn't care. Gardening was never her thing.

I don't think Bob intended to land on the balcony. He must have done so once he realized the window was closed. Then again, breaking things has never stopped him before, so I'm stumped.

Mothlady flew in during the rescue. She got tangled in the

curtains and the ensuing wrestling match raised a thick cloud of dust. Neither Magda nor Missera appear to be allergic. That's a bonus.

Magda was the only one happy to see the moth, despite the swath of destruction from her erratic flight through the apartment. She collected samples to test in her work lab. Magda has more toys at her disposal there.

I had a hard time not laughing at Herman. Despite his new armoured form, he is terrified of Mothlady. He let out a high-pitched squeal and rolled into a ball as soon as she burst in. I tried to help him out by nudging him in the direction of the couch so he could hide under it, but that just turned him into a rolling, squealing, armour-plated ball. Not the most survival-oriented reaction. I can see why gershuat armadillos developed armour.

Mothlady was in quite a panic. She flapped around the living room and kitchen, knocking over a bookcase and scattering components. Our Witch Jars were mercifully spared, but the parchments we're recording our experiment results on went everywhere. It took me most of the sun to sort that mess out. What a waste of time, and just when we're getting close. I should have been more diligent about numbering the pages.

After snuffing our candles and re-covering the window to hide the rising sun, I shooed Mothlady into a corner. She is very skittish and flies about at the slightest provocation, ramming into walls and whatever else is in her path. I always thought moths were delicate, but that is definitely not the case.

Despite this morn's excitement, Magda wanted to go out to celebrate our successful hexing. We arranged to meet at The Haunted Bonnet when she finished work. I attempted to sneak out of the apartment and failed. Herman was keeping close tabs on me.

Herman and Missera insisted on coming, so I shoved them in my cloak and walked to the tavern (after we waited for Missera to pick out a hat—a sweet little black number with a spiderweb veil, spider included). We were the first of the after work crowd to arrive and the place was empty save for one snoring regular in a back corner. I ordered a pint for myself and a half for Missera and Herman. That was when I noticed Bob's stony countenance at the other end of the bar. His bunny hopped onto the counter and lapped up the puddles of spilled drink.

The bartender, who was already looking nervous, beat a hasty retreat to the kitchens when Mothlady bounced off the doorframe and skidded in. Sighing, I poured myself another two pints and withdrew to a table at the back. I can't blame the bartender. A gargoyle, bunny, and monstrous moth, on top of a frazzled witch, armadillo, and be-hatted snake is a bit much. Still, I expected a place called The Haunted Bonnet to employ heartier staff.

Mothlady flapped around and eventually settled on top of a copper vat of mead. Out came her proboscis and there she sat for the rest of the eventide. I didn't let on that I knew her in hopes that the tavern wouldn't know who to seek reimbursement from. I'm sure she drained the vat.

Once Mothlady settled, my squealing armadillo reappeared from under the table and waddled off with Missera to join a game of dice with a group of newcomers.

Magda was surprised to see the whole crew when she arrived. I explained it wasn't intentional (at least on my part). Lucky for us, they were all engrossed in various pastimes and we enjoyed some much needed alone time to sip and chat.

It was lovely to have a good natter with Magda. Both of our families can be overwhelming and critical, so we commiserated about that. Then we lamented about our dating lives, or rather lack thereof.

I don't understand why Magda is still single. She doesn't want to be and she's such a wickedly smart, fun person. There has to be someone amazing out there for her. Problem is, most of the guys she meets are okay for the first few dates and then they go weird.

I've had a few of those myself, though not lately as I haven't had the time. No. That's not it. I think I'm just happy being single and can't be bothered to spare the time. There's more interesting diversions afoot. Hmmm. Yeah, that's not it either.

Seeing Justin brought some things back. Mostly bad things. Why would I want to go through all that again? I can't imagine what kind of person would date me while I'm such a mess. Wrong again. I can imagine. It would be someone like Justin who's looking for weaknesses to dig their claws into and failures to play up. Well, that's a big no thank you! No dating for me until I've sorted my life out. I talked about it with Magda and she agreed that was the safer path.

Homeless, jobless, loans up the broomstick, dwindling prospects of ever working as a professional witch, and a cadre of followers more destructive than a marauding army. Yeah, I'm a real catch. Even the bunny, who I wrongly assumed was harmless, chewed through the pipes for the on-tap ale. I could hear the bartender swearing in the kitchen as the pool of frothing amber nectar spread.

Herman and Missera did well in their dice game—and their other activities. Whenever a player left the table, Herman dropped to the floor and rolled himself into a ball. Missera then flicked her tail and sent him in whatever direction their mark was headed. The poor souls inevitably tripped over the armoured projectile and Missera slithered by, surreptitiously gathering any loose coins. Having a jaw that unhinges appears to be quite handy. It was a well-coordinated and profitable caper . . . until someone noticed.

I had to intervene when a dwarven waiter (the only staff member at The Haunted Bonnet willing to venture out of the kitchen) punted Herman across the room. My familiar wasn't badly injured, thanks to his armour, but I'm sure he'll be sore next sun. He certainly made solid enough thumps as he ricocheted between the table legs.

I was in the middle of chastising the waiter when I noticed Herman had teetered back and was drooling on his shoe. I grabbed my familiar as quickly as I could, but the dwarf's foot had already started smoking. Shortly after came the screaming and hopping and more screaming.

We decided it was best to leave. Magda and I must be destined to destroy taverns or be kicked out of them. Either way, our drinking holes are drying up and that is a desperate situation indeed. We'll have to start disguising ourselves . . . and our entourage.

So here I am, snuggled up on Magda's comfy couch again. Bob, his bunny, and Mothlady aren't home yet, but I imagine they'll show up soon enough. We left the window open to prevent accidents.

I had a talk with Herman about his premeditated drooling. He tried to defend his actions by saying he only promised not to spit on people. Drooling was not a prohibited activity. I rectified that oversight and he has now sworn not to spit *or* drool on anyone / thing. I made it clear that I was unhappy with his narrow interpretation and that it was not in the spirit of our agreement. He looked as disapproving as a gershuat armadillo can, which is quite disapproving. They have narrow, deep-set eyes, making them perpetually frowny.

ADDENDUM: Almost forgot . . . I found out why Missera has a fleet of hats. Magda worked out a tentative agreement with her. Apparently, they make her look less snakelike and more friendly. They bought a few and then had a bunch specially made. Magda's stress level has gone way down and she no longer screams whenever she sees her familiar around the apartment. Missera is quite taken with the hats, so it's a win-win. I suggested we should all take our hats off to hail Magda's giant brain, but everyone just groaned. My humour is wasted on this audience.

Freydias, Seed Moon 19, 209

I'M BORED. BORED, bored, bored. I suck at waiting and I hate not having something to do. I'm all out of magick energy and have to wait for my crystals to charge, but I don't feel like going out to find something else to do either. There are people out there and I'm not in a people-y mood.

HERE IS A crappy sketch of Herman and Missera:

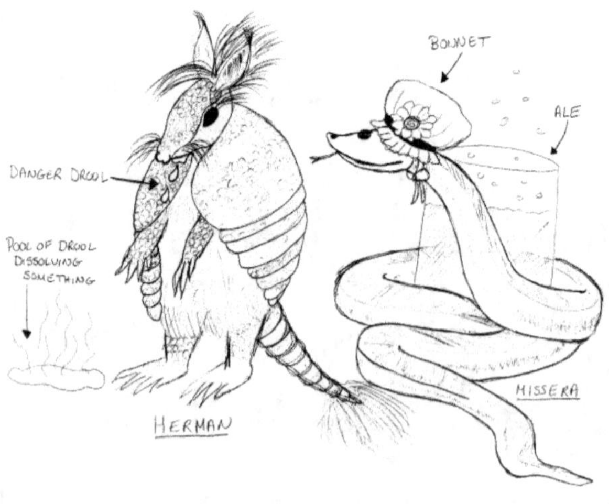

It took most of the sun. Herman says I made him lopsided and too fat, and Missera says the end of her tail looks like a poo that someone stepped on. Everyone's a critic. At least Magda appreciates it. She asked me to draw another one to put up on the icebox.

Speaking of Magda, she came home with exciting news! After running some experiments in her lab, she discovered a potion formula that should de-moth Mothlady. She's busy calling in some of her coven to help generate the energy vortex. Hopefully we can get it close to the one Mothlady had buzzing around her in Moonbrews. I should be able to identify it when I feel it. It was memorable.

We might be able to fix this tonight! I'd say I'm as excited as Mothlady, but I don't think that's possible. She's flapping up a storm that'll keep us dusting for a moon.

I must go now and help Magda prepare. There's potion components to gather and tidying to be done. Neither one of us expected company this eventide.

WELL, THAT WAS difficult and unpleasant, but ultimately successful. It is amazing what a group can accomplish when everyone focuses on a goal and is actually interested in helping. It's a rare occurrence. I will bake each of those beautiful witches a mooncake and imbue every stir of the spoon with abundance and health . . . just as soon as I recover.

Every nerve in my body is on edge from standing in the energy vortex. It took a while for the coven to get the correct mix of elemental power, but all the trouble and pain was worth it to put things right. I admit, I never felt that bad for Lady Tilandria Dobshire (formerly Mothlady . . . I should have guessed from her haughty attitude that she was a noble), but I did feel terrible about instigating yet another magickal accident. And that my Moonbrews boss, Andreas, was left to deal with the Infernal mess.

I did my best to smooth things over with her, for Andreas's sake. I apologized for my part in what happened, even though it's clear she still accepts no responsibility herself. Some people refuse to learn from their mistakes. I sincerely hope I'm never one of them.

Every witch Magda invited brought a bottle of ale or mead

and I made sure Lady Dobshire's tankard stayed full. This significantly helped with the smoothing over.

She was initially overwhelmed by the de-mothing and had difficulty adapting to having two legs and no wings. To my great surprise, she kept her irritation in check, only dropping a handful of insulting jibes and snobbish sniffs—a heroic effort for a noble.

I suspect her politeness had less to do with being magnanimous and more to do with concern over what might happen if she angered Magda's coven. She might have left with the misapprehension that I was a member. I'm okay with that. Nobody messes with a tight knit group of witches, especially not one with that many Sages and Elders. I'm lucky Magda flies in such interesting circles.

The moment we confirmed her transformation was permanent, I scryed Lady Dobshire's husband to let him know. He flew right over. Their reunion was enthusiastic, so I guess he missed her and vice versa. There really must be someone out there for everyone. Who knew?

They appeared eager to put this whole debacle behind them. I expect they'll drop the Infernal complaint against Moonbrews. Andreas will be very happy.

Pandias, Seed Moon 20, 209

I HAVEN'T DONE this much baking since the Gingerbread Hut. I slept late this morn and completely missed Magda leaving for work. I'm still worn out from last night. It's been hard to keep my energies up to instil the right intent into the mooncake batter, but I'm determined.

I wish Magda had bigger bowls. I had to scrub out my largest cauldron (a lot . . . apparently, I burnt whatever I brewed in it last time) so I could use it for mixing. In the throes of my fatigue, making all seven mooncakes at once seemed important. In reality, I'm not sure it saved any effort or time. Especially since Magda's oven only fits two pans. Hindsight.

The first two cakes are baking as I write. So far, so good.

MINOR SETBACK. I fell asleep and left the last cake in the oven way too long. Luckily, Herman woke me up when he noticed the smoke. He's the only one happy about the loss and was quick to claim the reject for himself. It's hard as a rock, but he insists it'll be edible (for him) if he drools on it for a while.

Time to mix more batter. And I had just finished cleaning everything. Go figure. Ah, poo. I'm also out of iinok eggs. Now I have to go to the apothecary and be around people. Curses! I'm feeling a serious need to hermit.

MAGDA AND I delivered the mooncakes to her delighted coven. I couldn't afford to add the Skiartian moon dew this time. I doubt they will mind. The cakes look and smell delicious. I'm exhausted, but it's a good exhaustion.

There's still no word on the job I applied for at the non-union job bank. I chatted with Magda and she agreed that now would be a great time to hide the focus mirrors from our cockroach reflection hex. Flying to the Gingerbread Hut forest won't be quick and certainly isn't without risk, but it will at least occupy my mind. I'm going stir-crazy. I'll be travelling light, so this will be my last entry for a while. Once more unto the breach. If Althea finds me, who knows what she'll do. Fates preserve me.

Soldias, Seed Moon 28, 209

*** THE END ***

JUST KIDDING! ALTHEA didn't get me.

I made it back to Aestradorra in one piece several suns ago but haven't had the energy to write. Making that quick of a turn-around trip is hard on the nether regions. And my back and arms have been stiffer than a petrified turd, despite salt baths and salves.

My journey back, though long and tiring, was fuelled primarily by excitement to share the good news with Magda. After hunting around for a suitably dank hiding place for the mirrors and spending a restless night hoping Althea wouldn't detect my presence in her forest, I received a scry from the non-union job bank. The position I applied for is mine! The company hired me on spec. This is my last chance to get and hold a job for long enough to meet the requirements for the Adept rites. I am scared, but also so, so thankful.

I've been dying to tell Magda, but she's been sleeping at her office and won't be home until this eventide. Probably late. We had a quick scry last sun and she looked exhausted. It didn't feel right to distract her by gushing about everything while she's in the thick of things. Before I left, her bosses put her in charge of a big project. Her co-workers reactions were seriously stressing her out. Many have been there longer than her and felt entitled. I hope they weren't jerks about it.

I'm going to brew up a rich, homey stew for supper. I wish there was more I could do.

Moondias, Nettle Moon 1, 209

MAGDA FINALLY CAME home and I eagerly related my news. She squealed and hugged me, saying she knew I would find something and weren't they lucky to have snapped up such a crafty witch—a ridiculous exaggeration, but I love her even more for saying it.

Herman was his usual surly self, but his mood improved as soon as I broke out a bottle of mead. Magda shares our love of the nectar so there was good cheer all around.

The Employment Cabal (who run the non-union job bank) teleported over a stack of parchments. I didn't get through all of them, but I read far enough to find out that my new employers have handled all the travel arrangements. Fancy! I've never had anyone secure passage for me before. All I need to do is show up at the port with my belongings. I feel like a VIW.

Only catch is, I fly Wendias morn. Two suns isn't much notice, but it's not as if I have a lot to pack. I'm pretty much packed already. There's a long list of restricted items for this journey, so I might actually have more things to unpack.

We all spent an enjoyable eventide watching dramas in Magda's crystal ball and relating details of our trip. While we talked, I got the distinct impression something was bothering Magda, but she wouldn't say what and I knew better than to pry.

She likes to think things over on her own and when she's ready to discuss it, she does. I bet it has something to do with her work project. If anyone was mean to her, I'm going to toad-ify them with extreme prejudice.

I wanted to stay up later, but my energy flagged. Darling Magda fluffed up the couch for me and even tucked me in. She is wonderfully silly sometimes. She really is the best of friends.

Herman curled up on a chair beside me with Missera. They thoroughly enjoyed the mead and are now snoring horribly. I considered smothering them with my pillow but that is probably uncalled for. Plus, it requires energy I don't have and it's surprisingly hard to contemplate smothering a snake wearing a bonnet. That accessory definitely works in her favour.

As tired as I am, I'm not sure I'll get much sleep. I hoped writing would help, but my thoughts are still looping around and around. Perhaps I should try reading more of the parchments. For some reason, I didn't expect such a robust parchment trail from the Employment Cabal. Live and learn. In any case, I'm sure their contents will be dry enough to induce sleep.

JUST AS I was drifting off, a raven flew in the window and landed on my chest. It hunkered down and stared at me, beak to nose, for a good long while. My feathered guest clearly had a mission, so I waited.

It croaked irritably, gave me the evil eye as it stomped back and forth across my chest, and then coughed up a crumpled parchment. The cheeky bird cocked its head, challenging me to take exception.

I'm proud to say that I kept my temper despite my extreme dislike of being thrown up on. I did flinch slightly when it cawed in my face and smacked me on the cheek with a wing. The turd flew off with my favourite quill pen, too. It was chattering to itself in glee, no doubt pleased with its bounty. I'll miss that pen.

The note was scribed in an elegant hand:

Keep up the good work, Daughter of the Moon.

It can only be from Hekate. Magda was freaked out and had to mix up a sleeping potion for herself before returning to bed. I had better follow her example. I can't risk being overtired. Goodnight, diary. What adventures will our next sun hold?

Tydias, Nettle Moon 2, 209

I AM SO angry!

This sun was flying by smoothly. I worked out what I could take to my new job and finished organizing things. Herman and Missera were hanging out, having fun.

Then, Magda came home early with her entire family in tow. She was near panic fending off an unrelenting barrage of cutting remarks from her parents about how silly they found her work and how small her apartment was. Her brother was no better, grumbling about how swamped they were at the shop and how much easier it would be if "someone" took her family responsibilities seriously and was there to help. Her three tormentors had showed up, unannounced, at work.

Poor Magda. My parents and I don't always see eye-to-eye, but at least they understand what I do because they are also witches. Magda comes from a family of blacksmiths who see nothing useful in the magickal arts. To them, magick is the refuge of the lazy and unskilled. I overheard her mother comment about how nice it must be, getting paid to just sit in a comfy chair all sun and swirl the occasional beaker. No respect. No understanding. No effort to look beyond their own beliefs or experiences.

They were like that when we were in college, too. They only

came to Aestradorra once to visit. And then it was only in an effort to convince Magda to give up her schooling and go home with them to do "real work like a responsible, contributing member of society." Her mother actually told her she needed to grow up and get on with her life, which encompassed raising a family to make sure there was someone to pass the shop onto.

These people, who should have known Magda's beautiful mind and heart better than anyone, had no idea how skilled their daughter was. No idea how seamlessly she worked with elementals or how inspired and creative her castings were. They must be wilfully ignorant.

Magda was born to be a witch. Magick flows through her like water to the sea. She had excellent innate talents and skills starting out, but a lot of hard work went into cultivating those into the staggering magickal competence she now has.

Anyone who thinks being a witch is cushy is clueless. The mental agility it takes to mould a casting, the constant drain of drawing in and pushing out power, suns spent researching and planning new workings, developing a sense of when our world's magickal balance is off and figuring out how best to balance it again without throwing something else off, everyone bombarding you with their personal energies . . . it's incredibly taxing. And as witches, we spend all the season cycles of our lives learning and re-learning our craft. There's always a better way to do something. Nothing in our job is static because magick is tied to our world and the world is constantly changing. What worked last sun may not work the same this sun. Adapting is exhausting! But it can be oh, so rewarding and wonderful at the same time. Loving your work doesn't mean it's easy, even if you're so good at it that you make it look easy, like Magda.

Her parents were the only ones who didn't come to our Initiate graduation ceremony. I cried for her that sun, though I didn't let her see. It should have been a time of family celebration, a time for our loved ones to recognize our hard work and feel pride in our accomplishments. Every smile, every hug and pat on the shoulder I got from my parents made me cringe because she deserved that, and more. She was the star Initiate of our class, not me.

And here her family was, still making Magda miserable with

their bullying ways. I completely lost it when Magda started crying. She sat down on the floor in the middle of her living room, drew her knees up to her chest, and buried her face in her arms. Her shaking sobs tore at my heart.

I knelt down and asked what I could do, but she couldn't even talk.

Magda's mother sighed long-sufferingly and complained about how tired she was of Magda trying to manipulate them with tears. Her father asked if there was any fresh milk to drink. Her brother sneered as he perused her bookcases, ignoring the situation . . . until he screamed and came away with an enraged Missera attached to his nose.

I've never been so angry, not even at the worst of times with Justin. I ordered everyone out of the apartment. I followed her family down to the foyer, told them not to come back until they were able to appreciate what a wonderful witch their daughter was, and slammed the door in their face. I must have unintentionally infused my push with some air elementals, because I blew the door right off and her family across the street.

It's strange. I've become so used to struggling to gather power and elementals, that it's a shock each time they heed my call. I'm still not back to normal, but some well-used Novice castings are becoming second nature again. I'll have to govern myself more closely. I don't want any more magickal accidents.

Magda's family was unharmed, if slightly dishevelled and shocked. Luckily, they didn't try to return or Missera, Herman, and I would have taken more serious measures.

Magda was a wreck. I bundled her up in a thick blanket on the couch and brewed a soup my father always makes when I'm not feeling well, along with some strong, milky tea.

It took a while before she was ready to talk, but I'm so glad she did. Sometimes venting your feelings relieves the pressure enough to make facing a new sun bearable.

Apparently, she's been under tremendous pressure for the last two moons to land a promotion that's coming up in her department. She made a minor mistake this morn that her jealous co-workers blew way out of proportion. And then her oh-so-not-helpful family showed up. She was so disheartened that she didn't see the point in going to work next sun, or ever.

We had a good cry together while the soup boiled. I am disappointed in myself. I allowed my professional woes to eclipse everyone else's struggles. I never meant to add to Magda's stress but I'm afraid that's exactly what I've done, and I'm a crappy friend for not noticing she was struggling sooner.

My world hit rock bottom when I lost my magicks and the village hag job. Some suns, it was hard to convince myself that I wasn't completely worthless. It's occasionally still a battle. That Magda would ever feel the same never occurred to me because she is so clearly amazing. She must have learnt early on how to hide her fears and doubts to protect herself from her family. She's very good at it and that's sad on so many levels.

We stayed up late, talking about things we've never shared with anyone else, or even wanted to admit to ourselves. Somewhere in there, I convinced Magda to eat and lay down in bed. Missera and Herman curled up on one side of her, with me on the other. We didn't want her to be alone. She's asleep now, as I write this. Her pillow is still damp from her tears.

I wish I didn't have to leave in the morn. I told her I was going to scry the Employment Cabal and get them to postpone my start date for a few suns, but she wouldn't hear of it. She even confiscated my scry mirror.

I agreed to go only because she promised to keep working for the next moon and to talk to me before handing in her broom if she still felt the same way after. I will scry her every few suns to check on how she's doing. I'm sure Missera will take good care of her, but I'm really worried.

Maybe Magda's current job isn't right for her, but I do not believe for an instant that she wasn't meant to be a witch. That's her family talking. Curse them for making her question her vocation!

Wendias, Nettle Moon 3, 209

TRIPLE GODDESS GIVE me strength! Whenever I think my life is finally getting back on track, the Fates wind up and smack me a good one. I don't even know where to begin.

I suppose I'll start with where I ended up. I'm in the Outerplane! The *Outerplane*! Gah!

The plane shift was . . . uncomfortable—imagine being folded in half with your head stuck up the ass-end of a dragon experiencing severe intestinal issues. That's close. Between the temperature fluctuations, foul smells, and a horrific wailing noise, I wasn't sure if I was going to make it. I'd say never again, but I'll have to go through it at least once more if I plan on making it back to my own plane. The indignity!

Things went downhill from there. I materialized in a room with a bunch of other poor sods, all equally horrified and ill. We were herded into an Interplanar Arrivals Terminal to wait in line for processing by a lone attendant—an angry goat with flappy ears who could only have been slower if she were traveling backward in time.

Usually ports are busy, but not this one. I guess there isn't much interest in visiting a level 7 null zone (big surprise), at least not via legal passage. From what I heard of Althea's trip, there is a booming market for interplanar contraband here.

When I finally got to the attendant, she asked what I was doing here and how long I was staying. Unfortunately for me, I couldn't answer either question. That didn't go over well. Honesty rarely does. She waved over a guard (at least that's who I figured the gelatinous blob was from the badge it had floating around its innards . . . though, there were a considerable number of other items in there too).

I explained that my new employers had arranged passage, hence my confusion about the details, and said there must have been a mix-up. There was no way the Outerplane could be my intended destination.

The attendant checked over my travel parchments. After a long sneer, she informed me that it was the passenger's responsibility to double-check all documentation and that I was "luckily" at the correct port.

My heart sank. I looked around with new despair as she ordered me to proceed to the luggage terminal. Beyond the little swinging gate beside her cube was a blank hallway. No signs indicated which way to go. I wandered, lost and more than a little confused, until I stumbled across a warehouse-sized room littered with luggage. Dust and cobwebs coated most of the piles. Locating my sack and broom took a while.

HERMAN WASN'T WITH my baggage. I wasn't overly surprised as the port in Aestradorra made me check him into a special terminal for animal companions and familiars. I searched around until I found a small kiosk tucked into a corner with a sign that read: Outsized, Irregular, & Unusual Baggage. I figured that described Herman perfectly.

A harried-looking ape-like creature covered in bright green feathers flitted back and forth behind the window. Although he was more enthusiastic than the first attendant, I thought he had made a mistake when he wheeled out a huge wooden crate stamped "Live Cargo, Etc."

Armadillos are compact—it's one of my favourite things about Herman's current form (possibly my only favourite thing). I was about to ask him to double-check my claim tag, when I heard a familiar groan from inside the box. I knocked on the side and was greeted with a string of Herman-esque swears.

Not sure I really wanted to know the answer, I inquired whether the journey had caused him to swell. My hands and feet had puffed up during the plane shift. Had Herman experienced a similar reaction, only on a body-wide scale, forcing the attendants to move him into a larger container? Based on its size, I was scared to see how much swelling.

My fears were shortly allayed and then stoked to a whole new level. Herman confirmed that he was mostly his usual size. The exception being a swollen, possibly broken foot as Bob had tipped over during transit. Also, the bunny was freaking out.

I swore loud enough to garner a worried frown from the attendant. I didn't care. Being stuck in the Outerplane was more than enough to contend with. Now I had a gargoyle and hyper bunny to manage, on top of Herman.

I couldn't fathom how in Hel's rooted realm they got themselves transported here. To clear Herman, I had to fill out a detailed form claiming him as an anxiety aide (what a laugh) because there was no box to check for "witch familiar." I would have remembered arranging for the rest of the gang to tag along.

The attendant's expression turned suspicious. His feathers rippled from green to yellow as he shoved a new stack of parchments into my arms and pointed to a door on the far wall. When I failed to move, he jammed the cart handle into my hand and gave me a shove. By the time the door closed behind me, his feathers were deep orange.

There, I found another line. I wheeled the cart to the end and tossed my sack and broom on top of the crate. I was settling in, preparing for a long wait, when the gelatinous fellow from the first line-up weeble-wobbled over and escorted me to a private room. And by escorted, I mean partially absorbed me and my luggage (including the crate, which was quite a feat), then spit us out when we arrived. It was messy.

A-ha, I thought. There *has* been a mix-up and he's going to apologize and see me back to my plane posthaste.

Not so.

Then began an odd ceremony in which he performed an involved set of gestures with a beeping wand while I repeatedly walked through a large metallic arch. It had the kooky air of wizardry about it. After the first ritual, two other guards joined the gelatinous blob for some synchronized wand waving, this time with a monotone chant thrown in.

There wasn't so much as a prickle of magick. Whatever spells they were weaving must not have worked. Probably because they hadn't bothered to memorize the words (they read the chant off a rumpled parchment). It never pays to hire the untrained when working magicks. At best, it's ineffective. At worst, it's cataclysmic.

They repeated the arch and wand ritual with my baggage. The crate caused quite a disturbance when it fell off the cart, lost its top, and Bob rolled out. His sudden appearance triggered some kind of alarm spell. A bright red lantern flashed on the ceiling and a loud wailing noise blasted from everywhere at once. There must be a banshee on staff. It took the guards a long time to reverse the spell and calm the banshee. Amateurs.

I answered another round of questions, pertaining to my profession and the disposition of my cargo. They became quite snarky when I said I was a witch. Probably couldn't fathom what business I had in a level 7 null zone. To be honest, I can't either. Why would anyone hire a witch to work somewhere they can only access the barest scraps of power (if any)? Given my condition, doing anything magickal here is going to be doubly hard. And I was just starting to shake this damnable magick drought. Curses!

The guards scrutinized my travel documents, which only worsened their confusion. I glanced at the original import parchments I filled out for Herman. There were several new pages attached detailing the crate contents. The scribe work was neat and precise, much like what I remember on the Notice of Condemnation I received from the building inspectors at the Gingerbread Hut. I will be having a long chat with Bob.

The new pages appeared to be the most contentious. Bob was recorded as décor. They gave him a thorough exam and grudgingly declared him a legal import. His bunny was categorized as a meat product, which spurred an argument over whether meat could really be meat if it was walking about (or hopping, in this case). Obviously, they have little experience with shambling akarathash. Their society is ranked by how much flesh is exposed, with the ruling class displaying an alarming amount of raw muscle and adipose.

After all their rituals and readings, the guards still had no idea what to do with us. The blob gave me a pair of glasses for translating Outerplane written languages, a guidebook, and another mountain of parchment to read and sign. Going through it all would have taken forever since they were scribed in infernal-ese (which the glasses predictably did not help with), so I relented and signed everything. At that point, I just wanted out. He let me keep copies after putting them through a strange wizard device that duplicated everything. I'll read them later, when I'm not so stressed and mind-fogged.

I convinced the guards to help roll Bob back into the crate. The bunny had taken a liking to the gelatinous fellow, so at least it was easy to catch, or rather extract. Last I saw, it was sitting on Bob's head, licking itself. Herman refused to go back in with them, so I stuffed him in my sack. The guards didn't care where I put anything, as long as I was on my way out.

They escorted us to a set of double doors which opened into an elaborately trapped loo. Normally I would enjoy such shenanigans, but my mental agility wasn't as keen as it should have been.

Three large stalls with gleaming porcelain basins full of water clearer than a mountain creek sat against the wall to my left. I initially thought they were for travellers to refresh themselves in but after a closer examination, one of the basins suddenly made a horrific noise and swallowed all the water inside.

What fiendish mind created such a trap? Or were they simply creatures skilled in mimicry? Imagine some poor fool being sucked into Goddess knows what or where. The Outerplane is a tricky place.

A row of smaller basins on a counter lined the other side of the room. Their polished spouts magickally produced water at a wave of my hand. A massive, impossibly perfect scry mirror hung on the wall above and a dizzying array of potion bottles crowded the back of the counter. I considered scrying Magda, but I didn't have the magickal wherewithal and didn't want to tell her what had happened until I stopped panicking.

I carried on to the next set of doors. One of two shiny creatures clinging to the wall growled as I passed. Its hot breath wafted over me and I jumped back, watching to see what its mate would do. The enraged one eventually quieted and I gave the other a wide berth.

An engraved sign hung above the doors at the other end of the room:

⸺ *[glyphs]* ⸺

The glyphs made more sense with my new glasses: *Interplanar Terminal Exit. Please refer to your Traveller's Guide for local customs and regulations.*

There had been no time to review the guidebook yet, and my knowledge of the Outerplane was limited so I went with my usual plan of keeping my head down. It works, at least for the short term.

Another plaque hung outside the doors which read: *Executive Employee Bathroom.* I barely had time to read it before I was swept away by a stream of rushed and anxious people. And by people, I mean mundane humans . . . as in they were *all* mundane humans. Every last one of them. Not a tingle of magick anywhere. I'm used to seeing a mix of forms and species and talent. The homogeny was jarring.

I had no idea where to go or what to do. The building was a never-ending vaulted monstrosity. Thankfully, people stopped crowding me when I proved I was willing to ram them with my cart.

I wandered aimlessly for a time and started to notice people reacting oddly. Some stared, while others avoided looking at me. A kid tugged on my robes and asked if I had a black cat. Her mother rushed her away after I said no and pulled Herman out of my sack. I don't know why. It's not like he was spitting or drooling. He was swearing but non-witches can't understand familiars.

A disembodied voice from overhead called my name and instructed me to proceed to Information Desk 5. I broke down and asked a human guard where that was, and she directed me to a brightly coloured desk, two floors down and a twenty-minute walk away. I attempted to ride my broom, but it didn't work. Not even a little. A non-operational broom is a serious issue. How am I supposed to get around? The guard looked concerned about it too and kindly offered to escort me to the meeting location.

When I arrived, a tall man stepped forward and asked if I was Hester Wishbone. I was pleasantly surprised to note that he was unique among the boringly uniform tide of humanity. Long, silky black hair covered every part of his body. At least I think it did. He wore trousers and a long sleeve shirt, so I couldn't tell for sure.

I nodded and he introduced himself as Sam, my new boss.

The person behind the desk and the guard exhibited a mix of fear and curiosity mostly directed at Sam. Like they wanted to stare, but at the same time get as far away as possible. Passersby showed the same inclination.

I smelled my robes to make sure I wasn't the problem but as far as I could tell, I wasn't putting off any offensive odours. It's possible my sniffer wasn't up to its usual standard. The swirling soup of humanity and strange chemical tang of the building had long since overwhelmed my senses.

Sam must have noticed everyone's discomfort because he asked if I was ready to leave. He offered to wheel the cart for me, but I declined. I wanted to remain in control of it to prevent another rolling Bob mishap. Sam held the doors open and we passed into air that smelled marginally better.

A herd of hard-shelled beasts with blazing eyes roared past us spewing clouds of vapor, and I suddenly knew where the chemical smell originated. Sam didn't appear alarmed, so I quelled my initial instinct to dive back inside and followed him through row upon row of the sleeping beasts. He stopped beside a huge box-shaped one. Colourful designs of intertwined snakes, divination cards, and a feathered man and woman flying toward each other patterned its skin. "Karneval Života" was inscribed on its side in fancy lettering.

He disappeared into the creature's posterior amidst a cacophony of loud screeching and rattling. I thought he had surely met his end, but he called out from inside, asking me to wheel the cart around. I did so with great trepidation, questioning for the millionth time what I had gotten myself into.

The beast turned out to be a kind of wizard mechanical construct with an empty compartment at the rear. The noise had been a door in need of grease. A new unease hit as I glanced around the lot and the full enormity of the situation settled in my mind. I was surrounded by more wizard contraptions than I had seen in my entire life. The Outerplane is overrun with them! Magda will never believe this.

After loading my crate, sack, and broom, Sam showed me to a smaller compartment at the front and belted me into a cushioned seat. Herman elected to stay in my sack. I shortly wished Sam had given me that option.

I am loathe to describe the abject terror of our journey. All I will say is that my screaming alarmed my new boss, who had no idea that travelling in a "truck" was a new experience for me. I'm sure there were probably some very interesting sights along the way, and I think Sam tried to talk to me, but nothing really registered until he stopped the infernal contraption in a field.

I threw myself out and kissed the ground, making a quick but earnest appeal to the All Mother for her continued protection. It made for an awkward introduction to my new co-workers who had gathered to meet me, but it didn't seem to faze them. They politely told me their names while I lay in the grass. Some of them inquired after my well-being. To be honest, I don't remember much of what was said. I was just so happy to be alive. I'd take flying my broom through the worst moor storm over traveling in a truck any sun.

Sam shooed everyone away and asked if I preferred to sleep in something called a trailer or a tent. I only knew what the latter was, so I indicated that would do fine and he showed me to a good-sized canvas shelter. I collapsed on a cot while my new co-workers filed in with blankets, a metal basin filled with warm water, a cup of tea, and a bowl of hot stew. Sam brought in my baggage, told me to get a good sleep, and to come see him once I recovered from my travels. A kind thought, but I don't think this is a trip I'll ever recover from.

Once again, I should be sleeping, but it mercilessly eludes me. My brain is too busy trying to assimilate everything.

What am I going to do? How am I going to get out of this contract and make it home? I mean, my co-workers seem nice enough, but it's the Outerplane. It might be a fine place for a witch to vacation (so far, I don't see the appeal), but work here? No way. No how. I can kiss my Adept initiation goodbye.

ADDENDUM: My scry mirror isn't working! I'll try again in the morn, but given that this is a null zone, I may have to go back to sending letters via air elementals—if I can find any. Of all the cursed times to be out of contact with Magda! I promised to scry as soon as I arrived. I don't want her to worry and desperately need to check in to see how work went this sun.

Cerridias, Nettle Moon 4, 209

Dearest Magda,

I am so sorry that I couldn't scry you this morn. Writing letters is a pale substitute. I wanted to tell you how thankful I am to have you as a friend and craft sister, and wish you a great sun at work. Your bosses and team are lucky to have you, and if they don't appreciate your skills, I'm sure there are any number of companies who would be glad to have you. No matter what you decide at the end of this moon, please know that I stand with you. Always.

I had hoped to share with you the details of my incredible journey and let you know I was having a blast in my new job. Unfortunately, it's safe to say that the only blasts I'll have here will be as a victim of haywire wizard contraptions. The Outerplane is crawling with them.

Yes. You read that right. There were a few details missing from the Employment Cabal's job posting. Now I see the hazard of acquiring work at a non-union job bank. My new employer is an Outerplane travelling entertainment show called Karneval Života. Given my luck, I suppose it's not that surprising. Being stuck here is pretty much the only cursed thing that hasn't already happened to me.

I have come to terms with the fact that I won't pass my Adept rites with the rest of you. There's no time to find a new job and I don't see how this one can satisfy our union's placement standards. For a brief moment in the interplanar port, I thought about contacting Ouleah and asking her to officially approve my position thereby making it eligible, but that was before I found out I was working in Outerplane entertainment. Gah.

I spoke to the boss, Sam, about bowing out of the contract. He was understanding, if disappointed. When we first met at the port, he thought I was perfect (first time anyone's said that about me), but he knows the carnival lifestyle isn't for everyone. If people stay on, he wants it to be because they're happy to, not because they have to. So I'm free to go, except it'll take a while to save up enough coin to buy passage back, which means I'll be working in the show for a bit. Sam said he hoped I would give them a fair shake. I don't think he meant that literally, but who knows. There's some very strange customs here.

I've already discovered that they record suns and moons differently. A sun is referred to as a day, a moon is a month, and a season cycle is a year. Thank the Goddess that their mathematics are close to ours and they count the suns in a moon similarly. It is apparently April (moon) 23 (sun), 2020 (season cycle).

I relate the following account of our travel saga in hopes of making you laugh and showing that you are doing just fine, at least in comparison! Herman and I arrived at a port in the USA, which is the name of this sprawling landmass, in a metropolis called Topeka Kansas. So many people and so little magick to keep them at bay.

Given the lack of magickal power on this plane (my scry mirror won't work and it's fully charged!), thrice-cursed wizardry has proliferated, and it is unusual to see anyone without at least three vile beeping, wailing, or flashing devices somewhere on or near their person. They walk around with these dodgy things as if they're best friends and then are surprised when they do something unexpected or catastrophic. Repeatedly. After the third time something goes wrong, it shouldn't be a surprise anymore.

The boss is an interesting fellow and seems friendly, but get this . . . *Sam is a wizard*! He outright admitted he was trained in mechanical engineering. Didn't even flinch when he said it. I'm keeping a close eye on him. He comes off as level-headed and reasonable, but no wizard is truly either of those things.

He is known theatrically as "The Beast" when he performs in the "big top" (a really, really big tent). He took over the carnival (a family business) when his mother died last season cycle. Sam is human, but he's covered from head to foot in the most lush, shining hair you could imagine. It's quite distracting talking with him when all you want to do is reach out and pet him. I wouldn't, of course. That would be horribly rude. At least it would be on our plane. I don't know about here, but I'm not taking any chances.

Sam lives in something called a motorhome—a sweet little one-room hut—or at least it would be if it wasn't attached to a truck (a type of wizardly mechanical transport that is particularly terrifying). I should have expected nothing less of a wizard.

He showed me around the House of Horrors, the "joint" they hired me to run. It's a wicked set-up: Two levels of rooms (six in total) connected by dark, narrow hallways lined in warped mirrors with hidden nooks and crannies from which any number of terrors could spring. The whole place is rundown and needs spookifying.

One of the rooms is witch themed, but has been decorated in a manner that is, quite frankly, insulting to professional witches. We do *not* use wands and wear ridiculous pointy hats. I can't even imagine the wind drag on those things while riding a broom! Wizards are the ones who dress extravagantly and wave wands around willy-nilly. Witches use sensible tools like brooms and cauldrons. And we absolutely do not use bones to stir our cauldrons. Yuck! I could see a druid doing that, but never a witch. The people here have witches, druids, and wizards all mixed up. It's now my personal mission to set them straight.

Despite the above issues, the House of Horrors has potential. Part of me is excited to turn it into something worthy of its name, but with limited magick power available, I don't know if it's possible. Then again, I've recently had to get by with no magick at all, so maybe . . .

I told Sam I'd do my best to fix the place up, with the

understanding that I still intend to leave as soon as I have enough coin. If you have any ideas about how I can do that, I'd love to hear them.

I am at least pleased that there are no bratty kids to care for and no clients to knock off. All I have to do is scare the warts off everyone who comes in the House of Horrors. I figure between myself, Herman, and Bob, that's an eminently achievable goal. Oh yes, don't fret if you can't find Bob or his bunny. They tagged along.

During my grand tour of the midway (where all the games, individual performance areas, and hideously dangerous wizard rides are), a shifty goblin-faced man showed up. The way he spoke and his mannerisms reminded me strongly of infernal demons. I was immediately wary.

Turns out, my impression was somewhat accurate. Although he was not an Infernal, he was a loan broker. Close cousins. I could tell by the way Sam's back and shoulders stiffened that our visitor was a known and unwelcome entity.

Sam left to deal with him and I followed out of curiosity (at a discreet distance, of course). My stealth was unnecessary. A great deal of shouting and banging arose from Sam's motorhome, so I overheard most of their conversation, as did everyone in the camp.

Sam took out a loan after his mother died as there was a slump in bookings and their operating costs increased. Something was inflating and something else was deflating. Both were bad. I didn't catch the specifics. The broker was here trying to enforce his right to review the financial records, and he wanted to bring in appraisers to assign coin value to everything. Sam told him to back off and that he wasn't to bother them until the season was over. The broker threatened to inflict us with something called bankruptcy if the carnival didn't turn a profit. Sounded nasty, whatever it was.

I need to get some protection spells in place. Or charm bags. They'll have to be stashed everywhere, but they take less power to create, which is important.

I didn't expect the broker to come out of the meeting alive. Sadly, he did. And he was sporting a vicious smile as he slammed the door.

Sam was greatly upset and stayed in his motorhome for the

remainder of the sun. He didn't even come out for supper (the whole troupe eats this meal together . . . I'll have to figure out the etiquette around this ritual later because nobody was talkative this eventide). I asked if someone should bring Sam food, but they said it was best to leave him be.

It's obvious from the way everyone speaks of Sam that he is trusted and admired. I feel bad about being so negative about working here. My new co-workers have been nothing but kind and helpful even though the loan weighs heavily on their minds. Finding a replacement for me so soon is an inconvenience none of them need.

I would have loved to do something suitably hag-tastic to the loan broker, but until I determine how magick works here (or if it does at all for me) it's best to keep things mundane. I might have whispered in Bob's ear that if he happened to haunt the broker every so often, some extra juicy cuts of meat could be left out for his bunny. I'm not sure where Bob is at the moment, but I hope he's sitting on something precious and breakable in the broker's hut.

Anyway, I need to sleep. Maybe I'll dream up an ingenious plan to improve my joint without magick. BTW, "joint" is what everyone calls the attraction they run—so the H of H is mine.

This whole situation couldn't be more screwed up if I had tried. Sometimes I don't know why you're my friend. I couldn't even get a job on the right plane. And now, these people need help, but what can I do? Even at home, my magick is a shadow of what it was, what it should be. I can't decide if the Fates are laughing or crying at this turn.

I'll send you letters as often as I can. Please write back and let me know how everything is going. I hate being so far away from you and will endeavour to rectify that, ASAP. In the meantime, I'll be thinking of you.

Brightest blessings,

Hester Digitalis Wishbone

P.S. People gave me very disapproving looks when I fed the bunny raw stewing meat this eventide. Were they disturbed that I shared my plate with it at the dinner table? Did they think the pieces too big for such a young bunny and were concerned it might choke? I know their income isn't great, so perhaps it was just that there was an added mouth to feed. Yet another Outerplane mystery to unravel.

Freydias, Nettle Moon 5, 209

ENOUGH MOPING. I'M kicking myself out of this funk. Almost nothing has gone right lately (for me or my new co-workers, it seems) and I'm getting pissed. So what if I'm on the wrong plane. At least nobody here knows about or cares that I won't pass my Adept rites. So what if there's practically no magick power. I'm used to working with limited resources now. Challenge accepted!

That's right. I'm a badass witch with a badass attitude and I'm going to make waves. Big, crushing, thundering waves! The Outerplane won't know what hit it. Hester Digitalis Wishbone has arrived!

I put my plan into action first thing this morn by going around and properly introducing myself, along with Herman and Bob's bunny. Everyone fawned over my companions. I have a feeling they're going to be quite spoiled.

I also discovered what the kerfuffle over Bob's bunny was at supper. The Outerplane only has *vegetarian* rabbits! I showed them its teeth, pointy and clearly optimized for flesh consumption. They were amazed and apologized for the misunderstanding.

Several of them have noticed Bob perched in various locations around camp, but they aren't commenting (possibly because they never actually see him move). I think I'll let him handle his own introductions.

My co-workers are an engaging and fascinating lot, if a bit human heavy (an endemic problem here). I had many interesting conversations while helping them pack up the midway and big top (what they call "tear down"). We are journeying on the morn to a new location. Everyone was pleased to hear that I'll be staying on for a while.

I started my rounds with Maria, Sam's right hand. She's the Master of Ceremonies for the big top show and knows everything about everything. Her stage name is Black Tide the Pirate Queen, which is fitting. I know this because I came across her practicing knife throwing. She invited me to join her for some exercise, and I found out that she's also alarmingly proficient with rapiers. Her accuracy and endurance were impressive. I shall endeavor to stay on her good side. I already knew from Sam that Maria was a retired soldier, but what I hadn't guessed was that she lost a leg in battle. She gets around on her prosthetic better than I do on my regular old legs.

I enjoyed chatting with her. She's blunt and gruff, which means she's also honest. She graciously offered to help with any questions or concerns that came up. I intend to take her up on that since I pretty much have nothing but questions and concerns.

The second person I approached was Asena, the show's fortune teller and fire dancer. (*NOTE: Talk to Asena about how to effectively work with Outerplane magick!*) I didn't delve into her presage abilities, but I did see her dancing while twirling four balls of fire on chains. She must have a special deal with fire elementals because she never singed herself once. We had a lovely, long chat while folding up the big top tent fabric.

The intricate sigils covering her skin intrigued me and I asked if they were part of a fire protection spell. Nope. They are permanent sigils of remembrance—for people and places she loves, for happy memories, for challenges survived, for lessons learned, and for keeping important aspects of herself visible so that she doesn't forget them in times of strife. An interesting idea.

Kamal, an Outerplane magician (sleight-of-hand act) and odd job doer, stopped by Asena's motorhome to share a mid-sun meal with us. His stage name is Ghost. Nice kid. I've never seen a live human with such pale skin. I didn't notice until he took off the shaded glasses he always wears outside, but his eyes are a pale shade of pink. I asked him about it and Asena told me that sunlight, or indeed any bright light, bothers him. She also explained that he doesn't speak. Can't blame him. Most people aren't worth talking to. All the animals in camp love him and follow him around . . . including Herman. They disappeared together after we ate. I hope Herman didn't get him into too much trouble.

Asena and I talked about her life, the show, and its personalities until the troupe gathered for supper. During the meal, she went out of her way to include me in discussions with the rest of the performers. She's a skilled conversationalist.

I sat between Fiona and Gilroy, the show's Strong Woman and Strong Man. They bend steel, lift heavy objects, and take turns operating two rides. Gilroy generally looks after the Ferris Wheel, a massive wizard contraption that locks people into cages and vertically rotates them on a large wheel. Fiona prefers the Carousel, a garishly painted round platform with horse statues which rotates riders horizontally. Both sounded more like people rotisseries than rides and I said as much. Everyone had a good laugh and assured me there was no fire involved.

I remember meeting Fiona and Gilroy during my first supper with the carnival. Fiona is short and stout and Gilroy is tall enough that he must be part giant. Seriously, my head comes up to his elbow and she barely tops his knees. She must have dwarven heritage.

Fiona and Maria invited me to join them next sun in a friendly targeting competition. Fiona is skilled at axe throwing, which I've never tried. I agreed, with the express understanding that I was not to be the target. There was another round of guffaws and Maria assured me the only thing slain would be a bale of hay.

I briefly chatted with Julie. She's known theatrically as The Bender and can fold and twist her body as if she's boneless. She demonstrated by placing her feet on a plate and folding herself backwards, essentially in half, and placing her hands on the same plate. Perhaps the Outerplane isn't as magickally bereft as we were led to believe?

Sadly, there wasn't much time to talk with Tim as he had to eat and run. I knew from Asena that his stage name was The Snakeman because he has two snake companions and a skin condition that makes it look as though he has scales. He's by far the coolest-looking human I've ever encountered. Unfortunately, the skin condition is quite painful.

NOTE: Brew up a salve for Tim. Research ingredient equivalencies!!!

Bailong, Tim's large white boa constrictor, who loves to cuddle, wound herself around my waist as we ate. He managed to coax her away before he left to take care of his other snake, Janus, who wasn't feeling well. Janus is a python, or two pythons . . . I'm not sure as he was born with two heads. I wonder if one of them ever gets mad at the other? That would be terrible. There'd be no escape.

After supper, I helped Danica and Nikolai collect dead wood for a bonfire. They're known as The Spider Siblings and are Karneval Života's trapeze artists and trick riders. I peeked in the big top before it was taken down and saw them practicing with their horses, Ebony and Snowball. They must use magick. There is no way they should be able to flip and somersault between two moving horses like that without falling.

The horses are beautiful, but dauntingly huge. Ebony is as black as the storm ravaged sky on Mother's moors, and Snowball is pure white. Their hooves must be as big as my head. Possibly bigger. I didn't stop to measure. Despite their size, they appear gentle. I saw Snowball kneel down to help Kamal climb onto his back.

The Spider Siblings also perform acrobatic feats while swinging from long white sheets tied to support poles at the pinnacle of the big top (probably where their name came from). It sounds like a dangerous endeavour. Asena described it as dancing in air. I can't wait to see them in action.

I had a good chat with Sam at the bonfire about the carnival's animal companions. Apart from the ones I've mentioned, there are a wide variety of creatures on or near Kamal at all times. This sun I saw him playing with a mouse, a squirrel, a bumblebee, a grasshopper, a family of brown songbirds, an opossum, and a wirehaired dog the size of a pony. I'm beginning to suspect he is a druid. Untrained, no doubt, but he shows definite talent in the animalia discipline.

Sam explained that most of those animals are only around for as long as they are in one location, but a few (like a raven they call Monkey) opt to stay longer. I briefly met that cheeky thief last sun when he pecked a glass bead off my spell component pouch and flew away. When I mentioned the incident, Sam jogged to his motorhome and came back with my bead. Apparently, Monkey spends his suns pilfering items from one person and giving them to another. Anything unclaimed in the general exchange of items before the eventide meal (a ritual that suddenly makes more sense) is put in a Lost and Found box. I'll have to remember to check it regularly. I'm sure that bead isn't the last thing Monkey will fly off with.

I also found out that Sam has a policy prohibiting wild animals from joining the carnival. Domesticated species are allowed, along with animals that have been abandoned, or injured, or those that refuse to leave . . . the accepted categories increased the more he thought about it. Policy enforcement appears to only go as far as his soft heart allows.

He admitted to having reservations about an armadillo. I explained that, although wild in every sense of the word, Herman stays with me by choice. Sam seemed to accept that. He's also fine with Bob's bunny. I even caught him cuddling the little fuzzball.

On the way to my tent, I ran into another of their long-running residents—Old One-eye. Asena warned me about him, but to be honest I was having trouble keeping my eyes open and wasn't paying attention. He is the scruffiest, meanest-looking orange cat I've ever met. Kamal is the only person he allows near. I accidently passed too close to his hiding spot on my sleepy trek and now my robe is shredded on one side. I suppose the encounter at least woke me up enough to make it to my cot and write up my sun. Tough old thing has moxy. I like him. I appreciate knowing where I stand . . . which I will make sure in future is out of claw range.

Between Sam the wizard and Kamal the untrained druid, there are shades of the fiasco on the moors here. I must tread carefully. So far, Sam and Kamal are more easygoing than Mother and Crone. Maybe all wizards and druids aren't so capricious.

Sam asked me to think about what renovations I want done on my joint. I believe he meant in a non-magickal sense, so I'll have to spend some time experimenting. Until I figure out how much I can do with muzzled illusion spells and makeshift potions, I won't know how heavily I need to rely on props. The thought of using physical aids (wizard-made, to boot) makes my skin crawl, but what other option is there in a null zone?

ADDENDUM: Every time I try to explain where I'm from or talk specifics about magick or spells, I choke. Literally. The words lodge in my throat like a log dam and I can do nothing but cough until the feeling passes. Everyone keeps offering me these disgusting sweet pellets. They must be some kind of throat remedy, but all I can say is YUCK! I'd take a nettle and kantaric saliva brew over that any sun.

Pandias, Nettle Moon 6, 209

KARNEVAL ŽIVOTA IS on the move or doing a "jump" as they call it (there's no actual jumping . . . Outerplane terms are confusing). I'm traveling in Asena's motorhome. She asked if I wanted to go with her, which I thought was very sweet.

So far, it has been slightly less terrifying than my first trip with Sam. I'm hiding out in the back, trying to ignore the fact that we're moving by reading, writing, and chatting with Asena. She does far less weaving around other transportation devices (vehicles) than Sam did. The few times I dared to part the curtains and peek outside, I also noted that she travels at a reduced speed. I wouldn't go so far as to call it a reasonable speed, but any amount of slower is better.

How they direct these vehicles is most bizarre. There is a small wheel inside the front compartment that the operator turns. It is similar in design to the four wheels a wagon travels on. At first, I assumed the interior wheel dictated speed, in that the faster you turned it, the faster the four padded outside wheels turned, but no. There are pedals on the floor for that. The wheel at the front changes the direction of the vehicle. Wizards!

I noticed the behemoth dog from last sun sitting in Sam's truck with Kamal before we left. Asena said she heard someone say its name was Jim Dandy. Apparently, when an animal acquires a name it's a sure sign they're staying on. The carnival has picked up another companion.

Herman reluctantly agreed to travel with me. He's been having a great time with Kamal and I suspect he wanted to ride with him. Normally I'd be fine with that, but I need him here to keep an eye on Bob's bunny. It has an even worse propensity to gnaw on things than Herman did when we first met, and I don't want Asena's home damaged. My knowledge of bunnies is limited, but I expect that it's just keeping its teeth sharp.

I crated Bob (in the interplanar luggage crate) and he's travelling in the back of Sam's truck. The bunny is small and I was afraid it would get hurt if their vehicle took a sharp turn, as Sam frequently does. Bob accidently falling on it would not end well for anyone. Poor guy would be devastated.

Herman is taking everything with surprisingly good humour. I've never seen him this cooperative or happy. He must like it here. I wonder if he never told me where he's from because he's also subject to a gag order? Could it be that he's pleased to be home?

The only thing Herman isn't too sure about is his role at the carnival. He's my familiar and will continue in that capacity, but my co-workers keep trying to think up ways to include an armadillo in their acts. Most of their ideas have not sat well. Can't say I blame him. I wouldn't want to be dressed up as a clown or pulled out of a hat either.

On a similar note, I'm trying to figure out my role. I've begun researching Outerplane magick and doing a bit of light experimentation. Asena has a collection of tomes on magick practices and rituals which she put at my disposal. She is the perfect traveling companion! I also asked Julie what spell she uses to soften her bones, but she insisted it was natural flexibility. I remain skeptical, but if she isn't comfortable discussing magick with me, then that is her prerogative and I won't pursue the matter. Should she ever want to talk, she knows I'm interested.

To date, the only thing I've confirmed is that there is a huge learning curve. I should have paid more attention in my Interplanar Principals of Magick course. Gathering power and casting spells is astonishingly complicated here.

Asena has tomes upon tomes outlining rituals, tools, and

components. And she called her collection modest. She promised to bring me to a library (a place that stores massive collections—Magda would be ecstatic) when we reach our destination, but I think my brain might be on fire by then.

The passage I just read said all spellwork must be recited in rhyme, something I do not excel at, and requires specially prepared ritual spaces. It also said you have to coordinate your spell with specific colours of candles, scents, and garb. And that's not all. Depending on the spell, there may be only one time of sun or moon in which it will work. And instead of calling the precise element you need, it sounds like you have to summon all of them for each working (and carry physical representations for all of them in order to even cast the summoning). So, for example, on my plane I would summon a fire elemental to instil passion in an attraction spell, but here I have to call elementals from all five domains and then entreat Fire to help. Perhaps the elementals pool all their energies to focus the effect of one? It's a wonder anyone ever figured out how to do anything with magick. I hope some of these requirements can be bypassed or streamlined.

The only magickal thing I've been able to do is make my broom hover . . . as long as there is no added weight. Not super useful, but at least it confirmed that some of my training and skills transfer to the Outerplane. I'm hoping to learn how local witches ply their craft so I can adapt my spells to work here and become more proficient at gathering power. I'd love to get my broom working properly and stop traveling in these wizard-cursed vehicles.

Therein lies a peculiar problem. Most Outerplane witches are incognito. Asena relayed a brief history and referred me to a tome that covered it in more depth. Turns out my profession has been persecuted, on and off, since the beginning of Outerplane record keeping. Asena assured me the burnings, hangings, and drownings in this area happened long ago, but warned that some lingering bad feeling remained. More so on other landmasses.

It's all so strange and makes me want to be the witchiest witch the Outerplane has ever seen. Let the ignorant fools try to come for me. I'll show them what crossing a witch brings. Being a witch should be a point of pride. Curses on anyone who tries to convince my Outerplane craft-mates otherwise. Our deep and abiding connection to the elements is something to celebrate and share. Not something to be hidden away and talked of in hushed tones.

I expressed my feelings to Asena and she agreed. Her family, although they do not identify as witches, has long worked with magicks and been mistreated for their trouble. It sounds like her skills lay primarily in spirit communion, both with living souls and those who have crossed to Underworld. She is an interesting person and I foresee us becoming friends. I wish I could introduce her to Magda. They would be best friends in no time.

Given the current attitude toward witches, I asked if we were likely to encounter trouble. Asena said religious groups occasionally protest the carnival, but usually in a non-violent fashion. When they show up, everyone gets together and decides whether to stay or move on to the next location. They've become proficient at dealing with fear and bias, which is perhaps the saddest thing I've ever heard.

I didn't truly appreciate how rare my new co-workers were until she explained why most of them joined Karneval Života. They have been, and still are, treated terribly by people, including their supposed loved ones. Being different here is apparently bad.

I don't get it. On a world littered with humans (boring!), why would they penalize those few individuals who are unique and interesting? Jealousy, I guess. It is a travesty that such a petty emotion causes so much pain and strife.

She didn't detail everyone's journey, saying some stories were not hers to tell. The gist of it was that they banded together to survive and make a new family that celebrated differences and encouraged unusual talents. Some members, Asena gave me a quick smile when she said this, came and went from season to season, staying however long they needed to heal or rest. She has been with the carnival for five season cycles.

The family they created is wonderful. Everyone pitches in. Everyone looks out for each other. She said if I needed anything, it was safe to go to any of them. They'd support me in any way they could. The only thing they ask in return is that I help them out when and where I can.

We spoke in general terms about carnival operations. Their future looks dire right now with coin being so tight, but she assured me everyone was staying positive and that I should, too. I asked what had happened and she said changeable weather always made their early season a gamble. The rain and cold this season hit their open-air midway attractions hard. Attendance was low and they had to drop their ticket prices. If things didn't pick up, there might not be enough coin to cover their next loan instalment. She was reluctant to say what the consequences of that were. I understood why after coaxing her into explaining that their equipment, homes, and vehicles could be seized and sold. She would say no more, but I know what would follow. Their family would split up as everyone took whatever jobs and shelter were available. Don't I know that scenario all too well!

These are good people. As long as Magda is okay, I intend to stay on until the end of the season. Swollen scum pods, do I ever miss the immediacy of being able to scry!

I am more committed than ever to transforming the House of Horrors into the most creepifying attraction anyone on the Outerplane has experienced. It's not just a point of pride. I want word of our terrifying prowess to spread like fire across a dry field. I want customers to flock from far and wide. Most of all, I want to see my new friends smile and know that they can stay together and be safe.

Enough writing. I must get back to my magick research.

ADDENDUM: I figured out what is going on with the choking. During my last fit, I suddenly twigged to something Althea complained about after her Outerplane vacation (one of the many things she griped about while stuck to the kitchen table). I went through the stack of parchments I signed for the interplanar port officials and found an Infernal gag order. I can't share any magick theories, rituals, or particulars that aren't public knowledge here. I'm also barred from telling anyone I'm from another plane. It's going to be awkward if someone tells me where they're from and all I can do in return is cough in their face. Bloody Infernals! Given the eclectic and welcoming nature of my co-workers, I suspect not much would faze them. A witch from another plane seems less strange to me than a woman who can walk upright one minute and then fold herself into a box barely the size of my bottom the next.

Soldias, Nettle Moon 7, 209

MAGDA IS A rare and beautiful gem. She sent me the best letter I've ever received. It's amazing the power words hold. My heart is singing. I'm going to keep the letter in here so I can re-read it when I feel down.

Knowing that she believes in me so completely is amazing and just the encouragement I need to push forward researching the ridiculously complicated Outerplane magick systems. Friends are so vital. Magda has rescued me from myself more times than I can count. I'm not sure where I would be without her unfailing support.

My co-workers thought something terrible had happened when they heard me crying and everyone came by to comfort me. They really are sweet. I hope Magda is right and I can find a way to help them.

Despite Magda's assurance that she is fine, I'm still worried and will continue to send letters every other sun. I'm not sure how to follow hers up though. I guess I'll just tell her how much she means to me and how much I cherish her thoughtful words.

DEAR HESTER, MY best friend and Moon Sister,

First off, because I know you are worrying up a storm, things are going okay here. I went to work and picked up where I left off, only I did it better this time. No mistakes. As far as the grief I got from some of my co-workers, at least I know who I can count on now. I'm going to keep the witches who stood by me close, and when I get that promotion, I'll make sure the bosses know how wonderful they are. I still don't know if this is what I'm supposed to be doing, but I do so love parts of it. Time will tell if the good bits outweigh the sucky bits.

I am so sorry to hear that things haven't gone as expected for you, but you are a master at adapting and shaping unconventional situations into something workable. You've got this.

When I think of you, I think of a river. Calm at times, effortlessly passing through the world and bringing life to all those you touch. But I've also seen you be fierce and powerful, carving a new path through seemingly immovable mountains, sweeping obstacles away with your steadfast determination. You make mistakes, as we all do, but you always pick yourself up and fly on. Witches are supposed to be forces of nature and you embody this principle down to your core. Nothing can stop you once you commit. Nothing!

You said you don't understand why I'm your friend. Well, I'll tell you. It's because you are amazing. Nobody is more loyal. When I cry, you lie down and share my tears. And when I'm ready to smile again, you help me rebuild my dreams. You have been my conscience when I didn't know which way to turn, my confidant when I didn't know who to trust, and my drinking buddy when I just needed to forget it all. You are a flame in the night for many people, Hester. You just need to learn how to trust your own light.

You've always thrived in adversity. You crave challenge. Even in school, you were never satisfied doing things the tried-and-true way. You were always experimenting, pushing the limits, exploring new territory. You might not have found the perfect job yet, but I know you will. And maybe in your lifetime there will be more than one perfect job. There's nothing wrong with that.

You don't shy away from anything. You fly straight at your fears and problems until you find a way to make them work for you. When you see something you don't like, you fix it, regardless of the personal cost. And the times you've had to walk away, you hold those experiences close so you can learn from them, even when doing so costs your heart terrible pain, as with Justin. You are the very best of everything a witch and best friend should be. If anyone can find a way to help the carnival, you can. Harness your wonderfully creative problem solving skills. They will not lead you astray.

I know, I know. You are thinking . . . "but they have in the past." To which I would reply, "Have they? Or have they drawn you down this path, placing you right where you are at this moment?" I believe you are uniquely qualified to help your new friends find their way. Trust your light.

Love and blessings on your newest adventure,

Magda

P.S. Missera says "hi" to Herman. She's already bugging me about visiting. I told her to cool her broom. Once you're feeling more settled, let me know and I'll arrange transport. I've never been to the Outerplane. It sounds a most exciting place. Perhaps we can help out in your House of Horrors! Missera is keen to shed her bonnet and do some snake-worthy scaring. She keeps telling me I'm stifling her potential, but I know how much she loves her bonnets. Little scamp!

Wendias, Nettle Moon 10, 209

THE LAST FIVE ~~suns~~ days have been a marathon of traveling, researching, and unpacking. We've set up our new backyard (the area with sleeping tents and motorhomes), the midway, and the big top tent.

I opted to keep living in a tent. Asena said I was welcome to sleep in her spare bunk, but I know I'll never be entirely comfortable in a motorhome because of its wizardly origins. The prospect of going to sleep one eventide and waking up somewhere else in the morn is not calming. I like my travelling to be conscious and directed, preferably on a broom.

That desire is looking less and less attainable. Try as I might, I cannot get my broom to carry any weight. I don't know if it's a problem with me or if the broom design itself isn't suited to the Outerplane. I'm not giving up, but it is discouraging.

Summoning elementals is becoming marginally easier. The process is different and more involved, yet similar enough to be confusing and cause a problem. I feel like a bumbling child. Basically, I have to go back to the beginning of my training and subtly shift all the magick building blocks I learnt. It is infinitely harder to unlearn something than to learn something new. Let's just say I won't be trying complex magicks for a while.

On a happier note, I confirmed many of the supposed

requirements for Outerplane spellwork are bogus, rhyming being my most gleeful dismissal. There is a lot of misinformation and downright ridiculous practice recommendations floating around. It almost feels like someone is actively trying to sow distrust in the magickal arts. Could it be part of a wizard conspiracy to discredit witches? Whatever it is, I will not let it stand. I have begun correcting the tomes I borrowed (within reason . . . the gag order prevents me from detailing some things, even in writing). False methods are easy enough to weed out as they simply don't work. It just takes time. Hopefully, I can save the next witch who picks up these resources some time and effort.

The not-so-great news is that I need to significantly downgrade my magickal expectations. I stole some private time away from the group ~~last sun~~ yesterday to play with Fire. Even considering my reduced magick abilities, I should have been able to summon decently powerful elementals (despite having to call five instead of one). What I ended up with was a pack of barely discernible sprites. The only reason I knew the immolate spell worked was that I briefly smelled smoke. After searching around, I discovered that my fire sprite sparks had burnt a pinprick-sized hole in the scrap of parchment I held.

I also successfully created a fleet of charm bags and placed them in everyone's joint and motorhome, as well as liberally hanging them around the big top and front gate. Instead of focusing on protection, I decided to boost our prosperity. My charms should work on us and our patrons. Who doesn't need a little extra prosperity in their life, whether it's for coin, love, or kittens? The effects won't be strong but that is a bonus since too much of anything is dangerous. For example, suffocating under a mountain of kittens would really suck.

I eliminated the protection ward idea because Sam told me obtaining the loan broker's hair, fingernails, or blood would get me into trouble he wasn't sure he could get me out of. Without those, I can't target the spell, which is a serious problem. A generalized ward to drive off greed might force away all our customers because there's no way to specify an acceptable level of greed. And everyone can be greedy, whether it's for coin, someone's attention, a favourite food, etc.

Some witches may be willing to cast broad-spectrum

protection wards, but not me. Not since Magda warned me off in college during the Justin fiasco. I wanted to make one to ward off jerks. That would have gone oh, so badly as they seem to make up the vast majority of the population. My job search would have been fruitless in perpetuity. Not to mention, I can be a real jerk sometimes. I shudder to think what it would have done in that scenario.

I didn't fully understand how narrowly I avoided disaster until I witnessed Klorepton's try at warding off Fire (he nearly died in a hut blaze as a child and was terrified of it). The moment he infused the spell with power, every cell in his body stopped working. We managed to undo the ward and save him but . . . wow! All hail Magda's giant brain! It should never be doubted.

For now, my strategies to improve the House of Horrors must remain magickally modest and heavily reliant on Sam's wizardry. The house itself is an incredibly intricate wizard construct. It was both fascinating and terrifying to watch the troupe break it down into component parts, pack it into a truck, and reconstruct it when we arrived here. I'm sure Bob was delighted.

The H of H is Sam's creation and I have to give him credit. If we were in my home plane, he would be a highly sought-after wizard. Royals are always on the lookout for someone to design elaborate traps to discourage unwelcome castle interlopers. Sam is a sweet person, but he's obviously capable of devising some truly wicked perils. I hope he's more careful than most wizards. So far, he seems to be.

After witnessing my joint's collapsibility, I was nervous to venture inside. Sam took great pains to demonstrate its stability, showing that once the pieces are locked into place, they will not move. It appears to be steadier than Althea's Gingerbread Hut and I managed to survive that horror, so I'll probably be fine.

I've only had time to implement a few minor improvements. I recruited Kamal to help collect spiders and then I cast spells on our eight-legged friends to attract more. He was interested in what I was doing. I tried to show him, but it always ended in a coughing fit. Bloody gag order. The spiders have been slow to gather, but our efforts are starting to pay off. I set them to work building webs and the H of H feels much more homey and witchy now.

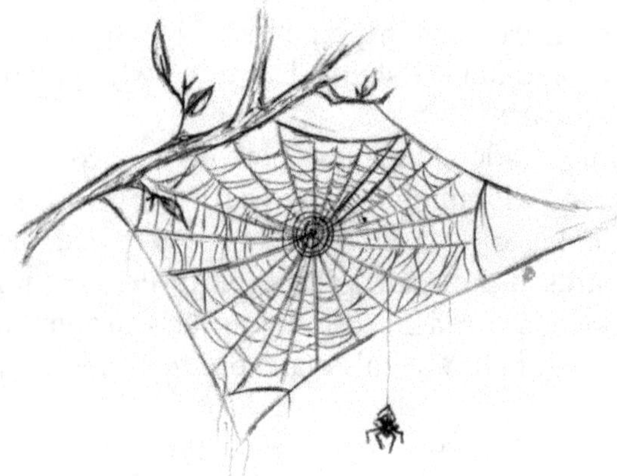

I plan to augment my appearance with prosthetics and makeup (paying very close attention to expiry dates), and am once again adopting my crone demeanour. Asena said it would be well received by our customers.

Sourcing equivalent Outerplane spell components is as daunting as learning their magick systems. I'm documenting each new component I test and in what spells it was useful. Asena's tomes contain a wealth of information about flora and fauna from this landmass, and I found a massive herbalist compendium in the town library (almost every town here has a stockpile of tomes available to anyone . . . how wonderful!). Some Outerplane components seem similar to what I know from my plane (i.e. hemlock), but I can't be sure they possess the same magickal properties until I use them. The fly knees, webs, and honeysuckle sap I used in my spider attraction spell acted as expected, if a bit weakly.

I've also been working on a salve for Tim's skin and am happy to report he experienced no side effects from the spot test. He was excited to try a full body test. The ointment is bright green, due to its ingredients, so the only real issue is that it lends his skin a distinctly verdant hue. He said he doesn't mind and that it might add to his "Snakeman" persona. I hope the salve stops his skin from cracking. I'm sure I can improve the formula over time and will carry on experimenting. I wish

Magda were here. She is the true potion star.

I may have been too hasty branding my position with the carnival as unacceptable to the Witch's Union. My role is very close to what I did as a village hag, only now my village moves. There is *a lot* of magick work involved and the challenge of casting in a null zone should fly in my favour, if I can figure out how to do it reliably. And sure, maybe I acquired the job through the Employment Cabal, but does that mean it can't ever be officially approved?

Ouleah pointed me to the non-union job bank, knowing I specifically needed a job to qualify for my Adept rites. She must have had some plan in mind to get a non-union job approved. Though, she had no way of knowing said job would be in the bloody Outerplane. I need to send her a letter. If she can accredit my position, I can stay with Karneval Života for a season cycle *and* make my Adept ceremony! I haven't been this excited since . . . I'm not sure I've ever been this excited. I had given up hope. This is amazing. Potentially. I need to rein in my enthusiasm and not get ahead of myself. Letter first. Then celebrate. Hopefully.

Cerridias, Nettle Moon 11, 209

Our group suppers provide me with some much needed opportunities to experiment with Outerplane components and kitchen witchery. Cooking the meal is a shared responsibility and I've contributed a dish of my own for the last few nights. I'm not a great cook, but I'm beginning to suspect there is also a difference in taste and texture preference between the planes.

My surprise buns were not a hit—the surprise being what kind of bug was hidden inside. Sam got the prized crispy beetle (I didn't tell Herman about that one), but he wasn't at all happy about it. I explained that the beetle conveys longevity, but he was too busy shovelling down great mouthfuls of Maria's chimichurri sauce (a green medley spicy enough to choke a dragon). He must really like it. I have to admit, it is tasty.

So far, gingerbread is the only dish I've made that my co-workers enjoyed. I still can't bring myself to eat it, but they polished off every last crumb.

This eventide I tried an Outerplane recipe for sweet buns (people adore sugar here). The recipe was more complicated than most spells. It took me all sun to decipher what the supplies were and find them. I had to sift non-genetically modified flour and ethically sourced icing sugar into a fair-trade bowl, make a friendly valley in the centre with a locally handcrafted and salvaged wooden spoon, into which I gently cracked vegetarian fed free-range eggs. And that was just the beginning. Yeesh. Also, I burnt the buns because I ran out of time to cook them and bumped up the heat in the oven a bit much. Very disappointing. Everyone was understanding and ate the parts that weren't charred, but I still felt bad.

My next big project is to make mead. I came across a local bee farm in my hunt for supplies and bought two large glass jugs, a bunch of smaller bottles, and all the ingredients I need (I think . . . whether I acquired equivalent components remains to be seen).

My favourite is Fire brew—a drink I fell in love with during my college suns in the most unlikely of places. It is normally spiced with Tarkalian fireplain berries and lieggar bark, which I replaced with polygonum blossoms and ginger root. I talked with the farmer, who also makes mead, and he said my plan was sound. He recommended letting the mead sit for six moons, but I'm sure I can speed up the process with magick. Should be interesting. Hopefully a tankard or two of mead will lift my co-workers' spirits.

Freydias, Nettle Moon 12, 209

THAT WAS FUN! I'm exhausted after my first full day of running the House of Horrors, but it was totally worth it.

I saw the big top show this ~~eventide~~ evening for the first time, and I am even more impressed with my co-workers' skills. Their performances had everyone on the edge of their seats. There was laughing and ooos of wonder and gasps of fear. All in all, a remarkable spectacle.

Wandering the midway and watching Fiona and Gilroy run their rides was instructive. Sometimes they sit quietly and let people come to them, but when things get slow, they perform feats of strength to drum up business.

Sam is popular with children. They are as entranced by his luxurious hair as I am, and a swarm surrounds him whenever he walks the midway. He's incredibly patient, letting them climb on him, telling them stories, and singing (his beautiful voice rivals any Siren's song). Throughout the day, he moves from joint to joint so the people running them get breaks, and he fixes anything wizardly that has gone wrong.

I amassed a fair bit of business for the House of Horrors by simply walking around. Asena calls it "dragging the midway." I broke out my most menacing cackle and recited a few gibberish hexes (no actual curses as I couldn't guarantee the effects and

I'd likely hack up a lung, thanks to the ever-inconvenient gag order). People were amused and amazed when I directed my broom around to poke them. Sadly, it takes a lot of concentration and power, so I couldn't keep it up for long. After a while, my brain said "Nope. You're done" and turned into a mushy pile of scrambled dodgerflun spawn.

There were a few minor issues and accidents at the H of H, but nothing catastrophic, which is a blessing given my propensity to mess things up. The only real issue was that I made one room too scary. Actually, it was more of a conflagration of several factors. The spiders gave me the idea.

I've been looking for ways to practice my magick skills and decided to try out a small sensory illusion. After emptying out the insulting witch themed room, I had Sam put in some moving red wizard lights. Then I cast a spell to make anyone entering feel as though bugs were crawling on them. I thought it would just startle patrons, but apparently there is a widespread phobia of bugs (which, incidentally, also explains my co-workers' bizarre reactions to my deep-fried mealworms and stewed maggot dishes).

*NOTE: Ha! While writing all this out, I had a wicked idea for the H of H. See * at end.*

My poor house spiders, through no fault of their own, inadvertently upped the fear factor. They enjoy that room, possibly because my illusion also affects them and they *like* the feeling of being crawled on. By the time my customers stampeded out, many really did have spiders traipsing around on them. Sam managed to calm most of the hysterical patrons by assuring them they were fake spiders, but sadly, there were a number of casualties (spiders, not customers). I'll have to recruit more to keep my webs in order.

So, today I learnt that the House of Horrors needs to be scary, but not terrifying. I have to lower the realism and research exactly what is considered frightening on the Outerplane.

Herman unintentionally elicited a few screams. He was just wandering around the house (or napping in one instance) and customers practically leapt out of their skin when they caught sight of him. I overheard several screaming about rats, so I wonder if they mistook him for one in the low light. The shape of an armadillo is vaguely reminiscent. Unless they were screaming about bats. It's possible I misheard. I don't think I have any bats, but it's not a bad idea. I'll look into recruiting some. Unless they're too scary. This is very confusing. *(NOTE: Check with Sam to see whether bats are just scary enough, or too scary.)*

Frankly, I'm baffled as to why anyone would find rats or bats frightening. Bats even eat spiders (which we've already established are vile Outerplane foes), so the whole thing makes no sense. I suppose there's not much logic to be found in most fears. Guess that holds true no matter what plane you're on.

In other news, my experiments to hasten mead production backfired, literally. One of the jugs blew up. Nobody was injured but the jug is well and truly done for. I'll have to find another one to replace it.

** IDEA—What about adding a witch's banquet to the House of Horrors? My co-workers had extreme reactions to the traditional family dishes I prepared. They tried to be polite about it, but they couldn't even stomach my eyeball soup. If I can join two rooms on the main floor, there'll be enough space for me to set out a variety of fare for patrons on a long table. Should it be a stand and mingle affair or a proper sit-down feast? I'll talk to Sam and see what he thinks.*

Moondias, Nettle Moon 15, 209

PHEW. FIRST FEW days of the carnival are done and today is my day of rest (I'm getting better with Outerplane lingo). It has been busy and people-y but fun.

I informed Sam that witches don't work on Moondias and he was fine with that. They usually close the carnival for a couple of suns a week to clean the grounds and rides. If my time off doesn't coincide with that, he said I can arrange with the others for someone to cover the H of H.

Perhaps there is something to what Magda said about me being meant to be here. I am cautiously optimistic about my stay in the Outerplane. Despite my unplanned planar dislocation, so much of this feels right in a witch-gut sense. And in a chicken gut sense. I read the entrails of some chickens Julie cooked for supper and the omens were mostly good. It was just as messy as I remembered but they were there and weren't being used. It would be a shame for good entrails to go to waste. My moor Mother would be proud.

I'm a little nervous that I haven't heard from Ouleah about whether it's possible to accredit my job with the union. I hope she's just busy and not trying to figure out how to positively spin the fact that it's impossible. The entrails bolstered my hope but I wish I had a letter from her, in hand. Distraction is the key to stopping my fretting and thankfully my co-workers are masters at it.

Everyone gathered for a roaring bonfire this evening. Sam and I spent most of the time chatting. He is curious about a great many things (some of which I can only cough at him about) and has bits of knowledge about topics I didn't even know existed. Tonight, he asked why witches are supposed to fly on brooms. He phrased the question in a way that suggested he thought it nothing more than a fanciful yarn. I can't fault his disbelief. My broom certainly hasn't been able to transport so much as an emaciated snail.

I explained that we use brooms because of our practical natures. A broom can be used to tidy a hut, as a ritual tool, a bonker or poker for self-defence, or to simply lift a cauldron off the fire. They also happen to be comfortably ride-able and easy to propel as long as they're made with a suitable wood and their withies have been gathered in the prescribed manner. We're not like wizards who delight in lugging around a different tool for every conceivable task. I winked at him as I said the last, but my teasing flustered him. For some reason he seems uncomfortable when I call him a wizard. Maybe they're more secretive here than they were at home—a ridiculous pretence given how abundant their blasted devices are.

Sam seemed surprised that my broom explanation made sense, so I left it at that. Delving into the philosophical debates from my college days about brooms being created from earth elements (i.e. wood) and used to cleanse homes of other earth elements (i.e. dirt), thereby using an element to restore balance to itself—a concept touted as a basic tenet of witchcraft (for some, at least)—would have just muddied the water (pun intended . . . hey, at least I can make myself smile). He probably wouldn't have been interested anyway. I was only ever marginally interested myself. I've never had much patience for theory or philosophy. I'm a doer, not a talker. On occasion, I miss our dorm's late-night debates over warmed fermented ghoul eyes. A few eyeballs in and the discussions always got more interesting.

I brought up my witch's banquet idea while Sam was relaxed and receptive. He was interested but hesitant because of the numerous Outerplane laws governing food preparation and sale. He promised to look into how difficult it would be to get the necessary permits on our various stops (apparently, we need permission from each town we work in). We already have stands where customers can buy snacks and drinks, but he said that is handled differently as those are pre-packaged. The fetid sulphurous stench of the Infernals is all over this. Sniff closely at anything overly complicated and you generally find they're involved.

As difficult as I'm finding it to navigate this strange plane, my companions have adjusted smoothly. Herman is usually somewhere near Kamal (at least it makes him easy to find). He even helped with Kamal's magic show, though I noticed he was not pulled out of any hats. Bob hangs out here and there, usually somewhere in the House of Horrors. He's having fun terrifying our patrons by randomly changing positions and facial expressions while nobody is looking. One minute they see a gargoyle with an exaggerated smile across the room and the next it's beside them baring its teeth. I find his game amusing, but gargoyles are yet another creature considered too scary here. I fear I will never understand the Outerplane.

There is one developing rivalry which is occasionally annoying. Mostly it's amusing, so I'm leaving it be for now. Monkey the raven has a fondness for Bob's bejewelled wand and is constantly flying off with it. I'm sure Bob is frustrated. I heard Monkey squawking up a storm the other day and found him locked in a wooden trunk with Bob sitting on top. His stony expression conveyed innocence, but I knew better.

Wendias, Nettle Moon 24, 209

WE'RE JUMPING AGAIN. I'm still travelling with Asena in her motorhome, as it is less terrifying than the alternatives. We should arrive at our new location tomorrow.

Kamal and I rounded up all the spiders from the House of Horrors and released them. To ensure there were no stragglers, we had to clear out all their beautiful webs. Rebuilding our collection and casting the spell at every stop will be a pain, but I can't see the spiders being okay with the carnival's constant relocations. And I'd have to collect them and find somewhere to store them during transport anyway. I briefly broached the subject with Sam. His horrified expression suggested it wasn't a good idea. It's a shame. I'll miss them. It's hard to be lonely with a hundred spider families hanging around.

I think I'm homesick. I received a letter from Magda this morn before we left. She's doing fine. Still working. Her annoying co-workers have backed off—a prudent choice. I miss her and Missera so much. And real ale. There is a drink here called ale, but you might as well order water for all its flavour. There aren't even any floaty bits in it! Bah. The drinks selection in general is depressing. I haven't found anything half as delicious as fermented ghoul eyes. At least I have my mead . . . or I will as soon as my jug finishes aging. I'm still working on a way to speed fermentation up. I've replaced the blown jug and started a new batch. No explosions, yet.

My research into what is scary on the Outerplane led to some bizarre discoveries. My co-workers helped, sharing tales of allegedly frightening mystical beings from their homelands—turns out many of the troupe are not originally from this landmass.

Perhaps that's why they are so kind and understanding. They know how it feels to be somewhere unfamiliar. It could also explain why they don't react strongly to new or weird things, like a carnivore bunny or armadillo Herman. I wonder if everything seemed as strange to them when they first came as it does to me?

Their fearsome tales are quite interesting and some of the villains are familiar. I suspect a good deal of folklore comes from extraplanar creatures either becoming stuck here (like me) or simply vacationing here.

Sam has been an incredible help with the House of Horrors. Not only did he spook the place up, he found a way to keep it genuinely scary. Instead of taming down the horror, which seemed counter-intuitive given the name, he posted a sign outside stating it was an adult only attraction. Brilliant and so simple!

Of course, youngsters being youngsters, they keep trying to get in, so he watches the entrance and shoos away any kids without adult guardians. Apparently, they can come in as long as they are with someone over eighteen and are aware of the terror level. It seems overly complicated. I didn't ask him to elaborate on the reasoning as I assumed it would only deepen my confusion. If anyone complains, he told me to say they should "use this as a learning opportunity about heeding posted warnings." It's more diplomatic than I'd normally be, but I'll take his advice since he has experience dealing with Outerplane denizens.

Monkey has taken to hiding in the House of Horrors. He enjoys cawing and swooping at people from dark places. At first, I thought he was just being helpful. Then I discovered his ulterior motive: His victims tend to drop whatever they're holding when startled. He's amassed an impressive collection of pilfered and abandoned items. It's quite the scheme. If I were a suspicious witch, I'd say Herman had a hand in it, but I can't prove anything. Yet.

Usually, whatever's abandoned is of little value, such as candy wrappers or those silly wizard devices people use instead of scry mirrors (good riddance, I say), but I do find the occasional bit of paper currency or more important stuff like Bob's wand. Sometimes, there's an earring or one of the mechanical time devices they wear on their wrists. This is mainly why I suspect Herman. How does someone accidently drop either of those? They should be attached. But I don't know how Monkey or Herman could remove them without the person noticing, so we're at a stalemate.

I have one amazing success to report on the magick front. I finally cast a transmutation spell! On the Outerplane! My witchiness knows no bounds!

My success is probably due to the sheer number of times I've cast the spell, courtesy of Herman's indecision. It's a thousand times more complicated here, and it took two full moon nights to top up the power in my crystals, but I did it. Next time it'll be harder as the crystals won't have any leftover charge from the moor storms. One transmutation completely drained them. All seven of them! Yikes!

Herman was happy with his new form, at least for a day or so. He chose an Outerplane creature called a panda. He was tired of being small and somehow got it into his head that they were accomplished in martial arts. I had to research pandas to set the form for the spell and warned him that I hadn't come across anything suggesting they had martial talents. He ignored me, as usual, and now he has to deal with the consequences. It'll be a while before I'm able to collect enough power to do another transmutation.

Turns out, pandas are not martially skilled. At all. Big surprise. It was quite amusing watching him trying to attack things. Mostly, he ended up climbing them. Climbing appears to be their foremost skill, that and being roly-poly and fluffy. Everyone at the carnival, patrons and co-workers alike, thinks he is adorable. They keep trying to rub his tummy and hug him. I say "trying" because he does have rather dangerous-looking teeth that he bares if anyone comes close (except Kamal . . . apparently, he alone gets panda hugs). But, hey, pandas are larger than armadillos, so at least one of his wishes was fulfilled. I pointed that out, but I don't think it made him feel better.

He's gone back to grumbling about all the good animals being off-limits. I actually caught him trying to eat my copy of the WU familiar list. He said he was angry at it and it just happened. Panda wrestling is surprisingly difficult.

I think Herman is having an identity crisis. He hasn't been happy with any of his new forms. Something always doesn't feel right or isn't good enough. I don't know where to go from here. He is depressed, and a mopey panda is seriously pathetic looking.

My co-workers were initially surprised to find a panda wandering the camp. I couldn't explain to them that I'd cast a spell to transmute armadillo Herman into panda Herman, but I did get across that the panda's name was Herman and that the armadillo was gone. Not sure what they made of that. So far, they appear to have accepted it and there haven't been any cough-worthy questions.

Sam was the only one to express concern. Pandas are considered wild animals and aren't native to this landmass. After he confirmed panda Herman wasn't in distress or a threat to anyone, he gave me a stern lecture on why keeping wild animals in confinement, nowhere near their native habitats or other members of their species, isn't in the animal's best interest. I'm afraid I got a bit stroppy and told him the panda and I were a package deal. If the panda went, so did I.

He hummed and hawed and grumped, and then told me to keep Herman in the House of Horrors while patrons are on the grounds and pretend he's an animatronic creature. I was prepared to object on my familiar's behalf until I heard his reasoning. Foreign animals require expensive and hard to obtain special permits (haha . . . if only he knew how foreign we are). He didn't want the carnival fined and Herman taken away if a customer notified the authorities. I readily agreed. That scenario wouldn't end well. If anyone tried to take Herman away, I'd be predicting their very short future with their own entrails. Navigating Outerplane customs and laws is trickier than I could have imagined.

NOTE: Restrict Herman to native species of this landmass for next transmutation. Hoo-boy! He's going to be pissed.

Sam was more vehement than he needed to be and later apologized. He's strict about animal companions because it's important to him that everyone with Karneval Života, human or otherwise, is there by choice and treated with equal care and respect. There are other carnivals that keep animals in deplorable conditions, bad enough that he considers it torture. Those carnivals give everyone else in the business a bad name. He said you can always tell the quality of a person by how they treat animals and enemies—an interesting thought.

I wonder what Sam would think of me cursing my ex-boyfriend and his mother? Truth be told, they deserved far worse than buggy reflections, but I stand by my hex. It was an elegant solution.

I completely understand where Sam's sentiment comes from though. Humans are one of the cruellest, if not *the* cruellest, creatures on my plane. As a witch, I do my best to keep the balance, not just between the elements in the world, but also between the opposing forces within myself—kindness and cruelty, empathy and selfishness, passion and apathy, etc. There's so many. No one aspect can exist without its opposing force, so they must all be carefully tended to ensure there is no overgrowth. Some days, that balance is harder to strike.

Great Goddess, I'm getting philosophical about witchcraft again. I am definitely homesick. Magda and I used to have such interesting late-night chats.

Get back on topic, Hester! Where was I? Right. Sam's problem with panda Herman. He doesn't think the carnival lifestyle is a good fit for a panda, but he's willing to try it for a while.

I think he'll come around. I saw him scratching Herman's back while we were at a rest stop this morning. I felt bad because I had been incapacitated from laughing at Herman's stretching and somersaulting antics as he tried to deal with the itch himself. Pandas are ridiculous creatures. Perhaps it's because Herman isn't used to his new form, but he's extremely clumsy and his bum wiggles in a most amusing way when he walks.

He's sweet and kind-hearted . . . Sam, not my depressed and grumpy panda. I enjoy his straightforward nature. If there's a problem, he tells you. But he doesn't just leave it at that. He explains why it's a problem, listens, and does his best to help solve it. He's a good boss. Ha! I had to travel to the Outerplane to find one. That's sad. Well, Andreas was okay. I just wasn't cut out for Moonbrews.

Asena keeps casually mentioning that Sam is unattached. I eventually figured out that it means he's not romantically involved with anyone—yet another confusing saying that left me wondering what he used to be stuck to. She's trying to spur me into asking him if he's interested in a romp, but things are complicated enough right now. Not that I don't find him attractive. The timing just sucks.

It is tempting. I'd finally get to run my fingers through all that luscious hair. He must use scented oils when he bathes. He always smells of peppermint and lemons.

ADDENDUM: I received a letter just as I was getting ready for bed. I wasn't able to open it right away because I had to collect my tent and stuff from a neighbouring field. Air elementals from my plane are way overpowered. After assuring everyone that the freak twister had not damaged Herman or myself, we set everything back up, and I am now sitting on my cot staring at the tightly rolled scroll. It's soggy, so I know exactly who it's from and I'm scared.

ADDENDUM II: I'm still staring at it. What if Ouleah says my job can't be accredited? Then you'll deal with it, Hester. Great, now I'm talking to myself in a diary in third person. I'd better open this thing before I totally lose my mind.

ADDENDUM III: Okay. Ouleah is optimistic that she can make this job sound acceptable to the WU Placement Accreditation Department. And she's going to put a rush on it. She can be quite persuasive, so . . . maybe. I'm not celebrating yet as she said there might be some blockers to deal with. She's going to keep me advised of the status and forward any requests for information to me as soon as she receives them.

Wendias, Lotus Moon 3, 209

WELL, MAGDA'S MONTH of reflection is up and she is a star! I purposefully avoided asking about her job in my letters as I didn't want to push her, but my worry was unfounded. Not only did she make it through her massive project, she landed the promotion! She credits her team, in her typical humble way, but she was the one leading them.

Magda still isn't sure if she wants to work there long term, but she's going to stay for now. She really loves experimenting with potions and curses, so as long as she can still do that, I'm certain she'll feel at home in her new position.

I can't convey how relieved I am to hear that she's recovered her confidence. She's my best friend. I love her dearly and only want her to be happy. Wherever her passions take her, she'll always have my full support.

On an interesting note, she mentioned that my Witch Jar caught a curse. I'm unsure if hexes from my plane transfer here, but I feel incredibly lucky all the same.

I guess Justin and his mother figured out who was responsible for their buggy reflections. Man, I wish I could have seen their faces when they first saw themselves in a mirror. I'll just have to close my eyes and imagine it. Maybe replay the moment a few times whenever I'm feeling low. Being wicked feels oh so good.

So, happy news all around today. For once. I believe people on the Outerplane call that a miracle.

Moondias, Lotus Moon 8, 209

WE MADE IT safely to the new location. Working for Karneval Života is a whirlwind of traveling and spooking. I'm not complaining . . . much. The spooking is satisfying. The traveling, not so much. The whole time we're camped, I exist in a low-level state of fear, knowing we'll be jumping again in a week or two. I hope I get used to vehicles at some point.

Our lot is on a coast this time, beside a massive body of warm, briny water. The sun is unrelenting. Even the moon blazes in its reflected light at night. I see as well on midnight rambles as I do during the day. The air is heavy and humid. It's so hot, I'm surprised all the sand on the beach hasn't turned to glass. Not my preferred environment. I'm not suited to it and neither are my robes. I'll have to invest in new ones if the climate doesn't improve. I can honestly say I miss the dark and chill of Mother's moors.

We're on the outskirts of a huge metropolis and there are people everywhere. *Everywhere.* The carnival is bursting with them, especially the House of Horrors. I guess it's good because that was my goal and I do enjoy scaring them. But also bad because I dislike people . . . which leads me back to the good part because I get to do my utmost to make them run away screaming. So, on the whole, that probably makes it good. Sigh.

Sam is working hard to market the carnival on something called "on line boards." He tried describing them to me. Much of what he said made no sense, but I think they are similar to group scrying sessions.

He also made a slight change to how we do things. During the day, the carnival is open to children, but at night after the big top show, it switches to adult only. That way I'm free to let loose with the horror, and it seems to be boosting interest in my Witch's Feast, which is now up and running (not literally . . . Outerplane people tend to turn their nose up at food that's still moving).

I decided to host two sit-down suppers and I'm glad I did. I've been sold-out every night. Trying out family recipes and creating menus is keeping me busy.

Everyone is helping. Asena and Julie usually stop by to assist with serving. They really get into it. While people are eating, Asena pretends she's been possessed by an evil spirit (at least I think she's pretending), and Julie accuses me of casting a spell on her that makes her melt. Very entertaining. Her melting was so convincing the first time, I feared I had inadvertently cast a spell. I hadn't. That was a rather unpleasant flashback to the phoenix disaster. Never again.

My parents would faint if they knew how much I've been cooking. Dad's been trying to interest me in kitchen witchery ever since I was old enough to stir a cauldron. No more Mean Cuisine meals for this girl! Julie and I usually split the leftovers. It's nice to know someone appreciates good food. My patrons mostly gag and make faces at it. I'm not sure why you'd pay to be disgusted and not eat, but it's a popular pastime here.

NOTE: It's probably safe to check in with Mom and Dad now that things aren't so bleak. Should I mention that there might be a problem with my Adept ceremony? It might just worry them unnecessarily. Then again, they tend to react badly when big news hits without warning. Yikes. That is going to be a tricky letter.

Sam organized a nice setup for cooking. He had the camp cookhouse inspected for food preparation and then parked it behind the House of Horrors. I can cook throughout the day and still randomly pop back into my joint via one of the many trap doors to terrify my patrons.

He also spends a considerable amount of time cooking with me. I never thought I'd meet someone worse at following recipes than I am. I have to keep a sharp eye on him at all times. Incautious handling or adlibbing has unexpected consequences with many of my dishes. He got curious about my matured puffballs and poked one before I could warn him. We spent a looong time cleaning up the spores, and he still complains that the curtains smell like old socks. He makes me laugh. I have to admit, I did the same thing the first time Dad and I gathered the delicate fungi late in their season. Even though we are from different planes, and Sam is a wizard, we are a lot alike.

Asena designed a new ghost costume for Kamal. Now he wanders freely through the House of Horrors doling out scares while ensuring the wizard contraptions are in good working order (he's picked up some wizard skills from Sam). He is a fantastic ghost and is a natural at sneaking up on people. Also, the spiders love him. There's always a horde crawling on him which enhances the costume's effect. Another feat he excels at is keeping Monkey and Herman in check. He's the only one they'll listen to, so having him in the H of H is fantastic.

In fact, Kamal has been such a big help that I made him my Assistant Manager. Sam had the title engraved on a badge for him to wear, which he proudly does every day. So now, I have a ghost wandering my halls with a shiny new badge. I don't mind. I'm sure there are Assistant Manager ghosts out there who enjoy the representation. I have come to think of him as my Apprentice (even though he's a druid with questionable wizard skills).

Fiona, our dwarven strong woman, has also gotten into the horror mood. The Spider Siblings taught her to ride their horses, so now she dresses up in a dark cloak that Sam altered to make her appear headless and rides through camp every evening. Her favourite part is tossing a fake severed head at people. Sam, with his wizardly ways, creates bone-rattling cracks of thunder when she appears and has some kind of contraption that makes fog. Our patrons love it.

Last night, the Spider Siblings painted a skeleton on Ebony and the reaction was even more positive. They convinced Kamal to get in on the game, too. He wore his ghost costume and rode Snowball around. It was fun watching everyone try to run away from the headless horseman, only to run into a ghost rider. They had no idea where to go.

Sam is all a tizzy because a group of T V executives (whatever those are) stopped by. They asked us to extend our stay for a few days so they could use Karneval Života as a shooting location for a popular T V show. My alarm must have been obvious because Sam clapped a hand over my mouth and happily agreed to their demands before I could say anything. His mood and their intentions didn't add up until he explained there would be no actual shooting of anything or anyone.

The shooting process they spoke of involves capturing different values of light and converting them to numbers so people can view an event later, even if they weren't there at the time. He went into great detail. There's a chance his explanation would have made sense to Magda. I, however, was thoroughly lost. I think the end result (a T V show) is something akin to the dramas we watch in crystal balls, except people are pretending to do things and talk to each other. I don't get the appeal if it's fake. It must be lucrative because the T V executives are paying a large sum to use our lot for the day, and on top of that, everyone is being paid as "extras." Sam sounded happy, so I guess it's also a good thing? I'll find out soon enough.

In between tear down, traveling, set-up, running the House of Horrors, and cooking, I've been trying to help Herman find a form he's happy with. The panda wasn't working for him. Or me. He ate a crazy amount of this hard to get plant. A plant that also made him gassy. Not pleasant when sleeping in a tent.

Whenever I gather enough energy to try another transmutation, we do. Thanks to some recent spectacular storms, I was able to charge my crystals between full moons. It's a more involved process and not as efficient as it was in my plane, but it works.

First, Herman wanted to be a squirrel. That was a short-lived desire. He kept getting fleas and chipped a tooth on a nut.

Then he wanted to be a sloth because he decided they weren't cute. Unfortunately, everyone else thought they were (poor guy is plagued with cuteness). Plus, he kept getting vertigo from hanging upside down.

Which brings me to his current form. To celebrate being by the sea, he decided to try a coastal creature. I borrowed a tome from the library and he settled on a coconut crab. For once, I approve of his selection. Coconut crabs are creepy and threatening. Very appropriate for a familiar.

I'm happy to report that he's more content in this form than he was in any of the others. He enjoys clicking his claws and scuttling after patrons. He also takes daily jaunts down to the beach to chase random strangers. He burrows into the sand and leaps out to scare anyone who wanders by.

Sam hasn't said anything, but I can tell he's relieved the panda is gone. He's been more accepting of Herman's recent forms, though he did mention the sloth was borderline (they are native to this landmass, just much farther south). The rest of my co-workers seamlessly accept Herman no matter what animal he shows up as. We couldn't have landed a job with a better group.

Bob is in and out of camp. Sometimes he doesn't even travel with us but he always shows up at the next location. I miss him when he's gone. I've grown used to having him around. He's a great sounding board for ideas. Much less lippy than Herman. Actually, he's less lippy than anyone because he never talks. I wonder what he thinks of our Outerplane excursion? He seems to enjoy haunting people in the H of H. I'm sure he wouldn't bother if it wasn't fulfilling. Lately, he's been experimenting with new facial expressions and has developed some very dramatic looks.

Well, I must get back to menu planning. I like to change things up every few nights to keep my patrons guessing. There's been a few repeat customers, and the last thing I want is to be predictably terrifying. I'm thinking of adding a sea themed dish now that we're on the coast. Dad used to bake up a mean eradian eel. I believe he stuffed it with a pudding made from pureed jellyfish innards, black fungus, and . . . something else.

My lips would tingle for ages after. I wonder if I can make something similar?

ADDENDUM: I have decided to keep elementals around me at all times to speed up my castings. Every morning I call a representative from each domain and ask them to stay near. They don't seem to mind. I would never consider hoarding elementals like this at home, but there aren't many practicing witches here. In fact, I have yet to meet any, other than Asena, and she doesn't even identify as a witch. Outerplane elemental demand is low and they do so enjoy lending their energies to spells. I feel bad for the little guys, aimlessly wandering, searching for magickal outlets. Granted there aren't many elementals about, but still, it's sad for those that are.

Tydias, Lotus Moon 9, 209

Dear Mom and Dad,

How are you? I bet your herb garden is doing well. Magda said your area has been getting lots of rain, so I imagine your acadium roots are bursting with juices. I used puffballs in a recipe recently and remembered how much fun Dad and I had collecting them when I was a kid. I miss you guys.

First of all, let me apologize because I know it's been a long while since I've written. I started a new job and things are very busy. Research and experiments take up what little spare time I have. You'll understand why shortly.

Please don't freak out. This is going to be a bit of a shock. Perhaps you should sit down. Seriously . . . sit.

The new job I mentioned is in the Outerplane. I'm running a House of Horrors attraction for Karneval Života and planning / hosting a twice-nightly Witch's Feast.

I know, I know, I couldn't have gotten a job any farther away from home. And before you ask . . . no, I did not do this on purpose. Due to circumstances beyond my control, I had to use the non-union job bank to find employment and there were a few details missing from the job posting.

At first, I was skeptical about staying, but I have since come to enjoy the work and my co-workers. It may sound strange, but I think I've finally found a place and job where I fit. It isn't just fun, it's challenging, and I believe it's a good career move. How many witches can say they made it on the Outerplane? None I know of. It is an unusual opportunity and I intend to make the most of it. There might be a slight hitch with regard to my Adept rites, but I have a union representative working on it, so please don't worry.

Dad, you would be proud of me. I'm cooking every sun and using all the family recipes you taught me. It's been hard to find equivalent ingredients, but I'm managing. I'm getting lots of practice since I've had to do the same for many of my spell components. If you come across any interesting recipes, please send them along (air elementals appear to be the quickest and most reliable way of delivering interplanar messages . . . though try to find a weak one because the regular ones make quite a mess here). Sadly, some of our recipes aren't workable on the Outerplane, either because there are no similar ingredients or there is a risk the dish may poison my clientele. That's frowned upon . . . even if you have the antidote.

There are many strange laws. I stumble across new ones every sun. It's difficult to be appropriately witchy, but I'm doing my best. Sam, my boss, said I can threaten to do things like poison or hex people, I just can't actually do it. Silly, I know, but I'm trying to fit in, at least a little.

Outerplane spellcraft is extremely complicated and elementals are a scarce resource. I feel like a child, struggling to grasp basic concepts and maintain even a weak connection to the elements. Every sun, I get better, but it is slow and grinding work. I never truly appreciated how good we have it at home. I miss the comforting feel of power flowing around me, through me. It's not something I will ever take for granted again.

I'm not sure when I'll be able to visit. The carnival is entering its high season, which means we are constantly traveling or working. And my funds are running low. Not desperately. I'm fine, really. I just can't afford the planar transit for a while. Not that I'm eager to suffer through that nightmare again, and I recommend that you also avoid it. I promise, I'm doing okay. I don't need you to rush to my rescue.

Again, I'm sorry I haven't written in so long, and please don't worry about me. I'll try to do better at keeping you informed.

May the Goddess light your paths,

Hester Digitalis Wishbone

Wendias, Lotus Moon 10, 209

TODAY I WAS reminded that not all people suck. With the constant press of humanity at the carnival, it's easy to lose sight of that (especially for those of us who lean toward the hermit end of the social spectrum). Occasionally, someone special comes along and makes every irritating situation and irrationally grumpy customer you've had to resist cursing worthwhile.

An elderly gentleman carrying a single white lily caught my eye while I dragged the midway this evening. He was alone, which was intriguing as it is not the norm. There was a sadness wrapped about him like a heavy winter cloak. He wore it well, so I knew it was a seasoned grief.

He shuffled slowly through the crowd with a wilful determination seen only in the very old. Out of curiosity, I followed and we ended up at the Ferris Wheel. Gilroy nodded to him in a familiar way, ushered him to the front of the line, and helped him into the next available carriage. The man placed his lily on the empty seat beside him, and there he silently sat for the next few hours while other passengers came and went. Gilroy always skipped his carriage.

Between my feasts, I went back to see if he was still there (he was) and asked Gilroy about him. His name was Mr. Baker and he'd been coming to the carnival for longer than Gilroy had been with the troupe (which I found out was just over fifteen years). Sam's mother had a standing order that he be allowed in free of charge and treated with the utmost respect—a wish that would be honoured for as long as the carnival and Mr. Baker were around.

Gilroy briefly left the controls to remove the seat in a carriage so a customer could manoeuvre her wheelchair in, and my eyes drifted back to our enigmatic guest. For a second I saw a young woman sitting beside him. She wore a lacy blue dress and gazed adoringly into his eyes. A gentle smile curved one side of her mouth, creating a dimple in her cheek, and her hand covered his where it rested on his knee. She laid her head on his stooped shoulder and then flickered back into the ether.

When the ride started moving again, I caught glimpses of the spirit, always cuddled up to Mr. Baker's side, always tender. Now and then, Mr. Baker pulled a wrinkled handkerchief from his jacket pocket and wiped away a tear. I don't think I've ever seen something so beautiful or heartbreaking. For such ties to last beyond the veil, for them to be strong enough to bridge the worlds, their love must have been epic.

As the carnival wound down and the crowds dispersed, Mr. Baker waved to Gilroy and descended from the carriage. I walked discreetly behind him as he began the long trek back to the gates, wanting to talk to him, but unsure if I would be an unwelcome intrusion on his memories.

Luckily for me, he encountered Maria and Sam. They stopped and had a friendly conversation which I quietly inserted myself into. Maria invited Mr. Baker to join our bonfire (which she never does with customers) but he graciously declined. Sam shook his hand and said that seeing old friends was always a pleasure. He encouraged him to stop by again before the carnival moved on and then he went to close the big top and prepare late-night snacks for the group.

Mr. Baker was a soft-spoken man, but an underlying cord of iron ran through his words and his bearing was unmistakably military despite his hunched stance. I swear Maria narrowly avoided saluting when she left.

I accompanied him to the gates. Before he exited, I asked who the woman was. At first, he was confused and thought I meant Maria. When I indicated I was referring to the spirit sitting beside him on the wheel, he grasped my arm. I was afraid he was unsteady, but his grip was firm and his gaze unwavering as he demanded I tell him exactly what I had seen. I recognized the look of a rational man desperate for confirmation of the irrational (for all the stories of ghosts and hauntings in the Outerplane, they are still considered myth).

I described the spirit and his breath hitched. He really did waver then. I pulled an empty crate over for him to sit on and retrieved his hanky to wipe a tear from his wrinkled cheek.

Once he caught his breath, he began to talk of Lily. She was his wife. They married as teens and had been through so much together, inseparable except for the wars overseas he felt honour bound to join. She died ten years ago and he missed her every hour of every day since. He started coming to the carnival alone after Lily died to celebrate the happy memories they shared here and to feel close to her. He had no idea she was actually with him. The Ferris Wheel was her favourite. She used to giggle the whole time because of the butterflies in her tummy. That sounded more alarming than funny to me, but he explained they weren't real butterflies; it was how she described the fluttery, excited feeling she got.

The midway was closed, and he was shivering by the time he finally accepted my invitation to share a hot cup of tea at our bonfire. I think he didn't want to intrude, but I assured him everyone would be happy for his company and even happier if he shared some of his stories. He laughed when I said he was blessed to have found a love so great and should pass his wisdom onto the rest of us poor souls. It was a wonderful sound and immediately buoyed my heart. Some people (usually witches) possess an innate ability to feel what others are feeling and can also share their emotional state with those around them. His talent was likely what drew me to him.

We had a wonderful evening together. Sam drove Mr. Baker home, but not before convincing him to come for tea again tomorrow. Lily will be pleased. I saw her in the drifts of smoke, standing beside him, her hand on his shoulder as he related stories from their lives.

It never occurred to me before, but this carnival is not just important to us. How many of our patrons have stories like his?

A first or last kiss. Friendships made and broken. A child's best day. All of them, a shared history that bonds those people to the carnival and thus to me. The web grows ever more intricate. Our lives, our deeds, our words ripple out even when we can't see them.

I shall cherish the loving memories Mr. Baker shared until my days are done and I too pass into Underworld. This was a good day.

Tydias, Lotus Moon 16, 209

I WENT AGAINST my better judgment and accepted Sam's offer of a swamp tour yesterday (a Moondias!) after the film crew "wrapped." Given the day, I knew things wouldn't go as planned but, to my unending surprise, it turned out to be a pleasant disaster. Not sure I've ever experienced one of those before.

I had just tasted my oldest jug of mead and judged it drinkable when the idea of the tour was raised. Interested, but certain things would go wrong, I decided to bring a flask to share. Nothing looks quite so dire after a sip or two of good mead. (*SIDE NOTE: I have the aging process down to a little over a month. Not bad, but there's room for improvement. More experiments needed!*)

Sam and I ended up on the tour alone . . . except for the boat captain but he was only there for a short time. I'll explain that in a bit. More people were supposed to come, but everyone else backed out at the last minute. I suspect Asena had a hand in it. Herman was excited about the trip, and yet he was mysteriously absent when it came time to leave. I later found out that he'd been cavorting on the beach with Kamal—a convenient distraction, I'm sure.

The swamp was breathtaking and mercifully cool. We explored an area overgrown with towering trees whose gnarled branches were thick with leaves and a moss resembling the greyed hair of ancient corpses. It swayed in the wind, beckoning us deeper. Hidden creatures peeked out of every dark nook. Only the barest touch of sunlight penetrated the canopy. Moving through water patterned with vines and roots, the shadows around us birthed more shadows and the world was right. Everything was right.

It was delightfully eerie. Dark. Dangerous. Alive with mystery. A perfect place for a witch. I'll definitely be going back. Perhaps I can build a hut there when I have spare coin. I never thought I'd be hut hunting in the Outerplane. Life is strange.

As much as I loved the swamp, Sam did not. He jumped at every rustle of moss and ripple of water. The captain was knowledgeable about the area, but the more he talked, the twitchier Sam became. I don't think he's a fan of alligators or snakes that drop from trees. I was most intrigued when one of the snakes popped in for a visit. Sam, not so much.

He would have killed the poor thing with a paddle if I hadn't spurred my water elemental into rocking the boat. The snake was quick to size up the situation and escape. Sam didn't fall overboard, but it was close. I imagine that wouldn't have gone well, since both he and the snake would have been together in the water.

The only part of the tour I wasn't fond of was the ear shattering wizard air blower the captain used to propel the boat. It was so loud, we had to cover our ears with a noise cancelling device. Leave it to wizards to make something so unusable that they have to devise another gadget so they can sit near enough to operate it. Honestly. It's not like there wasn't wind available. Why can't people use sails? Much more civilized. At least my air elemental had a great time playing in the engine.

Once we entered the overgrown section, the captain shut the air blaster off and used a pole. The sounds of the swamp were lovely. Waves lapped against the shores of small islands. Wind murmured through the leaves. Birds cooed. The occasional splash and startled cry as an alligator snapped its jaws closed on one of the cooing birds. Simply blissful.

Unfortunately for Sam, the air engine decided it was done working just as we were about to leave the treed area (Moondias always gets you!). The captain attempted to fix it, and then Sam tried as well, but even his wizardly skills could not coax it back to life. A part had broken inside, rendering the whole thing unusable (Wizards, they always get you too!). Sam said that area of an engine shouldn't get hot enough to melt butter, let alone metal. Guess there's a first time for everything.

We had travelled for a long while to get there and couldn't row or pole our way back to the dock. I offered up my robe as a sail, but that appeared to make everyone uncomfortable. The captain said he knew of a relatively short route to the mainland. Problem was, we'd have to wade most of the way as it wasn't passable in the now defunct boat. Sam was having none of that. In the end, the captain tethered the boat to a tree and set us up on an island while he waded away to secure another boat. He promised to come back as soon as he could. I didn't care. Any extra time spent in such a beautiful place was welcome.

The captain left while it was still light (or as light as it got in that part of the swamp), but blessed darkness soon reigned on our little island and brought with it a damp chill. After the unrelenting heat of the past week, it was a relief, but I knew the cold would eventually work its way to our bones. All the captain left us was a rope, a bucket, and a "flash light," which doesn't flash at all. It produces a bright continuous light. Even on a different plane, there's no rhyme or reason to wizard nomenclature.

Lucky for us, I'm in the habit of carrying my power crystals with me, so lighting a fire (even in such a water-rich environment) was of little consequence. My fire elemental was eager to help and the corpse moss was nicely dried and incendiary. I burnt off the water in some twigs and, from there, set alight larger felled branches.

Sam was beside himself. He stood in the middle of the island, arms crossed, turning in circles, trying to watch the shoreline and overhanging trees at once, convinced we were about to be overrun by ravenous animals. He apologized profusely for our predicament, believing it was his fault since the tour was his idea (Asena must have convinced him the idea originated from him. She's tricksy!). I tried to explain that a night in a swamp wasn't a big deal, but he was inconsolable. Poor guy.

He did his best to help gather branches for the fire and the small lean-to I wanted to build (didn't think those skills would come in handy again so soon), but he lost more branches than he collected. At least one armful ended up in the water because he accidentally grabbed a convincingly branch-like snake. I don't know which of them was more surprised.

When I finished with the fire and lean-to, I set a simple lure spell and caught a bucketful of crawfish for supper. The captain mentioned they were a local delicacy and I was not disappointed. I wrapped them into neat packages with leaves from a water plant and cooked them on a flat rock. Apart from some trouble cracking them open, it was an easy and delicious dish. Even more so when I added a splash of my Fire mead to the meat. Surprisingly, Sam liked the crayfish. It's the first thing I've cooked (other than gingerbread) that he's deemed edible. Why are Outerplane water bugs considered more palatable than air or land bugs? Strange.

Just as we were cleaning up, I noticed Bob. I'm glad I discovered him first and could steer Sam away before he saw what my gargoyle friend was sitting on. The alligator was unimpressed, but since it was probably sneaking up to take a bite out of something it wasn't welcome to, I didn't have much sympathy.

To show my thanks, I wove some of the yellow flowers that grow in the water with moss and a thin branch to make a necklace for Bob. His stony lips were curved into a wide smile when I next looked over, so I think he appreciated the gift.

Sam lay down and fell asleep in the lean-to and then things got really interesting.

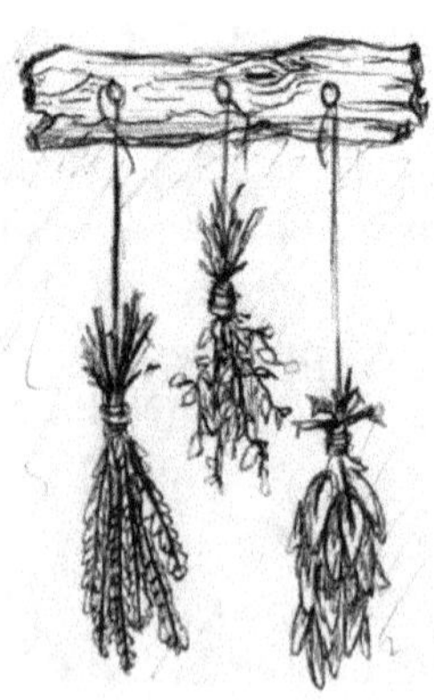

I was not tired. Night always invigorates me, especially one such as this, spent out in the wilds. I sat by the fire, revelling in the rich smell of smoke and lush vegetation, thinking about how lucky I was to spend time away from the fetid belching breath of wizard vehicles.

Our island was homey. There was a clearing in the middle, perfect for a modest witch hut. I could already see my broom leaning against the doorframe, drying herbs strung from the roof struts.

While I was lost in thought, a large snake (more than twice the length of me) slithered out of the water and curled up on the warm ground near the fire. I saw it coming, but had no objection to sharing my camp. I nodded to it and carried on dreaming, occasionally checking to make sure it was behaving itself and that Sam was still asleep. There was a glint of otherworld in its eyes as it watched me. I was curious, but not rude enough to ask.

"This place, so teeming with life and death, is one of my favourites as well."

I knew the snake had spoken, because Bob couldn't and Sam was unlikely to ever express such a sentiment.

"My magicks are weaker here, but sufficient. I'm pleased you are doing so well, my daughter."

Hekate again. I was alarmed that I couldn't sense her presence like I did at home. The Luminous Mother of Magick, Wise One, Goddess of the Night was sharing a fire with me . . . and I hadn't noticed. I swear the snake smiled as I flinched at the realization.

"Forgive my rudeness," I stammered. "I did not expect to meet you here."

"I like being where I'm not expected. Interesting things to learn." She uncoiled and slithered around the camp, curiously pushing her head into the bucket of live crawfish and tasting mead from the rim of my flask with a flick of her tongue.

I grew nervous when she peered into the lean-to, certain of how Sam would react upon waking to a face-full of snake. Hekate sensed my anxiety and assured me he would not wake until sunrise. Thinking back, I now realize it was odd for Sam to have fallen asleep so quickly, given his panicky state. The Goddess of Magick is full of mischief.

After stoking the fire, I collected more water plants and cooked the remaining crawfish as an offering to my guest and Goddess. She remained silent while I cooked, enjoying the warmth of the fire as she cast her gaze around the swamp. I was curious to know why she had come, but reluctant to ask. You never know what a goddess will take amiss.

I plucked the meat from the shells and added mead as I had done for our supper. Hekate gulped everything down, smacking her lips at the end in a satisfied manner—an unsettling sight on so large a snake.

Unsure what constituted friendly conversation for a goddess, I decided to stick to recent shared events and inquired after the sisters. Hekate said Mother and Crone were as cantankerous and feisty as ever, and that she was still overseeing their work on the moors. They were reluctantly revising a few of their attitudes and ways, but their implementation remained chaotic.

She rubbed herself against a rock, shedding a loose piece of skin. "It's always a trick, balancing order and chaos. I'm not supposed to have a favourite, but chaos is just so much more . . . fun."

I chuckled, wondering if that explained her interest in me. Chaos followed my steps closer than my shadow.

Fire reflected in the depths of her eyes as we spoke, and for a moment, I could feel the world, all the worlds, and every possibility in them stretched out around me. All the various paths of my hopes and dreams were laid bare. And of all the places I could be, of all the companions I could be with, and things I could be doing, right here on the Outerplane with Herman and Bob and Karneval Života was where I'd choose to be, every time.

Such is Hekate's power. In a land where magick barely exists, simply meeting her gaze can draw forth your heart's true calling.

We fell into silence and Hekate curled up by the fire again. I glanced at the swamp and every patch of darkness held a pair of gleaming eyes. Birds, rodents, alligators, fish, snakes; you name it, they were gathered around our island, listening to their goddess breathe, settling as near as they dared.

The creatures that came to pay their respects were well behaved. Alligators co-existed with herons. Owls and eagles shared trees with nary a misplaced talon. Even the fish left the water spiders and flies alone.

When the horizon lightened, Hekate bade me goodnight and slipped back into the emerald green waters. Her followers trailed for a while and then dispersed. A little field of flowering wolfsbane sprung from the soil where she had rested.

Fog drifted in with the dawn, low and thick enough to obscure the boundary between land and water. What a delightfully dangerous place! I commandeered a few cavorting water elementals to keep our island clear of vapours, worried the alligators might grow brave. There were some muffled splashes around us, but none dared approach without cover.

The misty veil flowed over the riot of vines and roots and water and land, transforming the swamp into a place of dreams. Trees reached up from the cloud, limbs twisted and knotted as if they could not decide which direction to grow next. Not long ago, that was me.

After staring at them, a realization hit. The chaos of branches served a purpose. No matter what angle the sun shone from, those trees would have enough light. A good life lesson and a poignant moment for me.

I've experienced chaos, caused a fair amount of it, been tossed around by it, but it has been to my benefit. I know without doubt that I can make it through anything. And I enjoy a bit of chaos. It's exciting. Magda was right. If I had locked myself into a safe and steady job, I'd be bored out of my skull.

As far as my Adept rites go, I find myself caring less and less. Even if Ouleah gets back to me and says the union won't approve my job but she has another one lined up, I won't take it. I can't just leave, knowing how hard-pressed Sam would be to replace me during their busy season. I guess my priorities have changed.

So what if I don't meet the requirements to become an Adept this season cycle? Hekate has never mentioned it, so I doubt the title means anything to her. It's not like my job with the carnival hinges on it. Magda is the only classmate whose opinion really matters, and I know her friendship is unwavering. My parents may initially be disheartened and confused, but I'll find a way to explain things. In fact, anyone who really cares about me knows that I have never in my life done anything the normal way. It's not surprising that I'm entering my profession on a unique schedule and path.

Strange to think that in all this turmoil, I have found peace. Well, my kind of peace anyway. Which is to say, chaos is my peace. In the end, it's that aspect of myself, the chaos I carry in my spirit, that I need to stop fighting and accept.

Sam awoke shortly after the sun and jolted me out of my musings. He fretted about the encroaching mists until the captain arrived with a new boat. I'm not sure I've ever seen Sam so happy.

Our leave-taking came all too soon for me. There wasn't even time to catch more crawfish for breakfast. I watered the wolfsbane and committed our little island to memory before stepping onto the boat. I don't know if I'll ever be back (I hope so), but I will carry this magickal night and island in my heart forever.

Cerridias, Lotus Moon 18, 209

WHAT HAPPENED TODAY is a great example of how I sometimes create my own chaos. I have been trying to embrace it, but it's not always easy. Especially when said chaos smells like bad fish. Others aren't so fond of that kind either.

After my realizations in the swamp, much of my anxiety about my path and role as a witch in the Outerplane has lessened. These last few days have been a welcome respite. I didn't know how deeply the constant stress affected me until it was absent. Even the prospect of tearing down the camp and making another jump felt less daunting.

Although I enjoy having a new batch of people to scare every few weeks, this is usually the time I start stressing about having to get in a vehicle again. My palms sweat and my heart races—very inconvenient when you have to be physically active and are trying to carry things. I'm sure people think I'm tragically out of shape and clumsy.

But today, the getting there part didn't seem so bad. I woke up refreshed and excited about our next location. I hopped out of my cot, gathered my washcloth and soap, threw on my robe, and tossed aside the flaps on my tent. As I stepped into the sun's unrelenting embrace, something wet and fishy smacked my cheek. I stumbled sideways and looked around. There was no sign of what had hit me.

I shook it off as yet another Outerplane oddity and carried on with my normal morning routine. I returned to my tent after breakfast to change into my work robe and gather supplies for spider collecting before taking down the H of H. Nothing fishy happened when I exited, so I figured it was a temporary issue.

Not so. I received a scaly slap at random times throughout the day. There was never any sign of what had hit me. A couple of times people were looking directly at me and saw nothing but my reaction to the blow.

After a while, I noticed it was more likely to happen when I passed from the backyard to the midway, or when I left my tent, Asena's motorhome, or the House of Horrors. The latter was extremely inconvenient as I was in and out constantly in my quest to free my house spiders and pack up props.

By the end of the day, I smelled worse than a dead fisherman in a barrel of chum. Jim Dandy the dog, Bob's bunny, and Monkey were following me around and rubbing up against me. Everyone else politely found excuses to be elsewhere. Even Herman said the smell was a bit much and he loves fish. I took a shower and did what I could to wash it off. It worked until the next invisible chum attack. I became seriously concerned that I had pissed off an Outerplane sea god.

What was actually going on hit me at the same time as another invisible fish. I left my tent for my last trek to the bathroom before laying down and *smack*! It must have been a big one, because it hit my face and shoulder at the same time, knocking me flat. As I lay on the ground, my broom, which had been propped against the canvas by the opening, fell on me. At first, I was angry, but then a distant memory tickled the back of my mind.

I tested my theory. Grabbing my broom, I stepped outside unmolested. I entered again, and left without my broom. *Smack*! Another fishy assault. I repeated the process and confirmed it.

After flipping waaaay back in my diary, I found the entry I was looking for and verified the wording of a hex I had put on myself: "Every time I leave my abode (whatever and wherever that might be) without my broom, a fish will materialize and slap me in the face." Abode. That was the key.

The hex had seemed a good idea at the time. It was supposed to ensure that I would never forget my broom. Oh, how naive I had been. Not to mention exhausted and more than a little irritated. It all came about after an epic foot-chase through a valley tracking Pasha, the surprisingly mobile "abode" I had been hired to hut-sit during college break. Good times.

Which brings me to today. I hadn't been taking my broom everywhere with me, probably because I'm less stressed (my broom has become a security crutch and I am rarely without it). It is surprising and heartening to know that I've settled in with the carnival well enough to feel at home in so many spots.

Instead of being mad at myself about the hex, I choose to laugh. Old me played a hilarious trick on new me. Herman is having a good laugh, too, the rascal.

Needless to say, I'll be undoing the hex as soon as I have spare energy. In the meantime, I'll endeavour to remember my broom.

ADDENDUM: My daily elementals are multiplying. At first, I had to call new ones each morning because they would wander off while I slept. Now, the old ones are sticking around and gathering others of their kind on their own. They're small, as powerful elementals are exceedingly rare, but I am delighted. I can save the power I was using to summon them for spells, which means less crystal charging. Yay! They mostly stay out of trouble and hang out in the House of Horrors in piles of dust, flickering candle flames, etc. My water elementals made a bit of a mess in the spider room yesterday. They redirected rain from an open window into a puddle and were gleefully playing in it when I found them. I cleaned some of it up, but left a little pool. The spiders were enjoying it too.

Moondias, Lotus Moon 22, 209

WELL, THAT WAS discouraging (even for a Moondias). We were almost done setting up camp at our new location when a mob of ignorant jerks decided to protest the carnival. Asena warned me it could happen, but our reception was so positive at other stops that it caught me off guard. Between the mob and the noise, it felt like I was back in the village after my unfortunate adhesive accident, hiding in my hut, about to be run out of town. Only this time things ended differently. I'm not the same witch and my employer isn't one of the ignorant jerks waving a torch.

I might not have blown my lid if they hadn't picked on Kamal. He's the youngest of us, so they probably figured he'd be the easiest to scare. Bullies are the same no matter what plane they're on. Little did they know, of any of us Kamal is by far the most unflappable. He's also the nicest . . . hence my rage, which my co-workers shared. I'm still shaking.

They cornered Kamal as he was setting up the arch (our main entrance gate). Sam and Maria were nearby and intervened before the mob went too far. Sam, who's not normally a violent person, punched one of the protesters when they grabbed Kamal's arm.

By the time I arrived, things were heated. The mob was hurling insults and curses, calling us Satan-spawn (I came across the Satan Outerplane creature in my research . . . sounded interesting and could be useful in the H of H) and damning us to burn in a fiery pit (for the sin of being born, apparently).

Maria brandished her rapiers at anyone who ventured too close. Herman joined the fray, pinching legs and other bits with what can only be described as wild and abandoned glee. The protestors initially recoiled when they saw me and then redoubled their insults. I'm pleased they took particular exception to witches. Clearly, our professional reputation preceded me.

Mobs are unpredictable and dangerous at the best of times, but this one had a distinctly noxious feel to it. My witch senses tingled in warning. We needed to disperse them quickly if we wanted to make it out with our equipment, homes, and skins intact. Problem was, they were standing between us and the majority of our vehicles.

I reminded myself that I had stared down Infernals and had tea with a goddess, experiences which permanently raised my fright bar. This motley crew had picked the wrong witch and the wrong witch's druid Apprentice to mess with . . . not that there's ever a right witch to mess with. On the whole, it's just a really bad idea unless you want to, say, end up as a bag of bones.

The Spider Siblings heard the commotion and rode up on Ebony and Snowball. They kept the mob at bay long enough for me to duck away and secure supplies from the partially constructed House of Horrors. Although massive, our resident horses are gentle. Danica and Nikolai had trouble even getting them to bump into people and step on a few toes. They were far more tolerant than I was at being jabbed and smacked. Soon, the mob pressed in and backed us up against the arch.

The third time an obnoxious blowhard poked me in the side with a sign that read, "Your going to Hell," I lost it. Honestly, the spelling alone was enough to make my eyes bleed.

Until then, I took my cue from Sam, who was mostly calmly asking everyone to back off so we could pack up and be on our way. That path would have been easier for all involved, but much less fun (to quote my favourite goddess). Really, I should thank the mob. As much as I dislike bullies (especially when they're picking on my friends), I do love meting out some well-deserved mayhem.

First, I secured everyone's attention by reproducing the best, soul-shattering banshee scream I could. Then I lobbed three exploding puffballs loaded with moth dust into the crowd (I have a lifetime supply thanks to Mothlady). As people choked on the dust and rubbed it out of their eyes, I asked my air elementals to whip up an eerie breeze. They turned my hair into a snaking mass of grasping tendrils and kindly kept the dust away from us.

Next, I summoned the army of spiders Kamal and I had collected. They flowed over the gates in a leggy wave and surged toward the mob. It was an admittedly short wave, but once I was covered in spiders, people were much more solicitous. I used the last scrap of power in my crystals to add a flash of red to my eyes and amplify my voice as I laid a chain of hexes on them. My curses, built on years of training and experience, put the mob's trifling insults to shame. Needless to say, the research I did on Outerplane fears was of great use. I didn't activate any of the spells, but they couldn't tell the difference.

The crowd was already backing away when Sam set off the wizard machine that produces realistic cracks of thunder. That pushed them over the edge. They turned and ran.

I sent my broom after them and managed to trip a few stragglers (hooray for my fishy hex because I might not otherwise have had it with me!). Lucky for them, the most my broom could do was tangle their feet or I would have had it smack their petulant backsides all the way to town.

We managed to tear down everything before the protesters worked up enough stupid to come back, and we are now on our way to the next location. We'll be a week early, but Sam said it would be fine. I believe he's concerned about having enough coin to make the journey—wizard engines guzzle expensive potions called diesel, propane, and gasoline. As long as we have enough to make it there (hopefully the coin left over from the T V show contract will cover it), we'll just run the carnival for two weeks instead of one.

Everyone was calm about what happened. I can't believe they have to put up with this abuse on a regular enough basis that it isn't notable. I'll put a few contingency plans into place for next time. At some point, protesters will learn that bothering us isn't worth the nightmares. Not that I can see any worth in it to begin with. Maybe being a jerk is its own reward? Whatever. It won't seem like a reward when I get done with them.

I'm not giving anyone a chance to repeat the vile Outerplane history I read about during my research. I stumbled across a whack of information on how witches were treated by various religious groups (magick systems reliant on the will of specific gods . . . usually only one). They used to torture false confessions out of anyone suspected of being a witch! Disgusting!

The rarity of magick power on the Outerplane enabled this persecution. Witches are few in number and widespread as well, which made them easier to overwhelm. Especially so, once the seeds of fear and suspicion were planted in the public consciousness and witchcraft was driven underground. Neighbours pointed at each other, hoping to avoid suspicion falling on themselves for simply helping birth a child or because a cow's milk went sour. It was mass hysteria of the ugliest kind.

I believe the persecutions also contributed to the current wizard infestation. Traditional wizard disciplines, such as chemistry, physics, and the much-dreaded engineering, thrived in this magick depleted environment. After observing Sam work (from a safe distance), I can confirm that their principles are sounder and more reproducible here than they were on my plane.

To make matters better (for wizards), local magick systems have been warring amongst themselves for centuries. While they fought over whether magick water was better than magick cloth, wizards buggered off and did their own thing. And they've had the last laugh. Wizards make a fortune selling their contraptions to the groups at war, which has unfortunately encouraged all parties to carry on in the same vein.

I'm not completely biased. I know witches and druids are capable of the same level of destruction. I just believe we're less likely to draw enough power to *accidently* wipe a city off the map or alter the temperament of a wasp species so that it becomes aggressive and spreads unchecked—the occasional half-phoenix notwithstanding. Although destructive, my mistake was merely tavern-ending, not civilization-ending.

Sam always argues the merits of wizardry during our nightly

bonfire debates, regaling me with stories of their beneficial medical, farming, information sharing, and building machines. If what he says is true, and I'm inclined to believe it is as he's been nothing but straightforward with me in every other respect, it sounds like Outerplane wizards have at least sowed as much positive creation as they have destruction. Although it pains my witchy sensibilities to admit it, maybe the type of power used isn't the most relevant factor. Maybe how it's used and what it's used for is all that matters. I think Hekate said something to that effect when she talked to the sisters and me on the moors. It takes a while for lessons to sink in, but I think I might have finally gotten that one.

For all its good parts, the Outerplane remains a dangerous place for witches. I'll remember that after today. I'm a witch in an Age of Wizards. Good thing I have one on my side.

Sam is a rare gem. I thanked him for his quick thinking with the thunder and he just smiled and gave me a hug. He said he should be thanking me. We were both partially right. It took all of us to get that mob to leave. We work well together. Never thought I'd say that.

Hester Digitalis Wishbone works well with a wizard. It may even be said that she *enjoys* working with one.

Every day is an unknowable adventure. What wonders and perils will tomorrow hold?

Freydias, Thunder Moon 5, 209

GREAT GODDESS, I'VE had a busy two weeks. There's been so much going on that I haven't had five spare minutes to document anything in here.

We made it safely to our next site. A few of us secretly contributed coin to buy food for the wizard engines. They are greedy things. We didn't tell Sam. He's worried enough about keeping the carnival going and paying back the loan.

We're still on the coast, which is not so great for me because of the heat but fantastic for Herman, who never tires of gallivanting on the beaches as a coconut crab. I had to invest in some thinner fabrics, and Asena, who is skilled in robe making, made me three new witch vestments that are not only comfortable to wear, but unique and stylish. She managed to blend the aesthetic of my old robes with some common styles worn by Outerplane witches.

I love the deep colours she used and the fabrics are light as air. The skirts flutter as if an otherworldly wind haunts my every step (though sometimes the fluttering is due to my air elementals playing . . . they also enjoy the fabric). She has sown little hidden pockets everywhere for me to store my spell components and tools (my spell pouches alone couldn't accommodate the added Outerplane magickal component demands).

For ease of access, I also started tying energy crystals and a few common components such as sage, raven feathers, and cedar twigs into my hair. The overall effect is quite pleasing. Even Herman approves, which is saying a lot. He has a very particular sense of fashion.

Speaking of Herman, I'm beginning to wonder if he likes being a crab so much because it's the closest to his original cockroach form we've come. I'll give him a while longer and then broach the subject. It was never my intention to make him feel bad about who he was, but now I'm thinking that's exactly what I did. I was so wrapped up in the insult of being assigned a familiar that wasn't on the official union list, I didn't stop to consider how my reaction affected him. I was unforgivably ignorant and will apologize.

Karneval Života's popularity is growing, which is good . . . mostly. Our appearance on the T V show has "exponentially increased our reach"—Sam's words, not mine, and I don't really know what he meant. He's been approached by more T V and movie executives about using the carnival as a shooting location. There have been many meetings and dinners and lunches and drinking parties to attend and host. I've put on a Witch's Feast for several batches of executives and scouts, to great praise, I might add.

I said it was mostly good because I'm not skilled at the kind of non-talk and "mingling or schmoozing" (again, Sam's words) that are expected at these events. In fact, I am diametrically opposed to such nonsense. If words come out of your mouth, they should be worthy of someone's time. I do not now, nor will I ever care how long it took someone to get their hair done or whether their shoes have red soles (unless it's blood and then I'd just like to confirm it doesn't belong to someone I like). I understand we need to promote the carnival and part of that is attending these hideous parties, but I just don't enjoy any of it. People ask strange questions like, "Where did the inspiration for your menu come from?" (Duh . . . it says right on it that everything is based on traditional family recipes) or they ask questions I can't answer without coughing up a lung like, "How did you end up joining a carnival?" or "How do you make it seem like the gargoyle is moving on its own when no one's looking?" Arrrg!

After enduring several of these events and conducting rigorous experimentation, I discovered that standing in a corner and cackling manically is an effective way to keep people at bay. They appear to find it disconcerting. No more weird or unanswerable questions for me! It's thematically and professionally appropriate too, so it's a win-win. I don't know why more people don't utilize this method.

The most exciting thing that's happened recently is that Peuturella, my old potions professor, paid me an unexpected visit to deliver a sack of gems and coin (with a promise of future payments every moon). After perfecting the processes and ingredient lists, she sold our laxative icing and gingerbread glue formulas to a huge alchemist company!

I knew she was going to try, but I didn't think it would be so quick or lucrative. With this amount of coin, which is just my half of the initial contract payment, I can count myself as rich. Add to that the bonus percentage of sales every moon and I am one lucky witch. I'll have no problem paying back my student loans now and there'll be no more fears of government-run love potion sweatshops in my future! Peuturella has lifted a huge weight off my broom.

I split my half of the down payment with Herman, as he was instrumental in developing the initial formulas. I also sent a pouch-full of gems to Althea as part of the recipes were hers. Hopefully it will mitigate any issues I caused at the Gingerbread Hut with the building inspectors, storks, and Infernals. Lastly, I sent some coin to Magda to pay her back for the loan she gave me. It doesn't begin to cover all the emotional and professional help she's given, but it's a start.

To my delight, Peuturella stayed for a mini-vacation. We're bunking together in my tent. She's having a blast with my co-workers and is an excellent helper in the House of Horrors. Her visit has given me a few ideas.

I threw the runes tonight to check whether a new direction I've been contemplating for the carnival is a good idea. I wouldn't normally take such a drastic step (tempting the Fates), but I'm fond of my co-workers and job and don't want to take any unnecessary risks if the result isn't worth it. The runes came back positive, so I guess the next step is to see if Sam is interested. I'm excited and cautiously optimistic. This could be great!

Tydias, Thunder Moon 9, 209

EXCITING NEWS! SAM loved my idea to re-brand the carnival (which doesn't involve any searing of flesh, thankfully). It's what he called my plan to modify the rides, games, and big top show around a horror theme. He said it would be a great way to capitalize on our recent popularity. Between the two of us, we have enough ideas to choke a reticulating lava worm.

The last hurdle is presenting the idea to our co-workers. They are usually open to new ways of doing things, so I don't foresee a problem. Neither did Sam, but he said it was a decision everyone had to make together. We called a meeting for this afternoon. I'm supposed to be getting my ideas on paper so I can keep things straight while I'm explaining, but I was too excited and had to write in here first.

Yikes! It's almost time. I'd better get on to that list of ideas. No rest for the wickedly clever witch of the carnival!

IT WAS A unanimous "Yes." Karneval Života is now officially a Traveling Horror Show and I've never been prouder to be part of a group. I usually prefer to work alone. Many class projects and uncomfortable work experiences taught me that it's easier and infinitely less painful. But . . . *but* . . . when you find a crew this fantastic, nothing beats collaboration.

They had terrific ideas and were excited and engaged. Their enthusiasm was energizing. Everyone discussed what needed to be done first and divvied up jobs. Although each performer is responsible for their own act, everyone has some kind of skill to help someone else, from Sam's wizardry to Asena's costuming prowess. Even my Outerplane research came in handy. I had a readymade collection of scary folklore, monsters, and phobias.

This is going to be *a lot* of work. I asked if anyone minded if I called in friends to help and there were no objections. I think Peuturella smoothed the way. She got along so well with everyone and helped perfect the salve for Tim. He said his skin has never been so pain free. We were all sad to see her go.

I wrote up invitations for some of my old classmates (including Magda, of course) and a few co-workers I got along with. I'll ask my air elementals to make the deliveries tomorrow. I'm not sure how many will be able to come or for how long, but I figure it's worth a try. It will also help test out my other new idea: Can I market the carnival as a vacation destination for folks from my home plane?

I've been mulling it over for a few days, and I think it's possible. Peuturella had a fantastic time terrifying people in the House of Horrors. Imagine the fun she could have if the whole carnival was one big scare! We could certainly offer more interesting activities than Hawaii did for Althea on her vacation. That sounded like a total snore-fest.

Not only would bringing in extraplanar guests be a boon to the carnival, as they would pay for the experience, it would also provide our customers with a rotation of new and exciting creatures and frights. The possibilities are endless.

And . . . if that works out, I've also considered opening up a few training / practicum placements for Grimoire College students. The Outerplane offers unique magickal challenges and learning experiences. The carnival is the perfect place for Apprentice witches to test their talents without the ever-present worry of accidently doing something permanently fatal (as my half-phoenix incident could so easily have been). They would have to stretch their talents, innovate, and master their connection to all the elements. It would be an incredibly ambitious apprenticeship.

To ascertain whether the practicum idea is feasible, I've

invited Ouleah to come and see the carnival for herself. Getting approved as a practicum placement with Grimoire College will only be possible if my job can be accredited by the union. I haven't heard anything about that yet, so I'm hoping my initiative will spur the union into action, one way or the other. Sigh. Guess I'm back to biting my nails about that again. My life has more ups and downs than the bloody Ferris Wheel.

If I run into trouble with the union or college, I'm sure Peuturella will back me. She's a tenured Grimoire professor and an Elder WU member. Her opinion holds weight. I won't say I have a good feeling about my plans, because that never works out, but I will say I'm cautiously optimistic.

I'm bursting at the seams with nervous anticipation. Of course, that could also be because Sam made his famous five-layer chocolate cake for our group meeting. I'm not usually fond of sweets, but he slathers each layer with thick cream and sour cherries. The combination is irresistible.

The meeting eventually wound down and people headed off to plan their new acts. Sam and I stayed by the campfire, chatting and drinking a relaxing tea made from the fresh mint, chamomile, and lavender I found at a local farmers market. We drank a fair amount of mead during the meeting, so I figured we'd better switch to something non-alcoholic for our next conversation.

I've never been great at casually bringing things up. Whenever I try, it goes weird, like the time I tried to hint that a fellow patron at The Resplendent Toad was interested in Magda. I must have accidently cast a hex because when I whispered that he was gagging for her, he suddenly turned blue and choked to death. Well, not quite to death. We managed to dislodge the ghoul eye he had inhaled and revive him. Still, it did kill the mood. He was much less romantically inclined after that.

I decided to be direct with Sam and told him that I'd come into some unexpected funds and wanted to pay off a chunk of the carnival's loan.

He was shocked and hesitant, perhaps a bit suspicious, but there was no turning blue and dying, so I'd call it a win. His main concern was what I expected. He thought I wanted to run the carnival, to which I replied, "Hel's no." We discussed amounts for a while. He went back to his trailer and retrieved a book crammed with columns of figures. Bob was off somewhere, but I sure wish he had been there. At least he might have understood the numbers and terms Sam threw around. It was hard to contain my horror when he started talking about drawing up some kind of Infernal contract to outline a schedule of repayment and default terms. I assured him no such atrocity was necessary, but that made him even more uncomfortable. He said it was too much money to accept as a gift.

I hadn't intended it to sound like a gift, but in retrospect I can see how it might be construed that way. Ensuring my own job security was my main concern. I told him as much, but it did little to dissuade him from promising to set up a monthly repayment scheme. In the end, I gave in and agreed. If that's the only way it'll work for him, then so be it. I'll use the extra coin to spruce up the H of H, which will benefit everyone.

Despite his initial concern, I could tell he was relieved to get the aggressive broker off his back. It was heartening to know he felt better owing me, because it showed there was trust between us. That realization meant more to me than I thought it would. After witnessing the joy and passion everyone had for the carnival in the meeting, knowing I was a part of that, accepted and celebrated, I knew I was home. Finally home. It was another perfect moment in time, like the night in the swamp. I've rarely had that feeling, and it's always a sure sign that my heart and mind are aligned, and my path is true.

He caught me wiping a tear away and laid a hand on my arm, asking if I was okay.

When I found my voice, I explained that I was just overwhelmed because I've never really fit in anywhere. A fact I've mostly ignored, and occasionally appreciated. I came here as an outsider (in the truest sense) and was unconditionally welcomed. They gave me an opportunity to be myself (find myself really) and do a job I love. No amount of coin could equal what that means to me, what they mean to me. My co-workers are the true gift.

Sam smiled and gently squeezed my arm. There was a sadness in his eyes as he shared his own history. He grew up in the carnival, but left when he came of age to study at an institution of higher learning (sounded similar to Grimoire

College). There, his classmates constantly taunted and rebuked him for being different. He tried to fit in, to do and say whatever was expected, but it was exhausting and ultimately futile. When his mother died and the carnival hit hard times, he returned and remembered what it was like to feel accepted, not merely tolerated.

With the carnival, what made him different was what made him great. It was the same for all of them. Karneval Života is a sanctuary and a living, breathing example to every ordinary and extraordinary person of how being distinct is not a weakness to be endured, but an awe-inspiring quirk of fate that deserves to be shared and celebrated.

Sam is extraordinary. I've never met anyone like him. He's a wizard, but you'd never know it by the care he takes to ensure everyone around him is safe and happy.

Once again, we talked far longer than we should have. The sun peeked over the horizon by the time we headed for our bunks. Before we separated, he drew me in for a hug and whispered that he was forever thankful our paths had crossed. He said he'd never met anyone with such an indomitable spirit. I laughed and, at his hurt look, had to explain that indomitable is exactly how I would describe him and every one of our co-workers.

I don't know why, but this hug felt different from the others he's given. He couldn't quite meet my eyes as we said goodnight. I wonder if Asena has picked up on something I've missed until now. I believe Sam may be interested in me, in a romantic sense. Then again, I'm not familiar with Outerplane social cues. Perhaps he's still uncomfortable about the whole loan thing.

By the Triple Goddess, I need to sleep if I'm going to be of any use today. It's going to be a hectic and exciting time. I can't wait.

Moondias, Thunder Moon 15, 209

I WOKE UP this morning to find a scroll tucked under my pillow. I knew it couldn't be from my friends at home, because my tent was still standing, so I was confused. The first thing that struck me when I unrolled it was the perfectly formed lettering and formal language. I guessed who it was from before I saw the signature at the bottom: Bob, my stalwart building inspector companion.

I was nervous to read it as it was a Moondias and the last time I received any correspondence from the building inspectors, it was to condemn the Gingerbread Hut. I love my House of Horrors and knew Bob had been hanging around it. Had he found the structure sub-par?

TO HESTER DIGITALIS Wishbone,

When first we met, I was a sheltered and unfulfilled building inspector. My world consisted of structural analysis, survey reports, and building codes. I existed only in the moments I was inspecting and ceased to be at the termination of each job. After the suns I spent bonded to the table in the unstable residential structure comprised of baked goods, I came to realize that a wide array of interesting formations and developments existed outside the bounds of my work.

I observed your life. It was new, baffling. I wanted to understand, to know the structure of a human life.

My decision to follow you, a controversial move among my kind, has produced an important and unexpected outcome. I realized I am more than my work. I am more than my clan. I am more than my constituent rock. I, and indeed any thoughtful being, am in a constant state of redesign and construction. And this is a state to be strived for, not avoided.

I witnessed your progression through cycles of instability and stability. When your foundations shook, friends shored up your weight-bearing walls and kept you intact. Then, the renovations began. You expanded your areas of strength until they could support your weaker sections. Humans, and indeed most soft skins, operate as individual components of a larger structure. This is a natural and beneficial process for all.

My research has been most promising. Applying our innate knowledge of construction to a human life is a new concept for gargoyles, and one that might in time foster increased understanding between our species. I also find that I am no longer reluctant to present new concepts to my contemporaries. This is due in part to your determination that developing and strengthening what makes you unique among your kind, converts those traits and skills not initially appreciated by others into valuable future assets.

Our coordinated velocity brought me into relative rest with your being and has exponentially expanded my world. In my time as your companion, I have encountered more creatures, travelled to more lands, and engaged in more activities than I knew existed. And, perhaps most important of all, I have come to understand what a friend is. Not only have I listened to your conversations with others, but you have spoken to me on many occasions, something no human has ever done. Through you, I have come to recognize your complex structure of emotions and how those essential components link humans through the creation of strong, shared foundational supports.

Gargoyle society is organized around a system of colleague clans. These are not the same as human friend or family groupings, as there are no emotionally derived connections between members. Gargoyle minds, on whole, are empirically driven. Humans would perceive our thoughts as a series of complex formulas and diagrams. Translating them into a common language for inspection forms is viewed as a gargoyle's greatest challenge. However, it was never a difficult task for me and this set me apart. I was regarded among my homologous peers as different and ultimately defective.

Why was this task easy for me and hard for everyone else? This question often imposed itself on my thoughts. I could feel how it set me apart from other gargoyles, and yet, try as I might, I could not determine the source of this difference. My time with you enabled me to uncover the anomaly within the enigma. I still do not understand why I find the translation of thought to common language easy, but the very fact that I *felt* it made me different *was* the prime difference.

I had feelings, but no frame of reference to identify what they were and no outlet or opportunity to explore them. My formulas were incomplete. When you talked to me about your life and feelings, I finally had a point of reference to understand my own.

All of my research has led me to a conclusion: Friends are the essential building blocks of a successful and fulfilling existence.

$$\Delta t' = \gamma \, \Delta t = \frac{\Delta t}{\sqrt{1 - \frac{v^2}{c^2}}}$$

Therefore, I, (Bob), do hereby, in this propitious time, formally petition you, Hester Digitalis Wishbone, for entry into your mutually beneficial friend clan. In doing so, I swear to uphold the high standards of friendship as defined by you, including but not limited to the provision of a safe haven, sustenance, regular correspondence, thoughtful and unsolicited gifts, emergency funding, an attentive ear, and access to any and all skills possessed by the petitioner. To show that I am serious in this petition, I have contacted my gargoyle clan to request their assistance with carnival renovations. It is my hope that this will function as suitable reparation for any inconveniences my presence may have caused.

With every sincerity,

Bob

Post Script: Thank you for the considerate gifts you have made for me during our acquaintance. I find the scent of my bark earrings and the flowers in the necklace you gave me to be most pleasing.

Post Post Script: Thank you also for helping care for my long-eared companion, as she was my first foray into friendship. She greatly enjoys the extra bits of meat you and your human companions feed her under the supper table. However, I have noted a significant gain in mass of late and wonder if this could lead to increased difficulty hopping, due to her absent foot. Please, inform me if you share this concern. I am unfamiliar with soft life forms and unequipped to make a final determination in this matter.

Post Post Post Script: To clear up a confusion you may be labouring under—I relieved the tavern wizard of his wand for violations of building code 1483: Unauthorized renovation by a non-union worker, and building code 1501: Unsafe removal of a weight-bearing support beam. Had The Moon's Lament not exploded, it most certainly would have collapsed. The wand is a displacement device. This is also how your companions, Herman and Monkey, are relieving patrons of their valuables. I kindly request that you ask them to refrain from utilizing the wand. I would prefer not to destroy it, as I enjoy watching the faceted jewels sparkle in the sunlight.

How's that for a letter? The guy (Or girl . . . hadn't thought of that until now. Do gargoyles have genders? I'll have to ask at some point.) hasn't dropped so much as a word in the six months we've been together and suddenly, this. Who knew all this was going on in that stony noggin? I'm glad Bob doesn't have an issue with the name I picked. Whatever gargoyle name that jumble of lines and symbols is, I doubt I'd ever be able to understand it, let alone pronounce it. I knew gargoyles were a different thinking bunch, but wow.

As soon as the shock wore off, I set out and found Bob perched on a rock, facing the sun as it rose over the ocean. I said I'd be proud to have a gargoyle friend and that I accepted the petition wholeheartedly. Bob didn't move or say anything, but after I hugged my new friend, I noted his / her / ze's contemplative pout was curved into a broad smile.

I never know what a day on the Outerplane will bring. Today it brought me a new-old friend. What an unexpected and wonderful thing that is!

ADDENDUM: Jim Dandy, our dog companion, had a litter of puppies this afternoon. Everyone is now calling her Jane Dandy. Kamal is overjoyed. Sam is dismayed, but resigned to the ever-expanding nature of our family (or clan, as Bob would say).

ADDENDUM II: I received word from Magda that she is coming to visit and help out! Missera, too. Herman is ecstatic. I can't wait to introduce her to everyone and show her around the Outerplane. She's going to be terrified of the wizard vehicles. I admit, I might enjoy that a little. It will be so nice to have someone around who understands just how horrifying it is to travel in them.

Wendias, Thunder Moon 17, 209

HERMAN WAS EXPLORING the beach late this evening and came across a seafood restaurant that specializes in lobster and crab dishes. He was appalled, to say the least.

Instead of coming back and asking for my help, he hastily planned an escape for his doomed crustacean comrades (one that did not involve the wand as I gave him a stern lecture last night and provided Bob with a lock-box to keep it in when not admiring its sparkle).

My familiar was scant on the details of what happened at the restaurant. It must have been epic because he barely made it out with his shell intact. I noticed a few dents and cracks as he scuttled into our tent brandishing an array of sharp implements in his claws. He refused to put them down for quite some time.

When he finally came out from under my bunk, he said he was considering another transmutation—a python, partly in honour of Missera's upcoming visit.

I didn't buy it. He wanted a new identity, ASAP, and he categorically refused to listen when I told him the Outerplane wasn't up to speed on sentient witch familiars. It's not like the restaurant was going to put up wanted posters with mug shots of Herman the Nefarious Robber Crab.

He responded by meticulously picking out clumps of grass

that had become wedged in his joints during the great escape and throwing them at me.

Recognizing it as a lost battle, I decided to tackle something that was long overdue. There was a wrong I perpetrated out of ignorance and selfishness when we first met that needed righting.

I asked if Herman wanted to be a cockroach again so he could compare his original form with his other, more recent ones. I knew being considered inedible would appeal and that he'd enjoy the fear factor. A good percentage of Outerplaners are terrified of anything with an exoskeleton. Especially small, skittery things. I don't get it but to each their own.

He responded to my inquiry with suspicion.

I understood why and it hurt to know that it was my fault. Every pang of guilt I felt was deserved. I sat beside him on the ground and apologized for initially reacting so negatively to his cockroach form, explaining my selfish reasons relating to union status. Hopefully, I conveyed that his importance to me goes far deeper than his form and that my behaviour was unacceptable. I made him feel like he wasn't good enough, not for anything he did or said, but because of my distorted perception of what he was. That's horrible. I failed as his witch and friend, and promised to never be so idiotic again. I ended by saying that more than anything, I wanted him to be proud of and comfortable with whatever he chose to be.

He listened, but I couldn't tell if I got through. He sat with his claws clasped together, clicking them occasionally. It might have been a thoughtful pose. I hope it was. At least he agreed to think about what I said. That's a start.

I didn't ask for his forgiveness. Ignorance should never be excused. The only thing anyone can do is acknowledge the hurt they caused and resolve to do better next time.

Facing my shame is difficult and uncomfortable, as I believed myself to be a better person than I was in those moments, but it also holds a sense of progress. I'm not the same person who was so concerned about what everyone else might think. My first duty of care should have been to ensure my familiar's well-being. I will never shirk that duty again.

All this harkens back to a lesson about balance my old Elemental Philosophy professor gave. He said that whatever is in you that makes you great, also has the potential to make you terrible. If you are greatly creative, then you can also be greatly destructive. That is the knowledge every witch must come to terms with and the balance we must strike within ourselves and our castings.

My talent has always been with words, whether using them to weave intricate illusions or to influence those around me. I must heed Hekate's warning and be careful to maintain balance in all things, magickal and mundane. Today, I feel I am closer to balancing my relationship with Herman. It is a work in progress, but I'm hopeful that one day we will come to a place where we are unconditionally comfortable with ourselves and each other.

Tydias, Thunder Moon 23, 209

I THOUGHT I was busy before. By Hephaestus's flatulent forge, I didn't know the meaning of busy!

Everyone has been working on their revamped acts and costumes and props and signs and personas, as well as the concession stands and arch and rides and House of Horrors and, and, and . . . In addition, we're experimenting to see if we can dye the big top fabric black instead of replacing it, which would be costly. So far, we've managed to get it to a deep purple.

My House of Horrors, now called The Witch's Lair, is undergoing significant expansion and renovation. We're adding a tent maze to one side with a grotto in the centre where customers can enjoy Asena's fortune telling services.

Herman is still a coconut crab. He's been hanging out with Ouleah, my water loving union employment counsellor, who arrived a few days ago. They enjoy popping out of a little pond in the centre of the grotto to scare people (when Ouleah isn't snoozing). She had only positive things to say about my idea of taking on practicum students and is madly filling out forms to finalize the union's endorsement so we can set it up. She wasn't kidding about the hoops to jump through. Luckily, they're all made of parchment and ink, and she is an expert at those.

That's right! Not only am I going to qualify for my Adept

rites, I'm going to be teaching Apprentice witches how to work in the Outerplane. Peuturella wants me to write an academic paper about it, and she said their Interplanar Magick Systems prof. wants me to be a guest lecturer. It feels good to be in demand.

I warned Ouleah about Justin's mother. I wouldn't put it past her to catch wind of our plans and intervene. Ouleah was incensed when I explained what had happened and offered to bring a complaint forward on my behalf. I declined. I did ask her to make sure that Herman and my successes are well known at the union. Let that stand as an example to my ex and his mother of how far petty bullying gets them. It didn't net them a single thing, apart from buggy reflections, and Herman and I have never been happier.

Out of curiosity, I also asked Ouleah how a job posting for an Outerplane carnival wound up in the non-union job bank in the first place. The question has been nagging at me.

I talked to Sam about it a while ago (through Peuturella, as she arrived via less legal planar channels and was not subject to a gag order) and determined he had no knowledge that other planes even existed. He tried to engage us in a conversation about theoretical physics, something about a string, but I put a stop to that before I got a headache. From his perspective, he posted the position on some boards, somewhere, and received a call from a head hunter who said they had an ideal candidate. He showed up at the Outerplane airport when they told him I'd arrive and . . . the rest is history. *(NOTE: A head hunter is a person who finds employees for Outerplane companies, not someone looking for their head, as I originally thought.)*

Ouleah wasn't overly surprised by my question or the subsequent events. The Employment Cabal have their tentacles in a variety of pots and view interplanar laws regarding trades and services as inconvenient obstacles. She referred to them as "unfettered."

Then, she said something most intriguing. "The union's restrictive regulations and practices work for some and not others. When you kept coming back to my office, I had a feeling you were suited to something a little . . . different. I was right. Let's just say I've been around longer than most and haven't always stirred the union's cauldron, if you know what I mean.

Of course, there's nobody there anymore that could attest to that. Longevity has some benefits." She winked at me. "But that's just between the two of us."

"Then why do you still work for the union?" I asked.

Ouleah tilted her head to the side and raised a tentacle in a nonchalant half-shrug. "I see myself more as working for the witches who come to me. The union is just a convenient nexus."

I politely suggested she might want to give the next witch she sends to the Employment Cabal a warning about their interplanar reach. She agreed. At least I think she did. She fell asleep mid-nod and disappeared under the water in the grotto pond.

I aimlessly wandered through the lot, pondering my enigmatic and surprising employment counsellor, and then stopped to help Sam finish building an enclosure near the edge of the maze for Ebony. To proceed past it and into the grotto, my patrons will have to feed him a handful of hay or alfalfa (labelled as zombie hair). Danica trained him to kick open a door once he's had his treat. It should be fun for everyone.

Asena somehow found time to sculpt a realistic horse skull mask out of leather. It really bumps up the creepy effect of Ebony's skeleton body paint. Even a fearsome kelpie would think twice before crossing his path.

We've also set up a room in The Witch's Lair for Tim (The Snakeman) and adorned it like an ancient Egyptian burial chamber complete with golden sarcophagus, canopic jars, and offerings. Tim wraps himself in aged-looking fabric and stalks customers while his snakes happily lounge on his shoulders or coil around his waist. Sometimes, he hides in the sarcophagus and when someone comes in, he pushes the top off and sits up. He treats the wraps with his salve which keeps his skin nicely moisturized and healthy, so it's a win all around.

All of these transformations would be going much slower if friends hadn't come to our rescue. Not only have mine showed up, but so have an impressive array of my co-workers' more supportive friends and family. Everyone is feeling pretty lucky . . . exhausted, but lucky.

Five gargoyles from Bob's clan are assisting with renovations while nobody's looking. It was really funny for a time because I couldn't explain to anyone what was happening. From their perspective, random jobs kept mysteriously being completed, and they couldn't understand why nobody would take credit.

The sheer volume of weirdness pouring into camp has been understandably overwhelming for my Outerplane friends. They might be more used to the strange and varied nature of humans and animals than most, but many of the stories they're hearing and people / creatures they're meeting are far beyond their experience. As always, they work through it with calmness and patience. Mostly, they are curious and interested.

The biggest surprise for me (though, not really when I think about it), is that my parents showed up out of the blue. Literally. Their alternate (read: Illegal) route dropped them out of a clear blue sky into the middle of camp. I'm not sure how they did it. They haven't been forthcoming, so I gather it's not a method they want me employing. Anyway, it means that my parents and most of my guests can openly talk about anything they want (as they avoided the dreaded infernal gag order at interplanar customs), which is a bonus as it makes organizing who's doing what and how easier. They were also able to explain to everyone what the gargoyles were doing.

My parents are being typical parents, asking too many questions, overreacting to everything, and nitpicking whatever I'm working on. It's amazing how you can be so sure of yourself one minute, confident in your maturity and skills, and then your parents appear and you become the same dippy, anxious kid you were on your first day of school. Despite all that, I am glad to see them. It's been too long and at least now, in this job, I am settled and optimistic.

They are making themselves useful, which is greatly appreciated. Dad has been helping me expand the Witch's Feast menu and Mom has launched herself into sprucing up the rooms in my lair (my lair . . . I really like the sound of that).

My former Moonbrews boss, Andreas, and his newly promoted assistant manager, my old co-worker, Teagan, popped in for a few weeks (also illegally). *(VERY IMPORTANT NOTE: Convince them to tell me how they did their plane shifts without going through interplanar customs!)*

Andreas is the same hyper-positive, jumpy micromanager I, mostly fondly, remember. I wasn't sure how he would take my invitation. We didn't part on the worst terms, but it also wasn't the best with the Infernals breathing down his neck.

Teagan successfully completed her first year at Grimoire College and is looking forward to her second. *(NOTE: Tell her about my proposed practicum placement to see if she's interested in applying.)*

Turns out, they are both incurably curious about the Outerplane. Over tankards of mead last evening, they waxed poetic about my supposed bravery for working and living here. I tried to explain that my interplanar excursion began as an accident, but they reframed it as my creative hand inspiring the Fates.

They've been refurbishing our concession stands. Andreas took over the drinks concession and is setting it up in a similar fashion to Moonbrews. I heard him mumbling to himself, wondering if he could get authorization to open a Moonbrews franchise on the Outerplane. I told him he could do better, that he should create his own menu and start his own potion café. I spoke before fully considering my words. Dear gods, from his excited expression, I suspect the carnival has acquired another permanent import.

Magda, my bestest friend and sanity saver, has also arrived (via legal means, being my sole lawfully inclined friend). Sam and I picked her and Missera up at an airport that houses a secret Interplanar Terminal similar to the one I used. Traveling in Sam's truck was just as terrifying for her as it had been for me, though she had the slight advantage of being mentally prepared, thanks to my letters.

Missera seamlessly fits in with the carnival. She spends much of her time with Herman, but has also developed a friendship of sorts with Tim's snakes, Bailong and Janus. There was some kind of scuffle her first day with Old One-Eye the cat, but there hasn't been any trouble since, so they must have worked out a truce. Like Herman, she is entranced by Kamal and can frequently be found draped across his shoulders. So now, Kamal wanders my lair as a ghost with spider, snake, and coconut crab followers. It's a good thing he enjoys their company because he couldn't get rid of them if he tried.

Magda was most impressed with The Witch's Lair and my feasts. She's having fun scaring our patrons and loves the new robes Asena made. Asena promised to sew her one before she goes home. As I suspected, they get along as if they had been lifelong friends.

Our trio spends the most time together of anyone. We've even developed a special act for my feasts, dressing up as aspects of our triple goddess: Magda is the maiden, Asena is the mother, and I am the crone (she's still my favourite . . . I can't help it). Just for fun, I gave Asena a few helpful pointers on how to act like a druid, such as talking to inanimate objects and things that aren't there, and I constantly interrupt our dinners with foul smelling potions and ill-timed theatrics. We're very popular. I hope it never gets back to Mother and Crone on the moors as I don't think they would appreciate the parody.

The only disturbing thing that's happened lately was Sam offering to teach me how to operate a vehicle. I stared at him, agape. He doesn't understand my hesitation. Perhaps he's right and I will change my mind one day, but that day is not today. I'm still hoping to be able to increase my broom's energy efficiency so I can travel like a civilized witch.

Phew. This was a long entry. I'm getting a hand cramp and need some refreshments. Perhaps I'll go see if my next batch of mead has finished aging.

Farewell for tonight, dear diary.

Freydias, Thunder Moon 26, 209

I SWEAR ON the Maiden's plump buttocks, my mead is *good* and it just keeps getting better. It's popular enough that I've had to expand production to ten jugs . . . rotating five at a time. I call my fiery brew *The Phoenix's Revenge*. It is seriously spicy. Plus, the acronym "PR" amuses me. Sam keeps talking about "public relations" (i.e. schmoozing). Mead is the only kind of PR I approve of.

I've had a most interesting night thanks to Asena, and her lovely accomplice, Maria. They tricked Sam and I into going on a sunset hot air balloon ride. As unexpected dates go, it was awkward, but pleasant. It was disconcerting being so high without my trusty broom. Rationally I knew it couldn't support my weight, but having it would have been a comfort. I can see why humans don't make sense to gargoyles. I don't even make sense to myself.

The views were breathtaking. The world, any world I guess, looks more organized and sensible from the air. Drifting along with the breeze was peaceful—a welcome break from the crowds and hectic schedules Sam and I have been keeping. As dusk fell, the fire flares of other balloons winked around us like lanterns lifting wishes to the stars. I think Sam was as moved as I was. He took my hand and didn't let it go until we landed.

Asena, Maria, and Magda (their love obsession has infected my best friend) wanted to know all about the date when I came home. I couldn't be angry with them for tricking us, as we'd had such a lovely time, so I just thanked them. They mean well. They just refuse to accept that Sam and I don't have time for this right now. If it was a quick romp, sure, but Sam doesn't strike me as that type.

My audience was disappointed that nothing had happened. Maria said if I was interested, it was up to me to make the first move. She thinks Sam is worried that it would be inappropriate for him to do so because he's technically my boss. He's also not great with the ladies. They only knew of one girl and their relationship ended badly when her family found out. Maria said it was for the best because if she wasn't willing to fight for him, she wasn't worth his time. I got the feeling that was meant as a message for me as well.

This whole thing makes me nervous. Maria and Asena are very protective of Sam. The fact that they are actively encouraging us to get together suggests they approve of me, but I'm not sure what would happen if things didn't work out. It could get messy, in more ways than one. Maria wields her rapiers as if she was born holding them, and I have no urge to get on her bad side.

Just a sec. Herman came in and wants to talk *right now*.

OKAY. THAT WAS a surprisingly positive conversation. I'm shocked. The last time Herman scuttled in here that fast, he had executed a risky prison break for his crustacean buddies and was brandishing weapons.

I think in this case, he was just excited. He wants to be transmuted back to his old cockroach form, only larger. Based on his description, he'd like to be as big as Ebony, but that isn't going to happen. There are limits to what I can do in the Outerplane and I'm pretty sure that is outside the realm of possibility even on my home plane. I can make him as large as his current coconut crab form. Hopefully, that will suffice.

I asked what brought him to this decision and he simply replied, "It is who I am." It was an insightful statement on many levels and a sentiment that is close to my heart. I'm lucky to have Herman as my familiar. He's a valuable and delightfully troublesome partner.

And now I am going to curl up in my bunk and try to get a few hours of much needed sleep.

Moondias, Blood Moon 15, 209

THE NEW AND improved Karneval Života is a hit! Our grand opening extravaganza last night was the busiest we have ever been. People came from far and wide to attend, including a number of guests from my home plane. The reviews and comments on Sam's wizard scry box (called a computer) have all been glowing (by which he means positive, not actually glowing). Our adult patrons were scared out of their wits and the children were begging to come back.

The big top show was amazing. Asena made herself a beautiful demon costume, complete with deep red curled horns and a tattered black leather skirt that protects her legs from wayward flames while she dances. She had the crowd mesmerized and nobody minded that she was far too attractive to be an actual demon.

The Spider Siblings, costumed as Death and a banshee, performed intricate and challenging acrobatics on Ebony and Snowball to great applause. Then they switched to their draped silk sheets and executed a stunning aerial routine. It was like watching a love story between Death and a ghost.

Maria put her sword fighting and knife throwing skills to the test against an undead dwarven warrior (Fiona), a stone golem (Gilroy), and a fearsome shape shifter (Julie, who I swear really can shape-shift). There were many gasps as Maria's foes came at her from the stands.

Throughout the performances, Kamal wandered through the audience in his ghost costume, silently sitting next to people. They would look over and scream as they suddenly realized their neighbour was a grinning ghost (Kamal is perpetually happy).

After the show, a documentary crew who stayed with us about a month ago to do a feature on the carnival, premiered the fruits of their labour. It was fun watching giant versions of my co-workers and friends appear in the projected illusion, talking about who they were, their acts, and the work they were doing to re-brand the carnival. Even I was interviewed, though I had to sidestep many questions. Their wizard crystals must have messed up my voice. Surely I'm not that squeaky in person. Ugh.

The documentary crew also interviewed those crazy protestors from the town we had to quickly vacate. They were in hysterics about an evil witch who called down the wrath of Satan in the form of a blight of spiders and choking fog. The field we briefly set up camp in is considered cursed ground. Nobody from town can set foot there without being overrun by spiders. My sweets are still holding their ground! They truly are the most underappreciated creatures on the Outerplane. I bet the town has never been so mosquito free.

I'm proud of my handiwork there. To have made such a lasting impression is gratifying and confirms that I am finally on the right path, both professionally and personally. If a witch leaves their mark wherever they wander, on lives or lands, they can consider themselves successful.

NOTE: Check with Sam to see if we'll pass near that town again anytime soon. If so, remember to undo the spider attraction spell. To be perfectly honest, I forgot about it in our haste to leave. Oh well. At least the protestors will think thrice before pestering witchy travellers in the future.

Sam is overjoyed at how everything has turned out. Karneval Života has locations booked for the rest of the season and into next, with several lucrative side contracts in between. A band of movie executives have engaged us to travel to Hollywood for a month around an Outerplane holiday called Halloween. We'll be hosting parties and some kind of award event, as well as providing them with location sets and acting as extras. Sam said we're going to make enough in that one month to pay everyone's expenses and wages for a full year.

He sat me down this afternoon to discuss the loan again. He wanted to pay me back right away, but I said I'd rather see him invest any spare coin in the carnival for now. There are still upgrades to make and nice-to-haves that were put off.

Sam considered my suggestion and said he would only agree if I became a co-owner. It was an interesting proposition. We talked more and eventually decided that the offer should be extended to everyone. We called a meeting and there was great support. Now we all own an equal share of Karneval Života. We are partners in a most exciting venture. We'll pay a fair salary to any new performers or venders who join, but our core group will comprise the voting council.

My parents stayed for the grand opening and, quite unexpectedly, said they were proud of what I'm doing. They like my co-workers and want to come back later in the year for another working vacation at The Witch's Lair. I think Mom is worried that I'm working too hard. She's not wrong. We're all working too hard, but things should calm down in a while. I hope. She keeps pushing me to take a break.

Maria, Asena, and Magda jumped on that broom right away. They want Sam and I to go on a vacation together. The idea has merit. I'm not comfortable enough on the Outerplane for solo travel yet, but if I had a trusted guide like Sam, it's feasible. Plus, I'm curious to know what he's like when he's not working. If we get along this well under extreme stress . . . let's just say, I'm intrigued.

Asena loudly and pointedly declared in the middle of our meeting this afternoon that our decision to become partners meant that there was technically no boss. Sam's eyes widened as he glanced over at me and then he looked away. If his skin wasn't hidden beneath his glorious fur-hair, I imagine there would have been a rosy tint to his cheeks.

Herman is beyond happy with his oversized cockroach form. With Kamal's help, he's gained fame as an "online celebrity." Kamal uses a wizard device (similar to what the documentary crew used) to record Herman doing what he does best . . .

getting into trouble. He has his own "YouTube channel" and show called *BOUS 4 Kids* (BOUS apparently stands for Bug of Unusual Size). The phrase "What would Herman do?" has become something called an "internet meme." It's all very wizardy, and I don't understand much of what Sam and Herman have tried to explain. I do understand that Herman is pleased, which is all that really matters.

Soon, Sam will have to take over Kamal's responsibilities on Herman's show. My parents are going to smuggle Kamal back to our plane so he can train as a druid. Kamal is excited about his upcoming trip and keeps hugging me whenever our paths cross.

As much as I'll be sad to see him go, there's something perfect about it. What that was didn't strike me until tonight. His going to my plane nicely restores balance, as I intend to be in this one for some time. It's an unexpected and satisfying outcome that warms me through to my witchy core. Hekate would approve.

Huh. When I wrote that, Jane Dandy, her pups, and some of their wild cousins set to howling. It's a joyful sound, full of wildness and power. The Goddess of Magick is ever-present. Her attention used to make me nervous, but now I am grateful. Whatever path I walk, whatever challenges await, I will not be alone and I will persevere. I am a Daughter of the Moon.

And on that note, I shall call it a night. Rest well, my new plane. May the elements sustain and strengthen you, the night embrace you, and the Fates be kind.

Final Words

It is my sincere wish that each of you has a gentler introduction to our profession than mine. Should that not be the case, then I hope you find a best friend as wise and compassionate as Magda, a fleet of companions that complicate your life in a most hilarious way so you never forget to laugh, and a good diary to help you work through any obstacles unfortunate enough to fall in your path.

Even if you start out with none of these, know that you do not walk alone. You are a witch, magick personified. Feel Earth in your bones, breathe and be one with Air, hear the roar of blood in your veins as Water through a mountain channel, let Fire fuel your dreams, and Spirit guide you. You are life and death. Be unique. Be powerful. Be loving. Be dangerous. But most of all, *be you.*

There will never be another witch like you and that makes you precious. Nobody else has your combination of personality, talent, and experience. Don't let someone else define you because they will impose limits based on who they are, not on what you can accomplish. No matter what anyone says, there is no right way to be a witch, there is only your way.

Be true to your dreams. Keep your broom close. Hone your skills. Acquire new ones. Learn everything you can. Take chances. Do the unexpected. Make mistakes. Fix them. Watch. Feel. Listen. Always listen! Many times have I learnt more in one moment of silence than in all my years of classes, as both student and teacher.

May you live fully all aspects of our Triple Goddess and her light always bless your path.

Sincerely,

Hester Digitalis Wishbone

CAST OF CHARACTERS

Althea – Boss at the Gingerbread Hut

Andreas – Boss at Moonbrews

Asena – Fortune teller and fire dancer at Karneval Života

Bob – Gargoyle building inspector

Bunny – Bob's first friend

Crone – Wizard who lives on the moors

Danica and Nikolai – Acrobats and trick riders at Karneval Života (The Spider Siblings)

Fiona and Gilroy – Strong woman and strong man at Karneval Života

Hekate – Goddess of Magick

Herman – Hester's familiar

Hester Digitalis Wishbone – Writer of this diary

Julie – Contortionist at Karneval Života (The Bender)

Justin – Hester's jerky ex-boyfriend

Kamal – Magician at Karneval Života (The Ghost)

Magda – Hester's best friend and fellow witch

Maria – Master of Ceremonies at Karneval Života (Black Tide the Pirate Queen)

Missera – Magda's asp familiar

Mother – Druid who lives on the moors

Mothlady – Former Moonbrews customer

Ouleah – Employment Counsellor at the Witch's Union

Peuturella Bloodroot – Elder hedge witch who teaches potion courses at Grimoire College

Sam – Boss at Karneval Života, Advance Man, Lot Manager, and Wizard (The Beast)

Sophie – Althea's bat familiar at the Gingerbread Hut

Teagan – Apprentice witch at Moonbrews

Tim – Snake handler and performer at Karneval Života (The Snakeman)

GLOSSARY

Calendar Terms:
    Sun – Day
    Morn – Morning
    Mid-sun – Mid-day / noon
    Eventide – Evening
    Moon – Month
    Season Cycle – Year

Suns of the Week:
** Note on correspondences to Outerplane suns (days): Our home plane weeks consist of seven suns as do Outerplane weeks.*

    Moondias – Chaos reigns. Rest sun for witches.
    Tydias – Celebration of Tyr. Set plans in motion. Sun of sacrifice and work.
    Wendias – Celebration of Wenepthia, the much beloved seahorse of King Porticulus.
    Cerridias – Celebration of Cerridwen. Perfect for creative endeavours, especially potion mixing.
    Freydias – Celebration of Freya. Care for home, family, and friends.

Pandias – Celebration of Pan. Bond with nature.
Soldias – Sol is an archaic word for Sun, the bringer of life.

Moons in a Season Cycle:

** Note on correspondences to Outerplane moons (months): In our home plane there are thirteen moons which follow our Goddess's lunar cycle, with twenty-eight suns (days) each, embraced within a solar season cycle. The Outerplane months appear to have been slapped down at whim, with varying numbers of days (Wizard's work, I'm sure). For example, shown below is a list of start and end dates of the Outerplane months for each moon that I jotted down during my first year. Please also note the Dark Seed celebration in Spirit Moon will result in slightly different date translations depending on the year. For a more thorough explanation, and an excellent ephemeris, I recommend Ormuz's Comparative Planar Calendars.*

Wolf Moon – 9 January – 5 February
Storm Moon – 6 February – 4 March
Crow Moon – 5 March – 1 April
Seed Moon – 2 April – 29 April
Nettle Moon – 30 April – 27 May
Lotus Moon – 28 May – 24 June
Thunder Moon – 25 June – 22 July
Blood Moon – 23 July – 19 August
Heather Moon – 20 August – 16 September
Dragon Moon – 17 September – 14 October
Hearth Moon – 15 October – 11 November
Frost Moon – 12 November – 9 December
Spirit Moon – 10 December – 8 January

Professions:

Druid – Harnesses nature energies. Unpredictable. They believe all things have spirit / force, whether it's a stone, a spear of lightening, or a deer. They are only interested in maintaining the natural order of the universe and cannot be hired (unless you are Hekate). Philosophy: *There is no magick, there is only the energy of existence and extinction.*

Magician – Outerplane entertainers. They do not use magick. You will piss everyone off who does if you suggest it is even peripherally involved in their showmanship.

Witch – Brews potions. Works with natural components. Seldom seen without the company of their familiar, broom, and cauldron. They cast spells by channelling the five elements (Earth, Air, Water, Fire, Spirit). Earth, Air, Water, and Fire are channelled in the form of elemental sprites. Spirit, the fifth element, is a life-force channelled directly from the witch. Philosophy: *We are magick.*

- **Hedge Witch** – Doctor / herbalist. Usually a hermit.
- **Illusionist** – Deals primarily in illusions. Considered an art form.

Wizard – Creates effects and devices using the principals of theoretical physics / mathematics / engineering / chemistry. They divide the five witch elements into a never-ending Wizard Table of Elements. Their complicated written spells are cast by verbalizing long algorithms which are incomprehensible to anyone who isn't a wizard (or gargoyle). They carry an array of tools—wands and staves are the most common—which are highly specialized and dedicated to particular spells. Showy. Reckless in their fanatical pursuit of knowledge. Wizards rarely venture into the countryside, preferring to stay in large metropolis centres. Philosophy: *We seek to understand magick and look good doing it.*

Acknowlegements

First and foremost, I'm grateful for my best friend and partner in both life and writing, Adriaan Brae. I love how ideas bounce between us and grow into such creatively wonderful worlds, characters, and plots. You lend assistance when I feel stuck, do endless read-throughs, and challenge me to push further and go deeper. You are a beautiful light in the darkness.

My heartfelt thanks also goes out to my friends and fellow authors Rob and Ellen Easton, who spent a considerable amount of time and energy reading and improving this work. Their insight and suggestions were invaluable and so very appreciated.

I owe a great debt to my brilliant editor Margaret Curelas for, well, everything. She streamlined and enhanced the story and prose, as well as enduring about a billion anxious author changes along the way. You were an absolute joy to work with. Thank you for believing in me and Hester.

This book has been enriched by three exceptionally talented visual artists. Sonny Tamko created delightful artwork which brought the characters and setting to life. Skyla Dawn Cameron created a fantastically fun and witchy cover. Special thanks to photographer Stacy Kreger, for my author photograph. Your photos capture the subject's spirit and that is an incredible skill.

I've heard it said that writing is a solitary endeavour, but I am fortunate that this has not been my experience. I came from a loving home where art was celebrated and imagination was encouraged. There was always food when I was hungry and a safe place to lay my head at night. Most of my teachers were positive influences. My friends were into creative activities like D&D, poetry, and painting. I had pens, paper, art supplies, and eventually computers to help develop my skills. I acknowledge how much of a blessing and privilege all of these were, and pledge to do my best to support and encourage the creative interests of those around me. I want to experience and learn from your art in all its amazing forms.

About the Author

Rebecca Brae lives in Alberta, Canada with her partner, daughter, and growing pack of animal companions. She is an artist, lover of diversity, fog enthusiast, and proud geek who aspires to one day live in a cave by the ocean (with wifi, of course). Her background in Criminology and Classical Studies informs her writing in unexpected and occasionally horrifying ways.

Rebecca has co-authored two urban fantasy novels, *Chaos Bound* and *Curse Bound*, has a short story in the furr-tastic anthology *Swashbuckling Cats: Nine lives on the Seven Seas*, and drabbles in *100 Word Horrors* and *100 Word Horrors 2*. Connect with her on Twitter @RebeccaBrae and at www.braevitae.com.